FROM TICKHILL, 1348

PAMELA TAYLOR

Pamela Taylor (signature)

Black Rose Writing | Texas

The author grants the final approval for this literary material.

First printing

This is a work of fiction. Names, characters, businesses, places, events, and incidents are either the products of the author's imagination or used in a fictitious manner. Any resemblance to actual persons, living or dead, or actual events is purely coincidental.

ISBN: 978-1-68513-520-1
LIBRARY OF CONGRESS CONTROL NUMBER: 2024943707
PUBLISHED BY BLACK ROSE WRITING
www.blackrosewriting.com

Printed in the United States of America
Suggested Retail Price (SRP) $21.95

From Tickhill, 1348 is printed in Garamond Premier Pro

*As a planet-friendly publisher, Black Rose Writing does its best to eliminate unnecessary waste to reduce paper usage and energy costs, while never compromising the reading experience. As a result, the final word count vs. page count may not meet common expectations.

To my loyal readers

CAPETIAN DYNASTY
Simplified to focus on this narrative

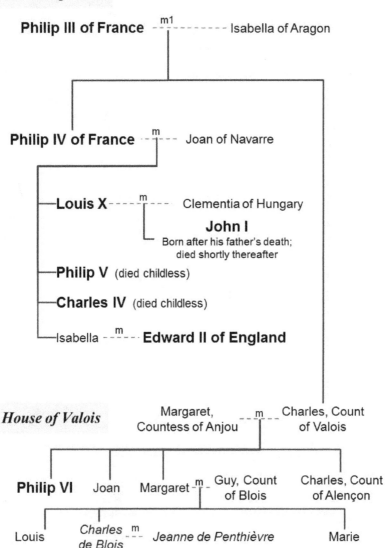

Direct Capetians

Philip III of France -- m1 -------- Isabella of Aragon

Philip IV of France --- m --- Joan of Navarre

—**Louis X** ---- m ---- Clementia of Hungary

John I
Born after his father's death;
died shortly thereafter

—**Philip V** (died childless)

—**Charles IV** (died childless)

—Isabella --- m --- **Edward II of England**

House of Valois

Margaret, --- m --- Charles, Count
Countess of Anjou   of Valois

Philip VI   Joan   Margaret - m - Guy, Count   Charles, Count
                                      of Blois   of Alençon

Louis   *Charles* --- m --- *Jeanne de Penthièvre*   Marie
        de Blois

PLANTAGENET DYNASTY
Simplified to focus on this narrative

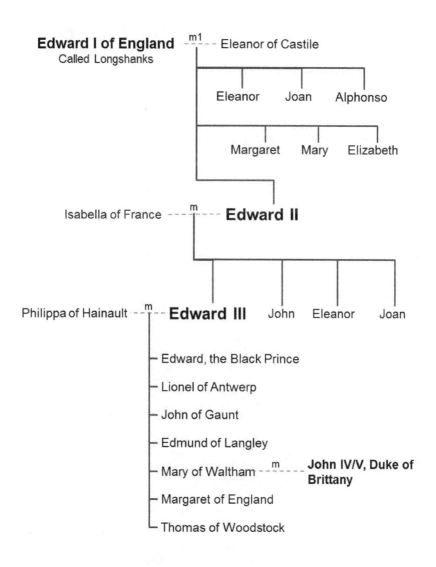

Edward I of England --m1-- Eleanor of Castile
Called Longshanks

Eleanor   Joan   Alphonso

Margaret   Mary   Elizabeth

Isabella of France ---m--- **Edward II**

Philippa of Hainault --m-- **Edward III**   John   Eleanor   Joan

— Edward, the Black Prince

— Lionel of Antwerp

— John of Gaunt

— Edmund of Langley

— Mary of Waltham --m-- **John IV/V, Duke of Brittany**

— Margaret of England

— Thomas of Woodstock

DUKES OF BRITTANY

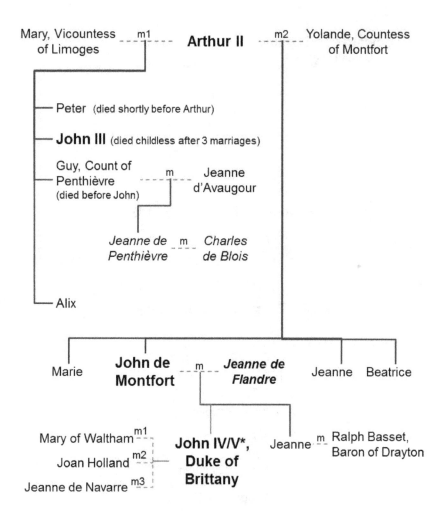

Mary, Vicountess of Limoges — m1 — **Arthur II** — m2 — Yolande, Countess of Montfort

- Peter (died shortly before Arthur)
- **John III** (died childless after 3 marriages)
- Guy, Count of Penthièvre (died before John) — m — Jeanne d'Avaugour
  - Jeanne de Penthièvre — m — Charles de Blois
- Alix

Marie — **John de Montfort** — m — *Jeanne de Flandre* — Jeanne — Beatrice

Mary of Waltham m1 / Joan Holland m2 / Jeanne de Navarre m3 — **John IV/V*, Duke of Brittany** — Jeanne — m — Ralph Basset, Baron of Drayton

* Known in French history as John IV. Charles de Blois is considered to be Duke of Brittany following John III. In many English histories, known as John V. John de Montfort is considered to be John IV, following John III.

FROM
TICKHILL,
1348

FROM THE WRITINGS OF JEANNE DE FLANDRE, DUCHESS OF BRITTANY AND COUNTESS OF MONTFORT
FOUND AMONG HER BELONGINGS AT THE TIME OF HER DEATH

Tickhill Castle, South Yorkshire, 1348

They say I am mad, but I know I am not. No more mad than those who confine me here in this wretched place for their own ends. Who would have me believe they fought on my side but whose motives were deeper and more self-serving than the mere pursuit of a rightful claim. Who were happy to champion my cause if it furthered theirs. And happier still to cast me away when my voice and my strength and my influence were no longer convenient for them.

But I remember everything that happened. Exactly as it happened. So I shall commit it to the page so that those who read my words will know.

If my words are not buried with me when I depart this earth.

CHAPTER ONE

30 April 1341

The old duke had taken ill in Caen on the way home from the siege of Tournai and was not long for this world, so the family rushed to his bedside – those that were left, anyway. His brother Peter died the same year as their father, when John inherited the duchy. And Guy had been gone for ten years now. But Guy's daughter was there, alongside her husband, Charles. So was John's half-brother, also called John, now Count of Montfort. The half-sisters didn't matter so much. One was a nun, and the others had made good marriages and gone their separate ways, more concerned now for their own children's inheritances than for what might be happening in Brittany.

From the beginning, the duke had shown little interest in his half-siblings. It wasn't that his father's second wife was unsuitable. She was, after all, dowager queen of Scotland and Countess of Montfort in her own right. It was just that John utterly opposed his father remarrying at all. And as the family grew, it seemed his father cared more about his living wife and their children than he did about John and his brothers. John began to feel increasingly protective of his brother Guy and of Guy's only child, a daughter named Jeanne. When Guy died, Jeanne inherited his title and lands, becoming Countess of Penthièvre in her own right. But, knowing that wasn't enough to secure her future, the duke arranged her marriage to a nephew of the French king.

Frustrated with still being childless late in life, John had once told his wife, "I'm sorely tempted to disinherit them all and sell the duchy to Philip."

She'd tut-tutted and continued with her stitching. "No less than they deserve," John grumbled. "Charles is a strange duck. All that piety. Jeanne says he has a priest hear his confession every night then sleeps on a pile of straw on the floor rather than in a proper bed. I ask you, how are they ever going to have children?"

"The same way everyone does, my dear."

"Pah! Jeanne says she's even seen him put pebbles in his shoes to atone for his sins. Why didn't he just become a monk? And how would he raise a son even if he managed one?"

"But you told me yourself, he sits a horse well and is not lacking in the skills of a knight."

"Like I said, he's a strange duck."

"Then what about John?"

"I hardly know him."

"He's a good man, dear." She paused to fuss with a stitch that wouldn't lie right. "And his wife . . . now there's a woman with spirit who'd serve him well as a duchess."

"Spirit, you call it? Sometimes I wonder if *that* Jeanne knows her place." He furrowed his brow. "Odd, isn't it? Both women being called Jeanne."

"Why odd? 'Tis my own Christian name as well. And quite a good one, I might add." A silence fell between them broken only by the crackling of the fire. "It's not too late for us, you know," she ventured at long last. "I still have my courses, so perhaps God will solve your dilemma for you."

But God, it seemed, was reluctant to intervene. At one point, Duke John held a feast in Charles's honor, even extracting from him an oath to bear the arms of Brittany and honor its customs. The future seemed a foregone conclusion, at least to Jeanne de Penthièvre and her husband.

As time wore on and Duke John felt the weight of his own looming mortality, his sense of heritage took hold. Brittany had always been independent of France – in customs, in language, in governance. His forefathers had fought to preserve that, and he himself had succeeded masterfully in perpetuating it by helping Philip with his endeavors elsewhere. Brittany's independence was paramount.

And so John vacillated again. Could he really trust a man so close to the French Crown to protect what Bretons held dear? Perhaps a rapprochement with his half-brother was in order. John had inherited the Montfort title from his mother, but he was Breton through and through and the ordinary people liked him.

When the two men and the two Jeannes were shown into the chamber where Duke John lay in bed, attended by a man said to be a physician, they were surprised to find another in the room – one they all recognized as the duke's lawyer. "What's *he* doing here?" Jeanne de Penthièvre said quietly to Charles.

"I summoned him," came from the bed, followed by a bout of coughing. "Help me sit up," the duke struggled to raise himself to lean against the head of the bed while the physician fretted with rearranging the pillows. Finally settled, the duke said "Good, you're all here. *He* . . ." He pointed to the other man in the room. ". . . is here to witness my telling you what he already knows. What he's known since I made these dispositions before I went to Tournai. In my new will, I've changed the provisions I've made for the duchy. John is to inherit. He's the oldest male heir of my father, and by rights, the duchy must be his."

Jeanne gasped and took a step toward the bed, Charles quickly putting a hand on her shoulder to restrain her. "But, Uncle, you can't."

"I can and I have. I've consulted the law and our customs. It's what's right by law. It's what's right for Brittany."

His niece couldn't stop herself from continuing to protest. "But, Uncle, you've already promised Charles. You accepted his oath."

The old duke succumbed to another paroxysm of coughing before sliding down to lie flat once again on the bed. When he caught his breath, he waved them all away. "For God's sake leave me alone and do not trouble my spirit with such things."

Venturing another step toward the bed, Jeanne was intercepted by the physician. "You should do as he says, my lady. Go and leave him to make peace with his God. I've sent for the priest."

Jeanne hesitated then turned on her heel and strode from the room. But not before she shot a withering look at the Montforts. Charles followed in her wake.

Having stood quietly at the foot of the bed during all the drama, John de Montfort stepped forward and took his brother's hand. "Rest in peace, dear brother. I will see your legacy preserved." When the priest entered the room, Montfort's wife took his arm and they stepped into the corridor without another word.

As the Montforts approached the top of the stairs, Jeanne stopped in her tracks. "What is it, my dear? Is something wrong?" her husband asked.

"It just occurred to me. Perhaps we should speak with Monsieur Bourhis."

"The lawyer?"

"Yes. Just to be sure of our position."

"Surely that can wait."

"John, you know how inconstant your brother's been over the succession. What if his pronouncement in there was just his latest whim and not something thought out beforehand? It's not out of the question he sent for the lawyer to create the new will on the spot. What's to say he didn't just make up that bit about having decided before he left for Tournai as a way to appease his niece? We need to know if we're to know how to act."

Her insistence was no surprise. Montfort had long known his wife's resolve was unshakeable when she deemed something important. In truth, he knew when he agreed to marry her that her father had faced something of a challenge in finding a match for his daughter. More than one man had withdrawn his suit after spending some time in the company of Jeanne de Flandre, declaring her willful and unlikely to ever be a proper, obedient wife. It was said that Jeanne herself had refused an equal number of prospects, labeling them variously weak-minded, boorish, a coxcomb, or, in the case of one unfortunate fellow, a complete cumberworld.

The old count had died in 1322, two months before his own father, leaving his daughter still unmarried and his son, Louis, the heir to two titles – Count of Nevers and Count of Flanders – and responsibility for his sister. So when word reached him that the Count of Montfort was seeking a wife,

Louis dared hope that this would be the right opportunity for Jeanne. It might, in fact, be her last chance.

"My father often said he had no one to blame but himself for the difficulties in securing a marriage for my sister," Louis had told Montfort on the evening when they sat down to a serious discussion of a betrothal over some of the count's fine brandy. "Much of this happened before I was born or when I was too young to be aware of things, so what I know is from the stories Father told. It seems that, when Jeanne was about five years old, Father paid a visit to the nursery one day and found her playing with a toy sword. Her nurse was scandalized and begged him to take the toy away. But he found the sight of a little girl playing at sword-fighting in her skirts rather amusing, so he told the nurse to let her be. I think perhaps he was, at that time, beginning to despair of ever having a son and so took some pleasure in spoiling his daughter.

"As Jeanne got older, Mother wanted her to read tales of courtly love, her tutors wanted her to read the Roman poets, but *she* wanted to read the *Chanson de Roland* and the exploits of the Crusaders. Father saw no harm in it, so he indulged her, and they had many a conversation about those long-ago battles and skirmishes. Mother, on the other hand, believed Jeanne's time would be far better spent learning the womanly arts if she was to make a good marriage. Father once opined to me that perhaps he should have acquiesced. But as I wasn't yet old enough to leave the nursery, he once again indulged Jeanne's insistence that she would only learn needlework and how to run a household if she could spend equal time pursuing whatever interest she chose for herself."

"That sounds like a fair bargain," Montfort had remarked.

Louis chuckled. "Apparently, Father thought so too. But Mother took it as an opportunity for a stern lecture on the merits of obedience in a wife and the importance that Jeanne look to her future marriage prospects rather than her current whims. I think it was around that time – maybe even as a result of that lecture – that she began to understand that different people required different tactics. Father said she quickly became quite adept at taking the measure of a person and deciding how best to deal with them."

"Well," Montfort said, "I haven't spent thirty-four years on this earth without acquiring some of that skill myself."

This time Louis had actually laughed aloud. "Nor I, my friend. But I rather think neither of us learned it at such a tender age."

"A man could do worse than having an astute wife as his closest advisor. Someone he knows he can trust without having to question their motives. Someone he can trust with the running of his affairs when events require him to be away from his estate. Someone he can converse with about things more consequential than a dropped stitch or the cook's shortcomings. Truth be told, I'm intrigued by your sister's mind and quite enjoy our lively conversations. Such a companion for a cold winter's evening would actually make a man's life far more pleasant, to my way of thinking."

"Are you forgetting, Montfort, that she's also seen thirty-four summers? She may be past her childbearing years. Aren't you concerned about having an heir?"

It was Montfort's turn to chuckle. "She's been quite forthcoming about that. Assures me in some detail that there's no reason we can't have children."

Louis rolled his eyes to the ceiling then smiled at the man seated across from him. "Holy mother of God." It wasn't an epithet but a sigh of resignation. "I suppose I shouldn't be surprised. Mother would be rolling in her grave."

"She's also told me she rides astride and the story of how she came to do so."

"Ah, yes. That, unfortunately, falls at my feet. When it came time for me to learn to ride, I was . . . shall we say, reluctant. Sure I'd fall off and break my neck. But I adored my sister and would do anything she asked, so when she promised to learn alongside me, that's all it took for me to overcome my anxiety and climb into the saddle. Another skill her mother abhorred, but one I fancy could stand her in good stead someday. And speaking of skills her mother abhorred, has she also told you she knows how to wield a sword?"

"From her nursery play?"

"From me, I fear. When I began learning, she begged me to teach her. Said it was fair recompense for her helping me with horsemanship. And, of course, I couldn't refuse her. But the day Mother came across us practicing swordplay in the garden, she almost had an apoplexy. And for once, Father took Mother's side. We both had to promise faithfully to give up the pursuit, but somehow, Jeanne managed to find places we could practice in secret from time to time. I was terrified we'd be caught, but she seemed to live an enchanted life, and no one ever saw us. Father, thankfully, never dared ask."

Montfort rested his chin on steepled fingers, apparently deep in thought, then reached for his brandy glass. Taking a sip, he remarked, "If we're to be brothers-in-law, then perhaps I'll get to enjoy this stuff more often."

"Are you saying, Montfort, that, despite everything I've told you, you still wish to take my sister to wife?"

"I'm saying I think we're a good match. We're the same age, we seem to enjoy each other's company, and I can think of no reason why she'd have cause to wield a sword as Countess of Montfort. Not only that, I find her quite beautiful."

"Beautiful? That's not a word I've ever heard used to describe my sister. In fact, most of the suitors who declined to marry her called her unattractive."

"Did you ever consider, Louis, that might have been just an additional excuse to refuse her hand?" Montfort sipped his brandy again before continuing. "Oh, she might not be the ravishing beauty that men languish and die for in the troubadours' songs, but then again, I have no interest in languishing or dying. Her face is comely enough, but her eyes. They're warm when she seems happy, you can see in them the depth of her thoughts, they sparkle when something catches her fancy ... and I can only imagine how they must flash if she's roused to anger. Some men might want a waif that reminds them of a girl-child, but I don't. So what if she isn't a full head shorter than me. I don't measure her beauty by whether or not I can look down on her."

"Then, if you're certain, John, it would be my pleasure to call you brother-in-law."

"Now I just have to hope she doesn't refuse me."

"If she dares, I'll simply have to order her to wed."

Montfort laughed aloud. "I think you and I both know, Louis, that *that* would be a losing proposition."

When they married, neither had expected anything beyond contented lives as the Count and Countess of Montfort. Now, twelve years later, with a young son and a baby daughter, to find themselves heirs to the Duchy of Brittany was quite a surprise.

But Montfort wasn't at all surprised by the fact that his wife had questions about the apparent change of fortune that had just landed in their laps. In the years of their marriage, he'd learned that satisfying her concern was the fastest path to restoring life to its normal rhythm, so he didn't hesitate to respond, "Very well. If it will put your mind at rest."

They stood facing one another, leaning against opposite walls of the corridor, studying their feet, their hands, the patterns on the floor made by the light from the small window at the opposite end, shifting their weight now and again from one leg to the other. At one point, Jeanne straightened her posture and smoothed her skirts, almost as though preparing to march back into the room to speak to the lawyer. But not a word passed between them. When it seemed as if they'd run out of ways to fidget, the door finally opened and Monsieur Bourhis made his way down the corridor toward them. John stepped away from the wall. "A word if you please, monsieur?"

"As you wish, my lord duke." Bourhis gave a small bow of his head.

"A bit premature for that, is it not?" John replied.

"Alas, your brother breathed his last but moments ago, so my words are in no way misspoken."

"Then all the more reason we should speak now," said Jeanne.

"Perhaps somewhere more private would be in order," said Bourhis. "Your lodgings, perhaps, my lord?"

"Follow us." John took his wife's arm and led the lawyer down the stairs, into the street, and past the market square to a small inn where the landlord had been only too happy to evict all his guests so the count and countess might have the upper floor to themselves. Once the threesome had settled in the small sitting room and the fawning landlord had made his exit after delivering a pitcher of wine and glasses, John came straight to the point. "My brother spoke of a new will, Monsieur Bourhis. A surprise to me. Even more of a surprise, I think, to others in the room."

"He did, sir. And it names you as his heir. Unequivocally. You inherit the title, the duchy, his property, and all his possessions. As from this moment."

"Just as important, monsieur, did he make the will before leaving for Tournai, as he said?" Jeanne asked.

"As he said, my lady. After all, a man doesn't leave for war without having his affairs in order." The lawyer turned his attention back to John. The sort of dismissive gesture that infuriated Jeanne, typical of almost every man she encountered. "Even more important, I venture to suggest, sir," Bourhis continued, "he reached his decision with the agreement of his most important advisors, so one must presume you will have their support."

"And the legal position is sound?"

"In both French law and Breton custom, sir. I cannot say your inheritance won't be challenged. It was clear the Countess of Penthièvre was much dismayed by her change of fortune. But as you are a living, direct male descendant of your father, your claim takes precedence over that of any woman. Even if the countess should decide to mount a challenge, it seems unlikely she would prevail. The Breton custom only permits a woman to succeed in the absence of a legitimate male heir, and French practice is even more restrictive."

"Very well, Bourhis, it seems the matter is settled."

"What about the burial arrangements?" Jeanne asked.

"Previously arranged, my lady, by the late duke himself. He's to be interred at the abbey in Ploërmel. I shall make arrangements for transport of the body and send the necessary invitations to the nobles to attend the burial. Now . . ." He turned his attention back to John. ". . . if there's nothing else, my lord duke?"

John downed the remaining wine in his glass, then refilled it and raised it in a toast. "Only this. To my brother." The others followed suit before the lawyer gathered his satchel and scurried out the door.

Montfort rose, walked to the fireplace, and rested an elbow on the mantel. "Satisfied?" he asked his wife.

"That your brother took the proper steps? Yes. That the inheritance is legitimately yours? Yes. But Bourhis is right. We *will* be challenged."

"You seem quite certain."

"I know Jeanne."

Montfort chuckled. "Hardly well. You meet on formal occasions, yes, but your acquaintance is not of the familiar sort."

"I know her. And I know her type. Right now, she's consumed with anger at being denied what she'd come to believe was her birthright. As the anger subsides, she'll start scheming to get it back. So there's one thing you must do straightaway – this afternoon."

"And what might that be?"

"Take possession of the ducal banner. Now, before anyone else thinks of it. So that when we leave here, we travel as the legitimate rulers of Brittany."

Montfort swallowed the last of the wine in his glass and made for the table where the pitcher stood, apparently intending to pour himself a refill.

"Now, John," his wife repeated. "Trust me on this. It's important."

He hesitated, then set his empty glass on the table beside the pitcher. "Perhaps you're right, my dear."

When the door closed behind him, Jeanne spoke to his retreating footsteps. "I know I'm right. And you know it too."

CHAPTER TWO

If Jeanne slept at all that night, she was hardly aware of it. She rose not long after sunrise – much to her maid's surprise – with her mind finally settled on the course of action they must take. All that remained was to persuade John of the merits of her plan, and that, she knew how to do. She also knew that, once he embraced it, he would execute it flawlessly. *He may not always be the most astute about the politics of a thing*, she thought to herself, *but once he's shown the lay of the land, there's no one I'd rather have on my side.*

By her side was where she wanted him at the moment, so she could apprise him of everything she'd thought through during the night, but he seemed in no hurry to start his day. She'd moved from the room that served as her bedchamber into the little sitting room that overlooked the street, but couldn't settle. Pacing back and forth beside the window, she went over everything one more time to be sure she had it right. Once she laid things out for John – once he understood her strategy – things would be in motion, and then it would be up to her to watch how the game played out. The little nuances that would tell her what their opponent's next move might be.

Just as she was contemplating sending for the manservant and asking him to wake her husband, John stepped through the door. "At last," she said.

"And God's good morning to you too, my dear."

Much as she wanted to chide him for spending too much time abed, she didn't want to get this day off on the wrong foot – too much was at stake. So she smiled and offered him her cheek for a kiss, which he dutifully supplied.

Not that it was really a duty to Montfort – he had a true affection for his wife. She was as beautiful as she was wealthy and thus a fine match for any man. That her brother was the Count of Flanders gave John connections far beyond his own in the Loire valley – connections that also gave him a buffer against the ambitions of the French king. But his affection for Jeanne went deeper than the advantages she brought to the marriage – he might even call it love. He was keenly aware she often used that affection to her own advantage, but, over the years, he'd developed a strong appreciation for her acumen and had learned to trust her instincts. And in his heart of hearts, he knew she cared for him too because she always used her insights to further his position.

"Would I be right in thinking your early start means you've much on your mind?" he asked.

"You know me too well, John."

"Then let's hear it all before you burst with the effort of holding it back." He sat in the nearest chair as she dragged another across the room so she could sit directly opposite him.

"I've been thinking all night about what we need to do – about how to make sure your position is unassailable. We need to make straight for Nantes without delay and establish ourselves in the ducal castle. You should send for your men-at-arms to meet us along the way so we arrive at the city just as your brother would have returned from his campaign."

"Aren't you forgetting something?"

"What?"

"My brother's burial. If I fail to appear there, then I forfeit all legitimacy to the title. That doesn't seem wise."

"Then we delay the burial."

"I think that's out of our hands. Monsieur Bourhis was quite clear yesterday that he'd been placed in charge of the arrangements. What difference will a couple of days make? Especially when I'll be seen showing respect for my predecessor."

"Very well. You make a good point. But we don't dally after the burial. We make straight for Nantes and your men-at-arms can meet us during that part of the journey." She paused and wrinkled her nose. "Though who will accompany us to Ploërmel?"

"You'll be pleased to know I already have that in hand. When I took possession of the banner yesterday, I also took possession of my brother's men-at-arms. Well, most of them anyway. I told them I was the new duke and offered them all the chance to transfer their allegiance and remain in my employ. Most accepted, so we have a contingent of a hundred men in our service already."

Jeanne clapped her hands. "Brilliant, my dear. So to Ploërmel then on to Nantes and by the time we reach the city, you'll have at least two hundred men at your disposal should we encounter any resistance from the officialdom there. Though we mustn't provoke them. Invite their homage. If they give it willingly, then you can have some amount of assurance of their loyalty. And the longer they're loyal, the stronger your position."

"Somehow I sense that's not all that's on your mind."

Jeanne looked at her hands in her lap. She'd already decided there was no need to overwhelm him with her entire plan at once. They'd have five days on the journey to Ploërmel for her to lay out the rest, and it would be easier for him to see the wisdom of her strategy if she painted the picture bit by bit. But there was one more thing that would be essential if everything else was to succeed. She looked up, straight into his eyes. "The ducal treasury. With that in our possession, we have the means to secure your position. And we must be sure we have all of it, no matter where your brother may have hidden bits away for safekeeping."

"And you think that might not come to us automatically?"

"You have to be sure, John. Sure no one else can get their hands on it."

Montfort placed his hands on his knees, a sure sign he was ready to rise from his chair. "How soon can you be ready to travel, my dear? We don't want to arrive late for the burial, and I've no doubt Bourhis has the transport of the body well underway by now."

"Does an hour from now suit you?"

John rose. "It will take me longer than that to get the men organized and the rest of our business attended to. Let's say midday."

• • • • •

A week later, the good people of Nantes had their morning routine interrupted by the arrival at the Porte Sauvetout of what looked like a small army. They rode three-abreast, and there was a richly decorated carriage among their ranks. The man in the center of the front rank wore a jupon bearing the arms of the Duke of Brittany as did the man to his right. To his left, the soldier wore the arms of the Count of Montfort. Standard bearers in the second rank carried the colors of both Brittany and Montfort. The column halted just outside the gate. "We'll not storm the town," Montfort had told his captains – those who rode on either side of him. "Better I accept their homage and we enter peacefully."

It took the better part of half an hour for the city officialdom to make their appearance. Eleven men in full ceremonial garb accompanied by twice as many men-at-arms as a modest show of strength, though no one would actually believe they stood a chance against the force waiting patiently outside the city walls. "By whose authority do you present yourself here under the ducal banner?" asked the man who was obviously the mayor.

"By the authority of our late, well-loved duke who, in his will, named me as his successor," said Montfort.

"And what proof do you have of this claim?"

"I'm given to understand, sir, by my late brother's lawyer that the will was properly drawn and witnessed and has been registered according to the law. In which case, you should be able to determine the proof you require from within your own records."

"And who is this lawyer you speak of?"

"Monsieur Bourhis. Who undoubtedly will return here on the morrow or the day after, once he's seen to the remaining details of the late duke's burial."

The mayor exchanged looks with a man behind him, who gave an almost imperceptible nod of his head. *Confirmation I speak the truth?* Montfort wondered. He hadn't expected this degree of hesitancy, though he understood the man's dilemma. If the city opened its gates and gave homage to an impostor, it could be the beginning of another bloody conflict that would be catastrophic for the prosperity Nantes enjoyed from the salt and wine trade and the tolls they collected for passage on the Loire. Time to give the man more assurances.

"*Monsieur le maire*, allow me to offer further proof of my authority. Among my men are many who will be known in the town. They departed with Duke John months ago to join King Philip's forces at Tournai and were returning with their master after the siege was lifted. When he died in Caen and was unable to lead them home, I offered them the opportunity to transfer their allegiance to me. Most did so. All who did, did so of their own free will, including Captain Kerveil here." He gestured to the man on his right.

"My lord speaks the truth, sir." Kerveil's deep voice was perfectly suited to his erect, military bearing and the scar on his cheek that said he'd earned his rank in actual battle.

"And the others?" The mayor pointed to the third man in the front rank.

"Durant – captain of my own loyal retainers who have peaceably joined with the ducal forces." The relaxed way Durant sat his horse and his complacent countenance might lead one to think he posed no threat, but Montfort knew there was strength of body and mind behind that calm demeanor and there was no one he'd rather have at his side if lives were at stake.

The mayor turned his back to the mounted men and huddled in conversation with the others, but they kept their voices low so it was impossible to discern anything beyond occasional hand gestures and nodding or shaking of heads. In due course, the mayor faced Montfort once again. "You and your men will remain where you are while I confer with my colleagues. We've much to discuss, and it's best we do so in private and not in the open air for any passerby to listen at their whim."

"We look forward to your return and your warm welcome to this fair city," said Montfort. *No reason not to plant the seed in the mayor's mind that we want his compliance.*

The cathedral bells tolled midday and still the mayor had not returned. The horses were growing restive from standing in one place for so long, so

Montfort gave permission for the men to dismount and walk the animals around a bit to relieve the boredom. He gave his own reins to Kerveil and walked back to the carriage, expecting to find Jeanne in a frenzy over the delay. Her cheerful "How nice of you to come keep me company" through the carriage window took him completely aback. "Would you like to join me in here where it's comfortable?" she asked.

He leaned on the window sill. "I'll stay outside. Easier to dash back to the front if I'm needed, though God knows when *that* will be. I thought I'd find you biting your nails with impatience."

Jeanne gave a little laugh. "I'll admit this isn't what I expected. But it's just a matter of time before they invite us in."

"You seem quite sure of that."

"Oh, they'd have closed the gates in our faces long before now if they weren't intending to admit us eventually. We'll sleep in the ducal castle tonight, my dear. Of that I have no doubt. And we'll do so with the town having declared their loyalty."

Montfort chuckled and shook his head from side to side. "You are really quite a marvel, Jeanne de Montfort. Most men would not know what to do with you."

"That's why I didn't marry just any man." She beamed and reached out the window to squeeze his hand. "Now, back to the front rank. You want to be exactly where they left you – sitting splendidly astride your horse – when those officials return."

Which they didn't do for another three hours. The bell in the nearby convent was tolling Nones when the delegation finally reappeared at the gate. "My lord duke," the mayor began, and the entire delegation doffed their hats and offered a bow. "My lord duke, the city of Nantes welcomes you. We offer you our homage on the presumption . . ." The man standing next to him nudged the mayor with his elbow. ". . . the condition, if you like – that the king will, in due course, recognize and affirm your claim. Our garrison is at your disposal for the housing of your men, and the staff at the castle has been alerted to your imminent arrival. I am Monsieur Allaire, and my colleagues and I would be pleased to receive you at the Hôtel de Ville at your pleasure." The entire delegation bowed once again.

"I accept your pledge of loyalty, Monsieur Allaire, and trust you will find us much similar to the late duke, my half-brother." The delegation stepped to the side of the street as Montfort raised his right hand above his head and signaled for the column to advance.

They were met in the entrance hall of the castle by what, to all appearances, was the entire staff. "Henri, my lord duke. Your steward." The man front-and-center of the assemblage was of average height, with a long face and a closely trimmed beard that came to a point at the tip of his chin. His long nose might have given the impression he was always looking down it in condescension had it not been for the kindness in his eyes and a demeanor that somehow conveyed authority and deference simultaneously. The steward bowed low then added, "I presume you shall be occupying the ducal apartments?"

"My wife will be in charge of household arrangements, Henri. You may take your instructions from her."

"As you wish, sir. My lady?"

"My trunks are in the carriage and the rest of what we have with us is in a small wagon at the back of the column. Please see that it's all unpacked, Henri. And yes, in the duke's private quarters. My maid will oversee the arrangement of my things. We can discuss the ordering of household affairs in the morning. It's been quite a long day."

"Yes, madame." He clapped his hands and most everyone else scurried away, the formalities having been attended to. "The evening meal will be served an hour after sundown in the dining hall. I'll send someone to fetch you and show you the way."

"If it's not too much trouble, Henri," said Jeanne, "might we dine earlier? We've none of us eaten at all today since the time for a midday meal came and went while we waited at the gate."

"I shall speak to the cook straightaway, my lady. If that's all for now?"

"Thank you, Henri. You may go."

He bowed smartly and did his own, somewhat more elegant version of scurrying away. Which left the duke and duchess alone in the entrance hall save for one man, who looked as if he had dined often and liberally from the late duke's largesse. The scarcity of hair above his shoulders paired with the profusion of fat below contrived to make his head look abnormally small. "If you please, my lord, allow me to show you to the duke's study." He inclined his head and gestured toward the corridor straight ahead.

Jeanne took her husband's arm as they made their way down the corridor led by their corpulent guide who kept up a constant banter. "My name is Raoul de Chartres and I'm the duke's personal secretary. Or rather I *was* the *late* duke's personal secretary. I'm familiar with all his affairs ... which, of course, will now be your affairs. I also kept his accounts ... which, of course, will now be your accounts. He trusted me to ensure everything was in order. With the exception of the household accounts, that is, which he assigned to the steward ... and which, of course, you will now oversee, my lady." He opened a door on the left and ushered them into a room where a large writing table sat in front of an equally large window that filled the room with light. Along one wall, shelves and cubicles held an array of scrolls, what appeared to be account ledgers, and various books. An elaborately carved mantelpiece graced the opposite wall, with comfortable seating arranged before it. "The duke's study, my lord. I trust you will find everything in order."

"I think, Raoul," said Montfort, "it will be easier to make that determination once you've given me a detailed accounting of the duke's affairs. So to that end, I trust you will stay on in your current position?"

"It would be my honor, sir. A very great honor indeed, my lord. One I can in no way refuse. Thank you, my lord."

"Very well, Raoul. For now, I'd just like to get the feel of the room. We can start in the morning – say, an hour past the cock's crow?"

"I ... that ... that's quite early, my lord. Quite early indeed."

"You have objections, Raoul? We've much to cover, so it seems to me the sooner we start, the sooner I'll know that things are in order."

The flustered secretary rushed to cover his blunder. "No objections at all, sir. None at all. An hour past the cock's crow, as you say."

"Then that will be all, Raoul. Until tomorrow."

"Of course, my lord." Raoul repeated the phrase with every bow as he backed out of the room and closed the door behind him.

"That man has turned fawning into an art form," said Jeanne when they could no longer hear footsteps in the corridor.

Montfort chuckled. "A strange one indeed. I only hope he doesn't find it necessary to tell me everything three or four times."

"Are you sure keeping him on is wise, John?"

"Well, unless you know someone else familiar with my brother's affairs, I seem to have little choice."

"For the moment, I suppose that's true. All that fawning, though. I wonder what he has to hide. Has he been feathering his own nest? Or is he just the biggest sycophant that ever walked the face of the earth?"

"I'm sure I'll know soon enough."

"There's something else to keep in mind."

"What's that?"

"His name. De Chartres. That means he's French. Was he truly your brother's man or does he have other loyalties?"

"That may take longer to work out."

"Until we do, we can't let our guard down. Your brother kept you at arm's length from his court for so many years, we don't know the ins and outs of how he navigated Brittany's relationship with the French Crown. But I shudder to think a French spy might have been in his inner circle."

"Let's not get ahead of ourselves, Jeanne."

"Neither should we let others get ahead of *us*."

Montfort smiled and shook his head in amusement. "No one will ever get ahead of you, my dear. Of that, I'm certain."

CHAPTER THREE

The scene that greeted Jeanne when she walked into the duke's study the next morning was a far cry from the time she'd just spent with Henri reviewing the management of the household. Henri's meticulous ledgers were kept in bound folios, his handwriting clear and easily legible. Separate folios contained the household inventories. "Which we verify once a year, madame," he'd told her, "by locating each item to be certain it's still in the duke's possession." In his strongbox with a sturdy lock were cloth sacks of silver coins, a different color cloth for each denomination, and leather bags for the gold florins. "I count the money at the end of each month to be sure it tallies with the ledger – before receiving and recording my next allowance from the duke's personal funds and from the ducal treasury. It has never been anything other than accurate, my lady. Though how it could be otherwise is beyond my ken as I have the only key, which remains around my neck . . ." He'd pulled a chain from inside his shirt to show her the key. ". . . day and night."

By contrast, what covered the duke's writing table appeared to be utter chaos. Loose pages, partially unrolled scrolls, two folios – one held open by a mazer that she prayed to God was empty and not half-full of ale and the other by her husband's dagger. A bag of coins spilled open on top of the papers – *deniers, sous, livres,* florins – all mixed with no apparent regard for keeping track of the value of the bag's contents. And on the floor at one side of the table, a large box with no obvious means of securing it filled with more sacks of money that she could only imagine were all as randomly filled as the one lying on the table top.

She stepped inside and closed the door softly behind her. "You're telling me, Raoul," Montfort was saying, "that you don't remember the last time you counted the money? How do you have any idea that what's here . . ." He pointed to the box on the floor then waved a hand over the mayhem spread all over the table. ". . . in any way matches what's on these pages?"

"My accounts are most accurate, sir, as you can see. Everything recorded. There can be no doubt that all is in order. The duke doesn't concern himself with such things. That's my job."

"Well, this duke *does* concern himself with such things." He glanced up briefly, acknowledging Jeanne's presence. "And since counting the coins doesn't seem to be to your liking, I'll have my wife do the counting, and then you can prepare a reconciliation with all of . . . this." Again, a wave of the hand over the disordered array on the table.

"It will hardly be necessary to involve your wife, my lord. Surely my lady's children will be arriving soon and her time will be fully occupied with their care."

Jeanne had quietly approached the table while Raoul's gaze was focused on his master. "Our children are safe in the care of their nurse, de Chartres. I shall send for them, of course, once we're well settled here. But even then, how I occupy my time is *not* a matter for you to concern yourself with."

Startled, Raoul jumped to his feet, doffed his cap, and bowed. "My lady, I didn't know you had joined us." Cap returned to his head, he continued, "Surely, I . . . I meant no offense."

Montfort lowered his chin and looked up at his wife from below his brow. Jeanne knew that look. It was his signal not to wake the sleeping hound. But something about de Chartres prickled the hairs on the back of her neck . . . enough that she didn't think it wise to allow him to feel too comfortable in his sinecure until they had taken the full measure of him. So she ignored his half-hearted apology and addressed herself to John. "I'd be happy to count the coins for you, my dear. After all, it seems only prudent to know precisely what resources we have before we start making plans for the duchy. I can assure you Henri has the household accounts and inventories in excellent order." She knew John was cringing at her subtle pitting of one senior servant against another, but it would serve to keep Raoul on his guard while they worked out where his loyalties lay.

"Thank you, my dear," said Montfort

"Shall I begin now?"

"As you wish." Then he turned to Raoul, who was trying hard not to fidget in his chair. "What you might not know, de Chartres, is that my wife is wealthy in her own right, so she's quite accustomed to dealing with financial matters. In fact, we share the management of the Comté de Montfort."

Dear, sweet John, thought Jeanne. *Keeping the peace for now. All in good time, de Chartres, all in good time. But I'll not trust you straightway.* Aloud, she said, "Is this the entirety of the treasury, Raoul? These sacks of coins."

His hesitation was exceedingly brief, but it didn't escape Jeanne's notice. "Ah . . . no, my lady. The plate and the gemstones . . . well, the gemstones that aren't part of the duchess's jewelry and the duke's crown . . . well, that would be your jewelry now, my lady . . ." A funny little nod of his head by way of a bow. ". . . in any event, the plate and the gems are kept at the cathedral. The duke . . . my apologies, my lord . . ." The same little nod toward Montfort. ". . . the late duke your half-brother, sir, thought that a safer place than here at the castle."

"Then here's what we're going to do," said Montfort. "Raoul, leave all this here." He gestured to the array on the tabletop. "We'll get back to it later. In the meantime, summon two servants to carry this box up to my bedchamber. Then after the midday meal, the duchess and I will go to the cathedral to inspect that portion of the treasury. And she can count the coins on the morrow."

"But, sir, with all due respect, is moving this box to your apartment really safe? Anyone could steal a few coins – a whole sack even – when you're not there."

"And where is the box normally kept?"

"Why, under my bed, sir. Day and night."

"And how is that any safer?" asked Montfort. "Surely you don't spend all of both your waking and sleeping hours in your bedchamber. And I see no way of locking the box."

"I do not, sir. But when the box is in my room, it's wrapped in a chain and secured to my bed. Someone would have to steal the bed to steal the box . . . and I rather think that might be noticed."

Jeanne struggled mightily to suppress a laugh, but couldn't avoid glancing at her husband and catching the sparkle in his eye that said he was equally amused and appalled. Nevertheless, he managed to keep his voice on an even keel. "Summon the servants, Raoul. My squire will stand guard until the count is complete."

Their meal finished, Montfort summoned Captain Durant, and the three of them made the short walk to the cathedral. The carvings above the entrance were not particularly noteworthy, but inside, the tympanum above the portal leading from the narthex to the nave was as elaborate as any Jeanne had ever seen, depicting Jesus sending the apostles out into the world to spread His gospel and all manner of fantastical men and women occupying that outer world in the lintel and in the surround of the main image. The builders had adopted the Norman style of replacing the tribune with a triforum, or narrow walkway, but the nave was no less majestic and evocative of man's aspiration to heaven. As the trio made their way toward the chancel, a priest emerged from the north transept. "It's our custom, monsieur," he addressed Montfort but gestured toward Captain Durant, who was wearing his sword, "that weapons aren't allowed within these holy precincts."

"I assure you, Father, our intentions are entirely peaceful. We've come to see the bishop."

"Alas, he's away and not expected to return for at least a week. I'm Canon Gregoire. Perhaps I can be of service."

Montfort took Jeanne's hand. "We're the new duke and duchess of Brittany."

"Ah, yes, I'd heard of your arrival but was not expecting to see you until mass on the Sabbath. What brings you here now, sir?"

"My secretary – well, my late brother's secretary, whose services I've retained for now – informs me that much of the ducal treasury is kept here in the cathedral. We wish to claim it on behalf of the duchy and return it to the castle where, in my opinion, it should properly be housed and secured."

"Your secretary is correct, of course. Come with me to the vestry." As they followed in his footsteps, the canon added, "I think you'll find everything in order, sir."

"Is there an inventory of the items entrusted to the bishop's care, Canon?" asked Jeanne.

"I believe that would be kept at the castle, madame."

If there even is such a thing in that mess Raoul calls records, thought Jeanne.

"This way, please." The canon stepped aside for them to enter the vestry then closed the door and crossed to the far wall where four identical chests stood side by side, none with any lock or visible means of securing them. "These two," he gestured to those on the left, "contain the vestments and other articles used in the mass. These," he opened the remaining two in turn, "house the items of the ducal treasury."

"And yet there are no locks? No means of securing those items?" Jeanne could barely keep the incredulity from her tone.

"This is a house of God, madame. We do not lock things away."

Jeanne and John stepped over to gaze into the chests. One was entirely filled with silver plate – chargers, platters, pitchers, goblets, eating knives, and spoons. The other held more goblets – these made of gold, some of them bejeweled – a silver ceremonial helmet adorned with a gold circlet resembling a coronet and indicating the duke's rank, and several caskets of varying size. Montfort opened one, revealing a collection of gemstones, cut and ready to be mounted.

John turned his attention back to the priest. "Very well. We'll move this back to the castle straightaway."

Anxiety swept in a wave across the canon's face. "But, sir, with the bishop absent, I have no authority to permit anything to be taken away."

"I'm the only authority that's required."

"But, sir ... I ... what will I tell the bishop?"

"These items were placed here by order of the Duke of Brittany. The Duke of Brittany is now ordering their removal. It's my right – my duty, even – to take possession of the treasury and see that it's secured."

The prelate seemed to shrink in stature in the face of Montfort's declaration. "Very well, sir. Whatever you wish."

"Then wait here, please, while I give instructions to Captain Durant and his men." Montfort made for the door and paused to hold it open for Jeanne to pass through. Turning back to Gregoire, he asked, "And you give me your assurance that this is all of the treasury that's not secured at the castle?"

It seemed to Jeanne that the canon shrank even further as he hesitated briefly before replying. "All that's not at Limoges."

When John joined her in the passageway, she whispered under her breath, "I wonder when Raoul was going to mention *that*."

"Indeed," was her husband's only reply. They walked back down the nave, with Durant following behind. "We'll wait in the vestry while you go get some men and a cart to haul all that stuff back to the castle," Montfort addressed the captain. "I don't want that canon deciding to help the Church to some of the treasure."

"What shall we transport it in, sir? We can't just take those chests too."

"My traveling trunks," Jeanne chimed in. "They can be locked and would be hard for anyone on the street to try to make off with. In fact, what do you think, John, of just leaving it in my trunks? Then, if we should ever have reason to change residences, it will already be packed in preparation."

"And what would you do for your belongings?" asked her husband.

"I think I have enough money to buy new trunks, dear." She gave Montfort a loving smile.

"It seems my wife has hit on a good plan, Durant. When you get the trunks back to the castle, take them straight to her room."

That evening, in the privacy of the ducal apartment, with the cash stowed in Montfort's bedchamber and Jeanne's trunks secured in hers, she turned the conversation to the remaining portion of the treasury in Limoges. "You really have little choice, John. You have to lay claim to it immediately." When his only reply was to take another sip from his glass of wine, she added, "Before someone else does."

"You mean before the other Jeanne does."

"Or Philip."

"And that's part of the problem, don't you see?" Jeanne cocked her head and looked at him quizzically. "Limoges is deep in French territory," he continued. "Philip could get to it just as easily as I can. If he hasn't already. All he need do is order some of his forces currently in Gascony to stop by Limoges on their way back to Paris and bring the treasure to him."

Now it was Jeanne's turn to sip her wine in thought. "In truth, John," she said eventually, "I'm less concerned about Philip than about the countess. If she has any of the ducal treasury in her possession, I've no doubt she'd use it as evidence that your brother had intended all along that she inherit. She might even assert he'd given it to her on that day he extracted the pledge from Charles to defend Brittany." Another thoughtful sip of wine. "Not to mention the resources it would give her to hire an army to dispute your claim."

Montfort smiled. "My dear, I think maybe you're getting ahead of even yourself at this point. What makes you think the countess even knows that part of the treasury is at Limoges? I'm not even sure Raoul knows about it. I had another look at his so-called records before joining you for the evening meal and couldn't find any mention of it."

"And what makes you think there aren't more of those so-called records than what he's shown you? It's far too soon to rely entirely on him. The wise move, John, is to take possession of the remainder of the treasury straightaway."

"What about the other wise move you've been pressing me about?" Another quizzical cock of Jeanne's head. "Securing the homage of all the Breton nobles. I can't be here to do that and collect the Limoges treasury all at the same time."

"You don't have to. How long is the journey to Limoges? Less than a week, I think."

"Five days at least. More likely six. Even more if the weather turns sour."

"So a week there and a week back. It will take that long to send the invitations to our nobility and for them to travel here. That settles it. You retrieve the rest of the treasury, and I'll attend to the arrangements for the accession ceremony."

Montfort shook his head and rolled his eyes – but with a smile on his face. His wife was clearly enjoying herself. "Very well, we'll do it your way," he said. "But just one thing. I'll not ride with a small army – just a few men for protection."

"But—"

"No buts. If the Limougeauds do homage and surrender the treasury, then we can be confident in that outlying part of my inheritance. But if they offer resistance, I won't fight. Not that deep in Philip's territory. No matter how many men I might have, we'd be no match for a French army. And every noble in Brittany would support Charles and Jeanne over a boy who's not yet two years old." Their son might be the heir presumptive, but he was as yet a toddler.

"You make a good point, my dear," Jeanne acquiesced.

．　．　．　．　．

As Montfort headed south, Jeanne ventured into Raoul's domain. She found him sitting at the duke's writing table fretting with the records spread on the desk – stacking a few pages, moving them to the side, aligning others in a row on the center of the table, changing his mind and stacking those as well, retrieving the first set and arranging them in three neat columns at one end of the table like an army about to march over a cliff. So intent was he that he didn't notice her until she was halfway across the room . . . and then, like a startled deer, he bolted from the chair and retreated from the table, bowing with each backward step. "Good morning, my lady. Forgive me, my lady, I didn't hear the door. I . . . I . . . wasn't expecting you, my lady."

"Calm yourself, de Chartres. There's no need to fret." Raoul stopped his retreat and took one tentative step back toward the writing table. "I need your help," Jeanne continued.

"Help with counting the coins, my lady?"

"I'll attend to that momentarily. Right now, there's something else we need to get underway. The duke and I intend to host a celebration of his accession, and we must invite all the nobles. *They* will offer their homage, and *we* will give them three days of feasting and entertainments to celebrate everything Breton. So I need you to prepare the invitations and arrange for them to be delivered. The homage ceremony on May 30th – that will be one month to the day since the old duke's passing – and the celebrations on the three days following."

"And this is what the duke wants, my lady?"

"Of course it is. Why would you ask?"

"Well...I...I'm accustomed to taking my instructions from the duke."

"The duke is away, attending to business in other parts of our domains, and he's left me in charge. So you'll take your instructions from me."

"Very well, my lady. As you wish. And then, I presume, you'll want me to organize the celebrations?"

"I've already spoken with Henri and he has that well in hand." Raoul couldn't prevent a scowl from coming to his face at the mention of Henri's name, so Jeanne decided to toss him a bone. "Food and entertainment is really a household matter, wouldn't you agree? No need for you to waste your time with it."

Apparently mollified, the secretary began stacking the marching-soldier ledger pages to make a workspace on the writing table. "I shall see to it straight away, my lady."

"And I'll go see to the counting." Jeanne started for the door, then stopped and turned. "Oh, and de Chartres?"

"Yes, my lady?"

"Don't dispatch the invitations until I've read them."

He bristled. "Do you not trust me, my lady? I've been secretary to a duke for years. I know how these things are done."

"It's not about trust, de Chartres. It's simply that I'd like to add a personal note in my own hand to each invitation." *But no, I don't trust you at all yet, Raoul.* "Just leave them in a stack there on the writing table and send word to me when they're ready. I'll attend to them this afternoon and then you can send your couriers on their way." She stepped back over to the table, scooped the scattered coins into the bag, and took it with her. "If my count is going to balance with your ledgers," she announced over her shoulder, "then I'd best count it all."

Her reluctance to trust was validated when she read the invitations later that day. There was nothing unusual in the first few missives, and she was beginning to accept that nothing was amiss when she reached the one addressed to the Countess of Penthièvre and her husband, Charles de Blois. The invitation was for them to arrive two days earlier than the others. *What's that about?* She crossed the room, opened the door, and called out to a servant at the far end of the corridor. "You there."

He stopped in his tracks and turned to face her. "Yes, my lady?"

"Find de Chartres. Send him to me at once."

While she waited, she dealt with the remaining invitations. There was nothing else out of the ordinary. *What's Raoul up to?*

More than a quarter of an hour passed before he came through the door. "You sent for me, my lady? You've finished your messages, I suppose, and are ready for me to send them. That was very fast indeed." He wasted no time approaching the writing table.

"I've finished all but this one. Perhaps you can tell me what it's all about." She handed him the page in question.

"It's an invitation, madame. Just like the others. I see nothing wrong."

"It's quite unlike the others, Raoul. The arrival date is two days earlier."

"Ah!" The secretary beamed. "The countess is family, my lady. I thought you and the duke would want to spend some time with your family before the formal festivities."

"And you didn't think to ask me if that is, in fact, what we *do* want?"

"I ... well ... you see ... it's quite customary for the duke."

"I fail to see how it could be customary for this duke when he's never before invited the nobles to celebrate with him." *Customary or not, it can't be permitted now. Jeanne must see that she's treated exactly like the other nobles. Her homage is required. So is her husband's. Anything else gives her reason to hope the old duke's final wishes could be overturned. Family ties will have to come later ... much later.*

"I ..." For once, Raoul was at a loss for words.

Jeanne rose from her chair and reached out to take the offending page back from the secretary. She couldn't risk that Raoul might send it behind her back. "Sit, de Chartres. And prepare another invitation, this time with the correct date."

"Would madame not like to prepare it herself? Just to be sure it's correct."

"No, Raoul. This is a very formal gathering. All the invitations must be identical. All in your hand. Now the sooner you have it ready, the sooner I can add my note and you can affix the duke's seal and send all of these on their way."

She walked to the window and surveyed the scene outside while tearing the unsuitable invitation into small pieces, to be burned later in the hearth in her bedchamber. *The duke's seal*, she mused. *How I wish I could take it away from this man until we know he can be trusted! But that would be too much of an affront to do in John's absence. All I can do is hope he gets up to no mischief in the meantime.*

Sooner than she'd expected, Raoul announced, "It's finished, my lady, if you'd like to see."

She returned to the writing table and he vacated the chair for her. The handwriting was even sloppier than his usual, but it was more or less legible and certainly recognizable as his. *How did this man ever get a job as a secretary?* she wondered, but kept the thought to herself. She quickly added a cursory note. "Thank you, de Chartres. Everything is ready now." And then she left him to his task.

· · · · ·

Over the next two days, she completed counting the money, organized it according to denomination, secured a large strong box with a sturdy lock in which to store it in John's bedchamber, and returned the original bag of mixed coinage to Raoul. "To conduct ordinary business as usual," she told him. "And here's my tally of the duchy's money. When will you have your reconciliation ready?"

"In time for the duke's return, my lady."

"Why not sooner? Say, the day after tomorrow. Or even a day after that if you need the time."

"I see no need, my lady. So long as it's ready for the duke when he requests it . . ."

Oh, no you don't, de Chartres. I'm not giving you a chance to fiddle your figures so you come up smelling like a rose. Aloud, she was more conciliatory. "Perhaps it would be better for you and me to compare our results in advance, Raoul. That way, if we need to recount the coins or find a discrepancy in the ledgers, we have time to deal with it. Don't you think that would be far better than incurring the duke's ire if there's a mismatch?"

"I see what you mean, my lady. Two days from now, immediately after the midday meal." Raoul's frown belied his words.

"Excellent!" She offered him a big smile in return before leaving him to what she was certain he considered a distasteful task.

And don't think you can fiddle with my figures either, de Chartres. I have an exact copy of what I just gave you stored in the strongbox along with the coin.

She still couldn't make up her mind about the man. Was he a fox? A weasel? Or just a toady.

Making her way through the corridors back to her pleasant sitting room, Jeanne allowed herself a moment of optimism. John would be back soon – perhaps even before Pentecost – with the rest of the treasury. The following week, he'd accept the nobles' pledges, and then all would be in order for him to make his own homage to Philip. Could it be that her worry about a challenge to the succession was all for nought?

Chapter Four

Despite her concern for what might go awry in the coming days, Jeanne's optimism was bolstered when Montfort finally returned late in the morning on Pentecost Monday. As the men-at-arms carried their laden packs up the stairs to deposit in the duke's bedchamber, she greeted her husband with a kiss. "I was getting worried you might not make it back in time. Was there trouble?"

"Not at all. We were welcomed, and the city leaders happily relinquished the treasury." He paused to remove his gloves. "Along with their meticulous records, I might add. It's entirely gold florins." Jeanne put her arm through his as they ascended the stairs behind the last man-at-arms. "Why my brother thought it a good idea to keep such valuable treasure so far away – deep in the heart of France and so near the Gascon border – is utterly confounding. I simply can't imagine what he was thinking."

"Well, it hardly matters now. But if things went so well, why so long getting home?"

"We stayed an extra day to accept their hospitality. It seemed only right after their homage was freely given. And I made a gift to the town of one of the bags of florins."

Jeanne laughed softly. "Buying their loyalty?"

"If that's what you want to call it," Montfort replied. "One never knows when having allies in unexpected places might be useful."

Their prospects kept looking up when Hervé de Léon arrived that same evening. De Léon was one of the most important vassals of the Duke of

Brittany in the west, his lands comprising a large portion of northern Finistère. That he was also a vassal of the French Crown for holdings in Normandy and even in France made his support even more valuable to the Montforts. His wife was Jeanne de Penthièvre's aunt and heiress to the Avaugur estate. That made the de Léons an important balance to the other powerful family in the west, the Rohans, whose loyalty had a history of fluctuating between Brittany and France.

"I do hope you'll forgive our early arrival, Montfort," Hervé apologized as he and his wife stepped down from their carriage. "One can never be quite sure how long the journey from Finistère might take. And as luck would have it, we encountered no delays."

Montfort and de Léon were a study in contrast. Montfort clean-shaven with a bit of gray starting to fleck through his carefully trimmed, straight, dark hair; de Léon sporting a short beard and curly blond hair that hung down to the tips of his earlobes. Montfort of a calm, almost controlled demeanor; de Léon possessed of what appeared to be boundless energy. Nevertheless, the two men took to each other straightaway, almost as if they'd been friends since childhood.

Propitious as the de Léons arrival may have been, Jeanne's hopes for a grand celebration were dashed when not a single traveling party arrived on the following day. "Don't give up hope yet, my dear," Montfort tried to be encouraging when they retired to their apartment following a pleasant meal with Hervé and his wife.

By midafternoon on Wednesday, there was no escaping the stark truth. No one else was coming. When the Montforts and the Léons met in the dining hall that evening, the mood was decidedly subdued. Hervé made his pledge, and then there was nothing for it but to take their seats for dinner. "Join us at the head table," Jeanne invited their guests. "There no longer seems any point in seating arrangements."

The meal was not what she had planned. Oh, the food was the same and it was delicious, but there was far too much for four people. Conversation faltered. The usual banalities of polite banquet talk seemed trivial in the face of the screaming reality of the vast array of empty seats. Jeanne knew it was her role, as hostess, to break through the doldrums, but her heart wasn't in it. At long last, she decided it might be better just to address the specter of their failure head-on. "I was honest enough with myself to know one or two might not come, Lord Hervé, but this is hard to understand."

"Not hard at all, my dear," Hervé replied. "They're all afraid of coming down on the wrong side. Philip hasn't declared himself yet, and no one wants to find themselves suddenly out of favor when he does."

"Then perhaps what this means," said Montfort, "is that I shouldn't waste another hour before traveling to Paris to make my homage."

"Perhaps, Montfort," said Hervé. "But consider this. Right now, what you hold is Nantes. The capital city, it's true. But it's only one town that's declared for you. That shouldn't matter. My own lawyers tell me your brother's will was all properly drawn and the succession shouldn't be in any doubt. But remember, my friend, this is Brittany. We have a long history of rocky transitions from one duke to the next. Before you present yourself to Philip, you should have more of the duchy in your control. Then you go before him in a posture of strength."

"That merits consideration, Léon," said the duke.

"It does indeed," Jeanne chimed in. "And it seems to me control in the east – in the marches and those areas where the nobles feel closer ties to France – puts you in an even stronger position."

"I agree with the duchess," said Hervé. "But don't overlook the west. That's where you have the greatest support from ordinary Bretons."

"So why spend time there?" Jeanne asked. "Why not give our attention to the places that might be vacillating?"

"The ports, my dear," said Hervé. "Control the ports and you control any opponent's ability to engage with the wider world. More importantly, you deny Philip any place to land his Genoese mercenaries. Right now, they're holed up in Normandy where they could be released to raid the English coast. But there's no reason to give Philip an easy path to send them here."

"I'm beginning to like your strategy, Léon," said Montfort. "But I do have a concern. The Rohans are quite formidable in the west – particularly in the mountains. And Penthièvre is just to the north of that."

"Ignore them. Take Vannes and Hennebont, then go on around the coast and take Brest. You can count on my help. Finistère is with you." Hervé raised his glass in a toast.

"It's a lot to do and little time to do it in," said Montfort.

"Not necessarily. I rather suspect most of the towns will simply open their gates and put their garrisons at your disposal. You should have enough loyal territory before the end of summer to satisfy Philip that he'll be riding the right horse by accepting you."

When the musicians arrived and the sound of their tunes could be heard from the great hall, conversation turned to how they would spend the next three days. "We're delighted for your company," Jeanne addressed her guests, "but I'm not quite sure how much dining and dancing four people can do."

"Don't despair, my dear," said Hervé. "What my irresolute peers have forfeited here can win Nantes irrevocably to your side."

Jeanne had initially taken Léon for something of a rogue, but – rogue or not – he was really quite shrewd. "What a brilliant idea, sir! Something I wish I'd thought of. I'll even prepare the invitations myself."

"Don't you think Raoul might get his nose out of joint if you usurp what he considers his personal duties?" asked Montfort.

"Oh, pish on Raoul! If he wants to sulk, let him. No one can read his scrawling anyway."

Hervé's wife, who had barely uttered a word since their arrival, suddenly burst out laughing, drawing three pairs of startled eyes in her direction. She blushed and covered her mouth with her hands to restrain her mirth.

Jeanne had begun to think Margaret rather mousy – one of those women who trail along behind their husbands like a shadowy servant, ignored until the man wanted something. So her laughter came as a pleasant surprise.

"Oh, dear," said Margaret "I'm so embarrassed. It's just that . . . well, this has all been a bit trying for me, stuck as I am between both branches of Uncle John's family, but . . ." She took a little sip of wine to catch her breath. "I just couldn't help myself. But you're absolutely right. Deciphering Raoul's missives has been the bane of everyone's existence ever since Uncle John took him on as a secretary."

As if on cue, Henri appeared just at that moment to announce that the musicians were ready and the evening's entertainments could begin. "I'm not sure how much we four can dance, Henri," said Jeanne. "Pay the musicians for the full night and tell them to be back as planned for tomorrow evening. We'll have the town officials tomorrow, the merchants the day after, and then, on Saturday, we'll take all the food and two casks of ale to the square in front of the cathedral and treat everyone in the town to the duke's hospitality."

When the town officials arrived on the following evening, some wore an air of skepticism and a few even acted rather grumpy, as if feasting in the duke's dining hall was something of an imposition. Their wives, on the other hand, all seemed delighted at the prospect of festivities that they hadn't had to organize themselves. But as the evening went on and a substantial quantity of wine made its way from the ducal cellar to the burgesses' bellies, even the grumpiest was applauding the mummers and joining the dances. The merchants' banquet was an equal success, and by the time the sun set on Saturday, the entire town was in high spirits from enjoying the duke's largesse.

From the Writings of Jeanne de Flandre, Duchess of
Brittany and Countess of Montfort
Found among her belongings at the time of her death

Tickhill Castle, South Yorkshire, 1348

The absence of all the nobles save one from our festivities was a profound disappointment. I did my best to keep John's spirits up – to encourage him on the path we'd discussed with Hervé de Léon. John was inclined to begin in the west, among the most Breton of the Bretons – those who held to Breton independence with an almost religious fervor, who spoke more Breton than French, and who were inclined to mistrust all things French. He wanted to believe that surrounding himself with those who already supported him would encourage others to embrace his position – to want to be part of the Breton identity, as it were.

But I knew better. I knew from my brother, Louis's, challenges in Flanders what it was like to rule in a place where men tended to identify with those who spoke the same language. And those in the east of Brittany were more likely to speak French than Breton. So I encouraged John to follow Hervé's advice – to consolidate his control in the east first.

In the end, I persuaded him to my point of view. And to this day, I believe it was the right strategy.

Now and then, when my spirits grow despondent, I revisit that time and wonder what might have happened had we followed a different path. Could it be I would still be in Brittany, by my husband's side, instead of locked away in *a foreign land? But such dark thoughts lead nowhere since we cannot turn back time.*

We chose our strategy and pursued it. And I know now that there were other forces at play. Forces far greater than the apparent whims of a childless man, the legal right of a man to succeed his brother by the same father, or even a woman's pique at being deprived of what she'd coveted.

Hervé was true to his word, leading his own men alongside John's, and Champtoceaux was soon ours, protecting the road to Nantes from the east. The ducal treasury was plenteous, allowing John to hire mercenaries to add to his own forces. The future was looking up. So I sent for our children.

CHAPTER FIVE

Nantes, June 1341

Why is it that a serving of good news seems always to be accompanied by an equal portion of bad? Is God really so perverse? More likely, it seems to me, it's men who are perverse. Or in this case, women. These thoughts and more wandered through Jeanne's mind as she handed her baby daughter back to the nurse. "I think she must be hungry, Perota. She won't stop whimpering."

"*Oui, madame,*" the nurse cradled the child in one arm as she reached for young John's hand with the other. "It's back to the nursery for us now, wee Johnny, before your sister puts up a howl for her milk."

"But I want to stay with *maman,*" the toddler protested.

"Your *maman* has things to do. You'll see her tomorrow."

Jeanne could see her son was on the verge of either tears or a tantrum, uncertain which would be more effective, so she intervened. "Nurse is right. I do have things to do. But if you'll go with her now, I'll come and have supper with you in the nursery later. What do you say to that?"

The little boy's screwed up face returned to its usual cheerful expression. "You promise?"

"I promise."

He reached for Perota's hand, and she took both children away. Leaving Jeanne with her ponderings, which were, in point of fact, the only thing she really had to do at the moment. The news from John was far better than she'd dared hope. Leaving Durant in charge of the garrison at Nantes, he'd made straight for Champtoceaux and installed his own men there, creating an outpost to control the approach to Nantes by land. His dispatch from Rennes had actually made her laugh.

My dear Jeanne,

I'm delighted to tell you that Rennes is now comfortably under our control and we march tomorrow for Saint-Aubin-du-Cormier. My delight stems as much from how the whole business played out as from the actual fact that my man is now in charge of the garrison and the former garrison commander rides with us.

We arrived to find the gates closed. In truth, I would have been surprised if every town had simply welcomed us without question. But what happened next was almost comical.

What appears to have been a rather intense quarrel between the ordinary townspeople and the more prominent citizens kept us waiting outside the town. The townspeople, it seems, were eager to open the gates, and now and then a small group would succeed in taking control of a gatehouse and opening the portal. Before we could advance, men-at-arms would arrive to break up the crowd and once again shut the gate in our faces.

From what we've been told, the dispute became something of a small civil war within the town walls. At one point, while we waited, the main gate opened and a troop of mounted men-at-arms emerged. They charged toward us, then pulled up short as we offered no sign of resistance. They then rode back and forth in front of us before retreating inside the walls.

Captain Kerveil and I both came to the conclusion that the man leading the sortie was the garrison commander and that he was undecided about which faction in the town to support. The purpose, it seemed, was to assess us. When they mounted another sortie, Kerveil and half a dozen men contrived to separate the commander from his troop and bring him to our ranks. Leaderless, the other horsemen made a dash back to safety.

It's completely unclear whether the capture of the commander forged some sort of unity within the town or if those who opposed us merely took advantage of his absence to assert their will. Whatever the reason, a few crossbowmen appeared on the parapets facing us along with what looked like ordinary citizens wielding spears. We advanced slowly, with the garrison commander between me and Kerveil in the front rank. Two of the bowmen fired, but their bolts fell short. Either they were the worst marksmen ever to wind a crossbow, or the intent was to goad us into an all-out attack. I refused their challenge and we maintained our slow advance.

Seeing we weren't intent on storming the town, the garrison commander finally made up his mind. "You on the walls," he shouted at the top of his lungs. "Open the gates." We kept walking slowly forward. The defenders appeared indecisive. Were they getting conflicting orders from someone inside? We never knew, and, in the end, it didn't matter. As we drew within ordinary hailing distance and the men on the walls still stood frozen like statues, the commander took matters into his own hands, riding out a bit ahead of us and shouting, "God's bollocks, men, someone open the godforsaken gates! I'm leading the duke and his men into the town, and we can't pass through walls like some specter from hell."

Once we were inside, we were greeted cordially by the town officials, and I received their homage almost as if they'd never intended to do otherwise. It wasn't even conditional on Philip's recognition, like that of our wavering friends in Nantes.

You would have enjoyed the spectacle, my dear. It's my fondest hope that this is the most serious resistance we encounter. I'm leaving loyal men wherever we establish our authority and gathering additional men into our ranks along the way. If fortune favors us, we shall soon be back in Nantes to prepare for the next phase.

Two days later, a fast courier had arrived with a message that St.-Aubin-du-Cormier had offered no resistance, and the duke was on his way to Dinan. Jeanne hoped he would be home soon. She wanted to see him, of course, but there was something more pressing on her mind.

Yesterday, she had been surprised when Henri announced the arrival of Monsieur Bourhis, who begged an audience with her. "Show him into the duke's study, Henri. I'll be down momentarily." She waited long enough for her guest to be settled in the study then took her time descending the stairs.

Everything was a matter of timing. It would never do to let the lawyer believe she'd treat his unexpected appearance as some sort of emergency. Neither would it be prudent to make him wait too long. Jeanne knew he wouldn't even be here if there wasn't something requiring her immediate attention – and in point of fact, she was quite anxious about what that might be – but an air of equanimity and confidence was an essential part of her role.

She found him seated before the hearth in the study. He looked over his shoulder at the sound of the door and quickly jumped to his feet. "My lady, thank you for receiving me."

"Please, monsieur, do be seated again." She took a chair opposite him.

Bourhis seemed hesitant. "My news is something I'd normally bring to the duke, but I'm told he's not here at present."

"He'll return soon – in just a few days, I hope – but you can discuss anything with me."

Bourhis hesitated again. "It's not of the most salutary nature I fear – perhaps too unsettling for a woman's delicate sensibilities. It might be better that I wait for his return."

"What would be better, Monsieur Bourhis, would be for us to come to an understanding. When the duke is away, I am his regent with authority to act for him in all matters. Whatever news you bring, you may share with me – with no fear of my swooning or fainting. The duke himself would tell you that I may have the body of a woman, but I have a mind and a heart equal to his."

The lawyer squirmed in his seat. "I . . . I meant no offense, my lady. I'm just not accustomed to . . ."

"Nor are most men, Bourhis. But if you can find it within your capabilities to ignore my skirts, then we should get on quite well and both of us can assist the duke with his business. Now . . . what news do you bring?"

"Very well, my lady." He cleared his throat as if preparing to start over from the beginning. "You'll recall that I made reference to the possibility that your husband's succession to the dukedom might be challenged, no matter how secure it seemed in law."

"I do."

"That is precisely what has happened."

"Tell me everything you know."

"From what I've learned, the Countess of Penthièvre has been completely unwilling to accept her uncle's decision and the terms of his will. She's written to King Philip, as has her husband – perhaps on more than one occasion. I'm given to understand that there's been no acknowledgment of the letters and no reply. In fact, one of my sources, who is now and then at court, reported that the king merely scoffed at the letters. It's said that he asked those who were with him, 'Does she think I have any concern at all for Brittany when England is running amok in Gascony and I'm running out of money?'"

"This is disquieting, of course, monsieur, but perhaps what it means is that once my husband's control of Brittany is an established fact, Philip will have no reason to question the duke's homage."

"If only that were the end of the story, my lady. The king's rebuff seems only to have made the countess more resentful. And so she has pursued another path. She's managed to convince a group of Breton bishops to hold a court to hear her claims. Quite an unusual ploy, I must say, but not entirely without precedent. And so we shall be forced to uphold your husband's position and his right to the duchy in this ecclesiastical court."

"And do you believe we'll prevail?"

"If it were simply a matter of law, my lady, I would have no doubt. Everything is properly done. Not only that, it conforms completely with French law, which prohibits succession through the female line. There should be no question. But one never knows with bishops. They subscribe to Church law, even when rendering judgment on secular matters. So it's my belief that the result is not a foregone conclusion."

At this point, Jeanne was growing concerned. "I trust we can count on you to represent our interests, Monsieur Bourhis?" She phrased it as a question, giving the lawyer an opportunity to decline or suggest an alternative.

"You can, my lady. No one knows more about the details of when, how, and with what advice the late duke made his decision."

"And will my husband need to appear before the court?"

"I can't say his presence won't be demanded, but absent such a demand, I advise against it. He has nothing to answer for. He's acting in accordance with the late duke's wishes. And . . ." Bourhis took a long pause. ". . . if you'll forgive me, my lady, it may be better for the bishops to see only a whining woman who can't accept the decision of the man obviously entitled to make that decision. I shall endeavor by all means at my disposal to avoid having the duke appear in this contrived court."

"Very well, then. I'll apprise my husband of the situation as soon as he returns, and we'll depend on your advice. Either of us will see you at any time if you have further news. And let's hope this puts an end once and for all to the countess's unwillingness to accept the will of her uncle."

Ever since Bourhis took his leave, Jeanne had been mulling the situation. She was more eager than ever for John's return, to learn if they also held Dinan. That would give them much of the Breton marches. Not Fougères and Vitre, but she understood why. The powerful families entrenched there were far more French than Breton, so it seemed prudent not to antagonize them until the succession was completely settled. Once Philip accepted John's homage, those families would have no choice.

What was more interesting was Philip's dismissal of the other Jeanne's petition, despite the fact that Charles was his nephew. This bought the Montforts some time – not much, but certainly more than they'd expected to have – to consolidate their control of the duchy. Assuming, of course, that the bishops didn't upset the cart.

FROM THE WRITINGS OF JEANNE DE FLANDRE, DUCHESS OF BRITTANY AND COUNTESS OF MONTFORT
FOUND AMONG HER BELONGINGS AT THE TIME OF HER DEATH

Tickhill, South Yorkshire, 1348

In truth, Jeanne's scheming was no surprise to me. It was completely within her character – as I understood it – to be what Bourhis had called "a whining woman." She had no lack of status. As Countess of Penthièvre, she was one of the leading nobles of Brittany. As the wife of Charles de Blois, she benefitted from his proximity to the king. In point of fact, she rarely occupied her seat in Penthièvre, preferring instead their sumptuous residence at Blois.

But she was like a spoiled child whose father had promised her a toy and who later decided it wasn't suitable for her. Rather than accept the father's – or in this case, the uncle's – wisdom, the child resorts to whining and manipulation to get her way.

I have to admit I found it amusing that Philip paid her no mind. Rather like the nursemaid who ignores the complaints of her charges when things don't go their way.

Philip may not have taken an interest. But there was someone else who did.

CHAPTER SIX

Palace of Westminster, mid-June 1341

"*God*, how I wish William was here," Edward moaned then emptied his wine glass in a single gulp. Philippa reached for the pitcher to refill it for him. She'd seen him like this many times since the Earl of Salisbury had been captured and held hostage by the French king. William Montagu had been her husband's best friend and closest confidant since William first came to court as a ward of Edward's father. Despite the eight years difference in their ages, the two formed an immediate bond. And during the early years of Edward III's reign, while he was still a minor and subject to the whims of his mother and her paramour, Roger Mortimer, Montagu had been a rock of strength for the young king, eventually leading the capture of Mortimer and Edward's assumption of personal rule. Edward had rewarded his friend for that and much more by creating him Earl of Salisbury.

"We all wish he were here, dear, not least Countess Catherine," said Philippa, replacing the pitcher on the table.

"Damn Philip for refusing to come to an agreement for his release."

"You can damn him all you like, Edward, but we both know it's a blessing Philip now sees William's value as a hostage. Otherwise, we'd be mourning his loss forever."

Edward was definitely in a mood. "Then damn him and Suffolk for getting captured in the first place."

"I have to admit, I still wonder why they ventured so close to Lille on the way to Tournai. They *had* to know they were tempting fate."

"And I intend to ask William precisely that question when he returns," Edward declared. "Why take the risk when he could have been safely here helping me with my current dilemma?"

Finally. The opening she needed to probe what was troubling him. "I know I'm a poor second, but ..." Philippa was nothing if not adept at how she advised her husband. She knew she was, next to William, Edward's most respected and trusted advisor, and she knew also that her husband would say the same if it were politic to do so. Her skill lay not just in her intellect but also in knowing when and how to present her opinion so he could embrace it without others casting aspersions on the source.

"It's France." Edward didn't wait for her to finish her thought. "As I'm sure you might have guessed. But not William's detention. It's painfully obvious now that trying to forge any kind of alliance in the Low Countries with Flanders, Brabant, and Hainault and with Emperor Ludwig isn't working."

"Well, Ludwig's never really been your friend despite his occasional half-hearted gestures."

Edward took a sip of wine and chuckled. "I guess I should be grateful William's not here to say 'I told you so.'" His wife just smiled. "So I've been thinking about Brittany. The last duke made a complete muddle of the succession, constantly wavering, seeming to favor his niece, and in the end, choosing the male line in his half-brother. My sources tell me that's left things rather unsettled, despite the fact that Montfort is taking steps to establish his position."

"Are you really thinking of getting involved in a civil war between two of Philip's vassals?"

Edward sipped his wine again. "Hear me out, my dear. Philip is completely disinterested in Brittany at the moment. If we were to support Montfort – help him to establish rule over the entire duchy – then we'd be in a perfect position to take back our ancestral lands in Normandy, Anjou, and Poitou. And from Normandy, it's an easy advance to take Calais, especially with the support of Robert of Artois. It will take time, but we'd end up with Philip surrounded – reduced to his hereditary borders."

Philippa sat in silence for quite a long time, her brow slightly furrowed in thought, gazing into the hearth as if transfixed by a blazing fire, though in mid-June, any flames were purely in her imagination. Her husband didn't press her. He knew she'd just heard in less than a dozen sentences what he'd been pondering and envisioning for the past three weeks. She'd take her time gathering her thoughts, and that was precisely what he wanted.

At long last, she looked back into his eyes. "It's a grand strategy, Edward – one worthy of a great king. And I think if William were here, he would say it holds far more promise than the fragile coalition on Philip's northeast border." Edward smiled. "But I do see one problem."

"Which is?"

"The whole strategy hangs by a single thread."

"Which is?"

"Does Montfort want our help? For that matter, does he even need it? Absent that, landing an English army on Breton soil would be nothing short of an invasion and bound to bring Philip running with his entire army."

"You're quite right. And to that end, I intend to send someone to offer Montfort a proposition."

"In complete secrecy, I trust?"

"Absolutely. A man from our household knights. He'll have my authorization to reach an agreement with Montfort that suits our needs."

"How much will this envoy know?" asked Philippa. "How much will you authorize him to tell Montfort?"

"Only that seeing the rightful heir on the ducal throne of Brittany is in England's best interests, and we're prepared to lend our support to that end. Anything more might cause a really astute man to imagine my larger purpose. For that matter, if Philip should get wind that we've even been in conversation with Montfort, it would be reason for him to turn his attention from Gascony to Brittany. So it all has to be done in the utmost secrecy."

"And you trust this person?"

"He's shown himself to be a man of honor. And to the broader world, no one knows he has any association with me. Not only that – he speaks excellent French."

"Then perhaps we should offer a prayer for his success."

It was Edward's turn to stare into the hearth in silence, but not for long. "There's one other question I wanted to ask you, my dear. If we turn our attention to Brittany, where will that leave Hainault? Will your brother the count feel we've abandoned him? And if he does, will he pledge himself to France?"

"In truth, Edward, I don't think it matters whether we stay in Hainault or not. My brother has no love for France. And despite being Philip's sister, what my mother wants is peace between England and France with Hainault left intact. She has no wish to see her son's inheritance subsumed into the French Crown. They've both watched the difficulties in Flanders with Louis trying to appease Philip while protecting his valuable cloth trade. If my brother should feel under continued threat from the French, it's Burgundy he'd most likely turn to as an ally."

"But Burgundy is a vassal of France."

"True. But a very strong and stalwartly independent one. Philip knows he can't threaten Burgundy without causing major trouble for himself." She paused for a sip of wine. "Besides, I can always pay my brother a visit and give him our reassurances, should that become necessary."

"I was hoping you might say that." Edward smiled and downed the rest of his wine. When his wife again reached for the pitcher, he shook his head. "No more tonight, my dear. I should go find my bed and leave you to your rest." Philippa had only recently delivered their fifth child, and Edward always gave her time to rest from the ordeal. Even though they'd have to wait until she was churched before resuming carnal relations, he'd return to her bed soon. They had that much affection for each other.

CHAPTER SEVEN

Nantes, July 1341

Montfort returned in triumph at the end of June. They were now in solid control of an important swathe of eastern Brittany, and he was eager to join with de Léon to secure the western ports. Jeanne felt a twinge of remorse at having to dampen his mood with Bourhis's news. He'd furrowed his brow briefly then seemed to shrug it off. "Well, you yourself suggested she would challenge us."

But they were both somewhat apprehensive when Bourhis requested an audience three days later. From the moment the lawyer walked into the study – before he even uttered his first word – it was evident the news was *not* what they'd hoped for. "I'm sorry to report, my lord duke, that I have failed to prevail. The countess's argument was flimsy, consisting of little more than an assertion that her uncle had once implied she might inherit and that she assumed his acceptance of her husband's pledge of loyalty to Brittany constituted a promise. She had no documents, she brought no witnesses . . . in truth, she offered the court nothing more than her opinion that she was the rightful heir."

"Did the bishops question Charles?" asked Montfort.

"In a manner of speaking. They seemed interested only in ascertaining that he really did offer a pledge of loyalty to the duchy." Bourhis paused. "I, on the other hand, presented your late brother's will and brought those who had witnessed its signing to attest to their signatures and to the timing of when the will was made. I was ready to bring other witnesses of the discussions that led to the creation of the will, but the bishops declared they had seen and heard enough and would not permit me to do so."

"I can't fault the manner in which you represented us, Bourhis," said Montfort. "But I must ask ... would it have made any difference if I had been there to speak on my own behalf?"

"In truth, my lord, I'm not sure they would even have allowed you to speak. It's my belief their minds were made up before the so-called hearing even began. Their deliberations were perfunctory – in fact, they called us back into the room a mere quarter-hour after asking us to wait in the corridor. Only two of the seven cast their vote to abide by the late duke's will."

"You seem quite distressed about the entire proceedings, Monsieur Bourhis," said Jeanne. "We, of course, don't hold you responsible. But do you have any notion of what led to this unfortunate outcome? I mean ... is it possible, for example, that the countess hand-picked the members of the court to get the results she wanted?"

"That, I can't say, madame. The Church would have us believe, naturally, that such a thing could never happen. But we're all three wise enough in the ways of the world to know that it can and does happen regardless of what church officials might proclaim. Whether she chose the members of the court or not, I think there's something else far more subtle at play."

"Oh?" Jeanne raised an eyebrow.

"The bishops fear being on the wrong side of the Pope – the *French* Pope. We all know Benedict is less beholden to the French Crown than his two predecessors, but we know equally that Philip would have no compunction about intervening in papal matters if he thought there were some advantage to him for doing so."

"You've actually hit on the most important thing, Bourhis," said Montfort. "As long as Philip continues to pay no attention to the countess, the decision really carries no weight. So I intend to proceed with our plans as if this little incident never happened. We're secure in the east and, as soon as we control the west, there'll be very little of Brittany for my half-niece to lay claim to. At which point, I'll make my homage to Philip and put her claims to rest."

· · · · ·

And then the winds shifted and the weathercock turned. A week later, Bourhis was back. "You've heard the news, I presume, my lord duke . . . my lady . . . that Philip has called a *parlement*."

"Yes, I've heard," said Montfort, "but I've heard no reason for the summons."

"It seems the king is almost out of money and can't afford to pay either his own soldiers or his mercenaries. I'm told he intends to demand a ninth from all his vassals and from the merchants and towns as well."

"That's extraordinary," said Jeanne.

"But hardly surprising," her husband added, "since he can't seem to decide where to fight. Paying the Genoese to sit in port and wait until he makes up his mind seems an enormous waste of coin. I'm told their services don't come cheap."

"Be that as it may, sir," said Bourhis, "the demand is to be made. And you'll be expected to attend, of course."

"And I will. But only after I've finished consolidating our position here. My presence won't make a rat's eyelash of difference in the debate. Philip will twist arms until he gets what he wants. So more important than *when* I go is that I go with Brittany under my control."

Bourhis cleared his throat, as if in preparation to speak, but then looked at his hands and said nothing.

"Is there something else on your mind, Monsieur Bourhis?" Jeanne asked gently.

"My lady is astute as always. I'm given to understand that it's widely believed among those closest to the king that he will also ask this *parlement* to consider the matter of the Breton succession."

"In which case," said Montfort, "it's more important than ever that I complete the consolidation before going to Paris. But why the sudden change? Has the countess been writing more letters?"

"It's not out of the question, sir, but I have no certain knowledge of it." The lawyer studied his hands once again while John and Jeanne exchanged glances. "There ... there is a rumor, sir," Bourhis finally continued. "I ... I don't like dealing in rumors. They're most often vile and hurtful things. The more they're repeated, the more they're believed ... and without any concern for whether they might contain any truth."

It wasn't like Bourhis to so assiduously avoid coming to the point. Clearly, he was trying to prepare them for something distressful. Jeanne took her husband's hand, undecided as to whether the gesture was intended to calm him or to calm herself. *It's just a rumor, after all*, she thought. *How bad could it be?*

"It seems, my lord, that this particular rumor has reached the king's ear. And it's for that reason that I find myself compelled to tell you. It is being said in some circles, my lord, that you have already done homage to Edward of England."

"That's **preposterous!**" Montfort lost all semblance of equanimity, slamming his boots on the floor as he rose from his seat and began striding about the room. "When am I supposed to have done this? When have I been *anywhere* except on Breton soil since my brother's death? Ask anyone. Look at where I've been seen and on what dates. When was there *any* time for a sea voyage to England and back? All my movements can be accounted for. Every last day can be accounted for. Who would *say* such a thing, much less whisper it in the king's ear?" His immediate fury spent, Montfort returned to his seat, but the expression on his face remained grim.

"That's the problem with rumors, sir," Bourhis resumed. "The source is so easily lost once the rumor begins to spread."

"Could the countess be behind it?" Jeanne asked.

"There's no way to know, my lady. But there doesn't seem to be any indication that either she or Charles has spoken any words *against* it. Their silence might be taken by some as complicity. Others might say they're simply trying to remain untarnished by the matter. I'm sorry to have to say this, sir ... madame ... but if I were advising them, that would be the course I would recommend. Remain aloof and leave the rival at the center of the controversy."

He paused and studied his hands once again. *He's going to know every vein and every line and every small blemish and the precise length of every nail before he leaves here today*, thought Jeanne.

"Alas, I can offer you no such advice, my lord duke. Your position is awkward, as defending against such accusations – even with abundant proof – is often taken as further evidence of the truth of what's being said. That's why I've come to the conclusion that your best course of action is the one you, yourself, propose – to establish yourself in firm control of your domain so that you arrive at the *parlement* in a position of strength."

Few words passed between the duke and duchess over the evening meal that day. Nor did they say anything beyond a quiet "Good night" as they parted company for their separate bedchambers. Both were deep in thought about the abrupt turn of events.

It was not at all the sort of setback either had imagined. A challenge in the field. A reluctant garrison that had to be subdued. Even a direct confrontation with Charles de Blois. Such things could be met head-on and conquered. But a rising tide of untruth and innuendo? One could no more hold that back than the rising seas that swept Brittany's coasts twice every day. The difference was that the sea tides also ebbed. Not so with a river of rumor.

· · · · ·

And then the weathercock turned yet again.

"There's a gentleman in the entrance hall requesting an audience with the duke, my lady," Henri announced. Jeanne looked up from her needlework. "But his lordship hasn't yet returned from surveying the city walls. What should I tell the visitor?"

"Did he give a name, Henri? Or a reason for his coming?"

"A Monsieur Corder, madame. It seems he's a salt trader. Apparently, he and your husband have a mutual acquaintance, though he would neither offer a name nor reveal the nature of the acquaintance."

Corder, thought Jeanne. *That's neither French nor Breton. I wonder what this is about?* Aloud, she said, "I agree it's out of the ordinary, Henri, but as

John and I have nothing in particular planned for tomorrow, it might provide a diversion to find out what this man could possibly want. Tell him to return tomorrow an hour past midday and the duke will receive him."

"As you wish, madame."

At the appointed time on the following day, Henri tapped lightly on the doorframe of Jeanne's sitting room where the Montforts were waiting, puzzling over what interest they might have in a salt trader. "Your visitor has arrived, my lord ... my lady. I've shown him into your study, sir." They followed the steward down the stairs and stood aside as he opened the door to the study and announced, "The Duke and Duchess of Brittany."

Standing beside the hearth, his gaze fixed on the door, Corder immediately bowed his head and held it there as the Montforts crossed the room. "I bid you welcome, Monsieur ... Corder, is it?" said John, taking his accustomed seat. "Do be seated." Corder hurried to comply. "My steward was somewhat vague about the reason for your visit. I'm in hopes you can provide some clarity."

"Henri did mention your profession as a trader in salt," said Jeanne.

"I am indeed, my lady ... my lord duke."

"And how does that concern us?" asked John. "Are your clients perhaps of my acquaintance, and you bring greetings?"

"I have numerous clients, sir. One in particular you might find of interest."

"Come, come, man. You have to be more forthcoming if I'm to understand the purpose of this audience."

Corder fidgeted in his seat and glanced into the empty hearth before returning his eyes to his host. "I ... with all due respect, sir ... I was hoping to speak with your lordship in private."

"Whatever you have to say, Corder, you may speak in front of my wife. She's privy to all the business of the duchy and is my regent when I'm away from these premises. Now, tell me what brings you here."

Despite these assurances, Corder seemed no less anxious, but Montfort had left him with no choice. "Very well, sir, but before I say more, it's my duty to state unequivocally that what passes between us must remain a closely guarded secret, not even revealed to your closest advisors."

"Then you should take comfort in the knowledge that my closest advisor is my wife. Now, out with it." John's tone said he was clearly growing impatient.

"My role here in Brittany, my lord, is indeed that of a salt trader, but I have only a single client. And while that client will buy my salt, he's far more interested in an entirely different sort of negotiation." He paused.

"This might be easier for all of us, Monsieur Corder, if you simply tell us who you represent." Jeanne hoped she sounded encouraging.

"I come on behalf of Edward Plantagenet." The Montforts exchanged a quick glance. "It has come to my lord's attention that your just and legal claim to your title is being challenged. And that the challenger has close ties to the French Crown. There is none who better understands the strong spirit of independence among the Bretons, feeling that same spirit for his own ancestral holdings. Nor is there anyone who better understands the French insistence on the application of Salic Law, since he himself is being denied the rights that should be due him as the grandson of Philip IV.

"My lord is therefore inclined to lend his support against any challenges to your rightful inheritance. Further, he has given me authority to come to an agreement with you regarding when and how such support might be rendered." Corder paused before adding. "Assuming, of course, that your lordship has an interest."

Montfort rose slowly from his chair and crossed to the window behind his desk to stare at whatever was happening in the courtyard. He needed time to collect his thoughts. Every word he uttered from this moment on would carry a weight and meaning beyond anything he'd ever thought to consider. This could be his salvation ... or his utter undoing. To accept it would be to throw the gauntlet at Philip's feet. To refuse it might mean putting his patrimony at risk.

But one thing was certain. In such matters, one didn't charge headlong into the unknown. And his current situation was not yet so dire that an immediate decision was required. After all, debates in a *parlement* were long, complicated, laborious political affairs. There was still time to consolidate his position, do homage to Philip, and render a decision by the *parlement* unnecessary.

Edward of England wanted something, else he would never have sent his envoy. Discovering what that might be was part of the delicate dance of negotiations. If Edward had chosen his envoy well, the man would be adept at the dance. The next step, then, was to buy time.

Returning to his chair, Montfort looked the visitor squarely in the eyes. "First, Monsieur Corder, we must have *mutual* assurances that any further conversation remains strictly between us – between the three of us, that is. You have my word of honor."

"And mine," said Jeanne.

"I give mine as well – and that of my lord in his absence," said Corder.

"Secondly," Montfort continued, "you will understand, I'm sure, that one can't hear such a proposal for the first time and reach an immediate decision. I must consider my position. And we must discuss the nature of your lord's offer in more specifics."

"In truth, sir, my only objective for today was to begin the conversation."

"Then I shall bid you God's good day for now. You've given us something to consider, and we will most certainly have many questions at our next meeting."

The duke and duchess rose to leave and Corder quickly jumped to his feet. "And I am prepared to give you answers, my lord. I'm lodging at the *hostel de l'Escu de Bretaigne* and available at your pleasure."

"I'll send the steward to show you out, Monsieur Corder," said Jeanne as they made their way through the door.

• • • • •

Late into the night, Jeanne and John spoke in whispers, reclining in her bed. Neither felt any inclination toward sleep. They'd been unable to discuss Corder's extraordinary proposition earlier as there was too much risk of being overheard. But when Jeanne ordered her maid to sleep in the servants' hall, they were finally alone.

It wasn't that she didn't trust Aaliz completely. They'd been together since Jeanne found the girl begging in the streets after she'd run away from the convent where her father abandoned her when her mother died. She was only twelve at the time, but Jeanne took her in and taught her to be a proper lady's maid. Even now, her small stature and delicate features masked the depth of her devotion to her mistress. Jeanne knew Aaliz would never repeat anything she overheard. But some things simply could not be heard.

"Do you think this is the source of the rumors?" asked Jeanne. "Has Philip somehow gotten wind of what Edward's up to?"

"Well, he most assuredly has spies in the English court. But the rumor is that I've already done homage to Edward. Any spy would know I've been nowhere near English soil. No, I think the rumors are far more likely to be some Frenchman's attempt to defame me." He put his arm around his wife's shoulders. "But Edward will have a price for his help."

"I don't think you should agree to do him homage."

"And what else do you think he might accept? Everyone knows his ambitions in France."

"Our treasury is enormous, John. And kings are always running out of money. That puts you in a strong negotiating position."

"Assuming I decide to accept his support at all. Edward may have his eye on Brittany, but *he* holds something that rightfully belongs to me."

"Ah, yes. The Honor of Richmond."

"We've held that ever since old Henry II's son married Duchess Constance and acquired all her titles. Those titles are intertwined – have been for a century and a quarter. If Edward wants my homage, then he'd best be prepared to return the lands he's confiscated – the ones that would entitle him to my pledge."

"I wonder if Corder knows the strength of our position?"

"It will be interesting to find out. For now, though, I won't change my strategy. But do you agree we should keep the door open?"

Jeanne didn't answer straightaway. There was a lot at stake. And she knew how much John relied on her acumen. Whatever she said would likely set them on a path. At long last, she snuggled closer and laid her head on his chest. "Yes. When storm clouds gather, it's best to have a shelter. And we don't know yet if we're facing a real storm or just a mild headwind."

In truth, the weathercock hadn't turned so much as started to waver ever so slightly in the breeze.

Chapter Eight

"I'm growing impatient, Raoul," said Jeanne, the tone of her voice leaving no doubt about her pique. "When are you going to hire the tradesmen for the repairs and refurbishments in the nursery? It's really not a suitable place for the children in its current state, and yet we have no other place to care for them properly."

"Oh, dear." Raoul managed to appear flustered. "With respect, my lady, I thought you understood that Henri is responsible for the household and that I deal with the duke's affairs."

"I'm quite clear on that, de Chartres. Just as I'm clear on the fact that maintenance and upkeep of ducal property is part of the duke's affairs and not of the day-to-day operation of the household. This is not the first time I've asked. So answer my question, please."

"Surely, madame, Henri has ample funds accumulated from the generous amount I give him each month that he can supply new draperies or whatever it is your nurse wants."

Jeanne's mood was on a downhill slope from impatient to angry, but she held her tone in check . . . for the moment. "It's not a matter of what Perota *wants*, Raoul. Have you seen the nursery recently? It's had no attention since . . . well, since my husband and his siblings were small children. There are cracks in the mortar around some of the windows and now and then a chunk falls on the floor. And one of the windows can no longer be closed completely. The chimney needs a good cleaning – Perota finds bits of soot in the hearth every morning. Repairs are needed, Raoul. So I'm instructing you once again . . . and for the last time . . . to hire the tradesmen and get the work done."

"With respect, madame, the duke has not given me his consent."

"With respect, de Chartres," the sarcasm dripped from Jeanne's tongue but she was unsure if the man would recognize it, "I am authorized to speak for the duke when he's not here." She scanned the room. "And I don't see any sign of him here."

"Begging your pardon, my lady, but he *is* in residence. The reason he isn't in his study at this moment—" Raoul stopped short.

Jeanne imagined she could see him actually biting his own tongue to prevent the escape of another word. "Do continue, Raoul." Her kindest and sweetest tone. Whatever it was he didn't want to say, she wanted to hear. "You were saying?"

"It's nothing, madame." He tried to extricate himself from the muck he'd almost stepped in.

"My husband and I have no secrets from one another. You may speak freely."

Watching the man's discomfort might have been amusing if Jeanne hadn't been so exasperated with him over the nursery repairs. Nevertheless, she let him fidget, shuffle his feet, wring his hands, and stare out the window until he reached the point where he realized she wasn't going to let the matter drop and he had no choice but to speak. "Are you aware, my lady, that the duke has gone into the town every day this week dressed in servant's clothing? It's never the same time of day and never to the same place."

Of course I'm aware, you stupid man. It's how he meets in secret with Corder to discuss King Edward's offer of support. But this was an unfortunate development. She still didn't fully trust Raoul, and if he'd observed the meetings . . . The possible consequences didn't bear contemplation. She needed to draw him out. "Why, yes, I know. It's his way of mingling with the people . . . hearing firsthand what's on their minds. But you've been following him?"

"Being near to hand when the duke needs me is my job, my lady. So, naturally, I . . ."

She gave him her warmest smile. "I think my husband might tell you the presence of a secretary might give the game away, and people wouldn't talk with him as freely. No doubt you've seen him chatting with all sorts of folk as he walks about – everyone and no one in particular." She desperately needed to know if Raoul had worked out that there was one man John met every time . . . one conversation that lasted much longer than all the others.

"I've observed him in many places indeed. He's been to the salt traders' hall. He likes to visit the bake shops. On the first day, he called at the *hostel de l'Escu de Bretaigne*. I asked myself, 'What business would he have at an inn?'"

"Innkeepers are townspeople too, Raoul."

"Once, he spent quite some time at prayer in Saint Catherine's Chapel."

But did you follow him inside? Did you see who he met? She couldn't ask him directly without revealing her concern. And any effort she might have made to draw him out was forestalled by a single knock on the door followed immediately by Henri's entrance to announce, "Monsieur Bourhis to see you, my lady. Shall I show him in?"

"Please, Henri." She turned back to the secretary as Bourhis entered. "That will be all for now, Raoul. But do see to the hiring of the tradesmen straightaway."

"Wouldn't Madame prefer that I stay, in case there is some matter that needs to be recorded?"

"I think, Raoul, that Monsieur Bourhis is quite capable of recording anything that might be necessary."

Raoul's countenance fell and his shoulders slumped. Clearly, he wanted to hear whatever might be said. *To report to John?* Jeanne wondered. *To report to someone else?* She said nothing further as the secretary left the room, his reluctance proclaimed by every halting footstep. When the door finally closed behind him, Jeanne couldn't suppress a sigh.

Bourhis smiled. "I take it you and de Chartres have an unsettled relationship."

"Do be seated, Bourhis. And you take it correctly. I don't know what to make of the man." She settled into her accustomed chair. "His manner is insipid when it's not insufferable, his records are inscrutable, and his handwriting is almost indecipherable. How he secured a position as private secretary to a duke is beyond my comprehension."

Bourhis allowed himself a chuckle at her outburst. "Your sentiments aren't misplaced, my lady. The late duke hired de Chartres on the spur of the moment – something he later described to me as a 'moment of lunacy' – when the previous secretary died suddenly. The man's shortcomings emerged slowly, and by the time Duke John recognized just how many there were, he'd been putting up with them for so long that he just continued to tolerate it all. If he'd lived longer, I think he might have been inclined to make a change, but as that didn't happen, your husband inherited Raoul along with the title."

"And my John has decided we have little choice but to keep him on until we have a strong command of all the business of the duchy. But I can tell you, Bourhis, there's something about that man . . . I can't put my finger on it, but I don't trust him. Just before you arrived, I learned he's been following John whenever he leaves the castle. Raoul claims it's to be at his master's beck and call, but I can't help but wonder if he's actually a spy in our midst."

"I can't rule that out unequivocally, but consider this. I think somewhere inside, Raoul is aware of his shortcomings."

"His incompetencies, you mean."

"Whatever you wish to call them. He's aware, but he also desperately wants to be important. And so he tries to disguise his inadequacy with constant attentiveness, excessive protection of his prerogatives, obsessive attention to protocol and formalities . . . all the things that are causing you to question his motives."

Jeanne furrowed her brow in thought. "That may be. But men desperate to be viewed as important can also be dangerous. If they think they're being denied the approbation they want in one place, they may look for it elsewhere."

"In truth, my lady, I never thought of de Chartres as dangerous. But neither have I spent time with him every day as you have. If it would give you some peace of mind, I can arrange to have his movements observed and report my findings."

"I'd be grateful, monsieur. Until our position is secure, we've no choice but to be cautious. But I don't think you came here only to listen to my misgivings about Raoul. I assume you have some news?"

"I do indeed, my lady. The *parlement* is proceeding slowly. They seem bogged down in the matter of the king's finances. According to my informant, there are quite a number of members in opposition to the levies the king is demanding and the debates are, at times, quite lively. At one point, I'm told, there was such a protracted argument that it was necessary to suspend debate for several days to allow tempers to cool. The king will no doubt get what he wants in the end, but it won't come without a price. And it will take time to convince him to offer the necessary preferments and inducements needed to win over the naysayers. For the moment, according to my source, there's been no mention of Brittany."

"And the rumors?"

"They persist. I'm given to understand there is now some whispering in the corridors that my lord duke's failure so far to make his homage to Philip is proof that he's already pledged himself elsewhere. The Countess of Penthièvre and her husband are in Paris – no doubt with the intent of pressing her case in the *parlement* – and it's said that the king has received them once, though only as a formality among many nobles paying their respects. What that *does* mean, though, is that Philip no longer considers the countess worthy of derision."

"All of which means we must use the time wisely," said Jeanne. "I'll inform my husband as soon as he returns."

"And I, my lady, will return as soon as I have any further news. In the meantime, I'll take steps to find out if de Chartres is up to anything untoward."

"Thank you, Bourhis."

Thank you indeed, Bourhis, thought Jeanne as she watched his departing back. But she knew he couldn't do everything that was required. He could mark Raoul's movements and who he spoke to, but not his personal correspondence. That would be up to her. And at the moment, she could conceive of no way to do that since Raoul controlled all the correspondence and all the messengers that entered or left the premises. *You're resourceful, Jeanne de Montfort*, she told herself. *You'll come up with something.*

·   ·   ·   ·   ·

That night, she and John spoke only of Bourhis's visit and the king's financial woes. She hadn't dared send her maid away again, lest that arouse suspicion. And suspicion inevitably led to gossip. But when, at long last, they heard Aaliz's soft snores from her pallet on the opposite side of the room, Montfort whispered directly into his wife's ear, "I told Corder he must wait for an answer until my return." She squeezed his hand in acknowledgment.

Jeanne wouldn't bother him tonight with her concerns about de Chartres. John had too much on his mind. On the morrow, he would march for Vannes to join forces with Hervé de Léon and secure the ports and the west to their cause. How that venture unfolded would shape their next move – whether toward Philip or toward Edward.

In the meantime, she was perfectly capable of dealing with Raoul herself, should the need arise.

CHAPTER NINE

"Brittany is ours!" Montfort's exuberance was contagious as he greeted Jeanne in the entry hall when he returned to Nantes late in the afternoon of Assumption Day. He wrapped her in a strong embrace then held her at arm's length, a hand on each of her shoulders, and planted his lips squarely on her mouth, seemingly oblivious to the man standing in the doorway with a huge grin on his face. Releasing the kiss, John turned his attention to his companion. "Come in, Hervé! Come in. Give her a kiss. She deserves to be kissed by *both* heroes of Brest."

As de Léon approached, Jeanne offered her cheek and he leaned forward to give her a brief peck. By then, Henri had quietly arrived in the hall.

Montfort clapped Hervé on the shoulder. "The best guest quarters for my best friend, Henri. Find someone to attend to his needs – whatever he wants. Then, once we've removed the grime from a month of traveling and fighting, we should feast."

"But it's a holy day, John," Jeanne reminded him.

"And by sundown, fasting is over. A fine supper, Henri. Fit for a celebration. The best of everything we have."

"I shall see what we can manage, my lord." Henri bowed his head to his master then addressed de Léon, "If you'll come with me, sir." He started up the staircase. "I'm sure we can accommodate whatever you may require."

John grabbed his wife in another embrace. Seeing her wrinkled nose when he released her, he laughed out loud. "Told you we were grimy. But we've done it, Jeanne." He put an arm around her shoulder and they started up the stairs. "Exactly as you said we should. And now I can make plans for my homage to Philip, which will secure our position at last."

Leaving her husband to his much-needed ablutions, Jeanne returned to her sitting room in a pensive mood. Could it be the winds were shifting in their favor once again? She barely dared to hope. But if it was, that would obviate any need to even consider the Plantagenet's proposition – which would be a huge weight off John's mind. Hers too, if she was honest with herself.

Bourhis still had no news from the *parlement* beyond the matter of the king's finances. Much as she wanted to believe that, once Philip was again flush with funds, his attention would turn to finishing what he'd started in Gascony, she knew something would be required to point him in that direction. I *must remember to tell John to offer his help in that conflict as part of his homage. That would almost certainly ensure our position is unassailable.* But as long as the rumors persisted . . .

Jeanne knew the very best way to quash a rumor was to start another one. And if she were in Paris, she wouldn't hesitate to do just that. But from here in Nantes, it would take a long time for the gossip to reach court, not to mention that the source would be immediately suspect.

Bourhis's surveillance had turned up nothing more sinister in Raoul's movements than visits to the cathedral for mass and the occasional confession. The lawyer was inclined to the view that the secretary was harmless, but Jeanne's gut remained skeptical. Neither she nor Bourhis had come up with a way to gain access to Raoul's private correspondence without his becoming aware of their meddling, so anything he might be up to on that front remained an enigma. Over the last few days, she'd reached the conclusion that the only way to the truth was for John to confront Raoul directly and see what happened. But that would have to wait . . . at least until the current euphoria ran its course.

Henri's "what we can manage" turned out to be a veritable feast. Freshly caught fish. Duck. Parsnips. *Haricots verts.* Paindemaine still warm from the oven with butter churned that very morning. A splendid Gascon wine. And after the main course, four different cheeses, berries, summer melon, and honey cakes.

John and Hervé took turns regaling Jeanne with their exploits. "Hervé was already in Vannes when we arrived," Montfort began. "He'd spent hours wining and dining with the town officials, spinning stories about how my late brother wanted a true Breton at the helm and how I'd sworn to protect all the ports from any threat that might come from the sea."

"Everything I said was true," Hervé picked up the story. "I just made it sound like they were the most important people in the whole duchy and the new duke would look after them like he would his own children."

"So when I arrived, the gates were wide open and the ducal banner flew from every tower. We spent two days there while I spread around some largesse—"

"He means spent a lot of money," Hervé interrupted and then laughed aloud at his own joke. "It worked, though. By the time John announced he was leaving his man in charge of the garrison, they were begging him to leave an entire troop."

"Which, of course, I did." John took a long swallow of wine before continuing. "Then when we reached Hennebont . . . What a spectacle! The gates wide open, the townspeople gathered in the market square, a formal ceremony for the officialdom to welcome us . . ."

"You'd have thought we were local heroes returning from a long war," said Hervé. "Come to think of it, maybe we *were* in an odd fashion. Sort of like your late brother returning from Tournai." He raised his glass. "To Hennebont!" They all drank the toast.

They're like young lads with their first wooden swords, reveling in their exploits, thought Jeanne.

"Two days of feasting and entertainments there," John picked up the tale, "and we left some men behind to round out their garrison."

"Along with some more of the duke's money." Hervé seemed to find it quite amusing that all the largesse was coming from Montfort's pockets and not his own.

"Then on to Quimper before we turned north to Brest. Now *that* was a different story."

"Biggest surprise I've had in a long time," said Hervé. "My own people, for Christ's sake! What in the name of God's goose feathers were they thinking?"

"I wish you could have seen the expression on his face, my dear, when we arrived to find all the gates closed, no banners flying—"

"Not even the arms of Léon, for God's sake!"

"Not even the town's standard, for that matter. And not a soul in sight. It was as if they had settled in for a long siege."

"So what did you do?" Jeanne asked.

"Made camp," her husband answered. "I thought surely once they saw Hervé's banner flying over his tent, they'd realize we weren't an invasion force." He drank what was left in his wine glass and refilled it. "Next morning, it was the same thing. So Hervé and a few of his men rode to one of the gates and demanded to be admitted, but there was no response."

"Unless you call the silence of the tomb a response. We waited for damn near an hour and repeated our request several times, all to no avail. John wanted to wait them out."

"Not showing aggression had worked at Rennes, so why wouldn't it also work at Brest?"

"So we waited patiently for another entire day."

It was John's turn to laugh. "Patiently? Pacing around my tent and voicing epithets at all the town officials is how you show patience?"

"You should see me when I'm *really* angry," Hervé shot back with a grin.

"Truth be told, Jeanne, my patience was running low too. We gave them one last chance. Hervé rode to the gates and demanded admittance one more time, and, when there was no reply, he announced we'd storm the gates if we didn't find them open when the sun rose the next day."

"And that's exactly what we did. Guess they didn't really want a fight, though, because as soon as they saw our battle charge coming at them, someone threw the gates open and we rode in."

"They put up a bit of a fight – for appearances sake, I think – but it was obvious they were no match for us. We replaced their garrison with our men and demanded homage from the town officials. And actually got it quite willingly."

"After you made a nice contribution to the town treasury for the upkeep of the garrison." Hervé downed what remained in his wine glass. "Too bad that half-niece of yours can't be bought off the same way."

Hervé stayed for three more days, giving his men a rest before the journey home. He and John had long discussions about the homage to Philip, often with Jeanne as part of the conversation. There was, of course, no mention of the overtures from England.

. . . . .

Hervé and his men left in the morning. The king's men arrived in the afternoon. Well-armed, their jupons bearing the Valois livery, they demanded an audience with John de Montfort. "They did not say 'the duke,' my lord," Henri explained when he informed John and Jeanne of the new arrivals as they were discussing the upcoming journey to Paris in her sitting room.

"Thank you, Henri. Bid them wait in the entrance hall. I'll be down momentarily."

As the steward left, Montfort's expression turned dark. "I don't care for the sound of that. What do you suppose they want?"

"Whatever it is, I'm coming with you to find out."

The three men snapped to rigid attention as the Montforts descended the stairs. Without waiting for John to speak, the obvious leader of the group said, "John de Montfort?"

John maintained an outward calm. "The Duke and Duchess of Brittany. And you are?"

"Sergeant-at-arms to King Philip of France." The man thrust a folded paper toward John. "This is a warrant from the king ordering you to come with us to Paris to await the king's pleasure."

Taking his time, John accepted the message, examined the seal, then opened and read it before passing it to Jeanne. "What the king could not have known is that I am even now making preparations to come to Paris to offer him my homage. So this warrant is really unnecessary."

"Nevertheless, our orders are to bring you with us. Shall we go, sir?"

"Very well. I'll come with you. But not until the morrow. I need time to pack for the journey. A man can't present himself to his king in grimy traveling clothes."

The sergeant looked annoyed, but didn't press. Apparently, he hadn't been ordered to actually make John a prisoner. "An hour after sunrise."

"And you may lodge with my garrison in their barracks until then."

"We'll make camp in your courtyard. I have no intention of having to answer to the king for letting you escape."

When Jeanne bid her husband farewell the following morning, she did her best to disguise her anxiety, but she knew he was feeling it too. He was right – Philip couldn't have known he was on his way to render homage. But no one could mistake a sergeant-at-arms with a warrant for a courteous invitation.

As she waved a final *adieu* and turned to go back inside, she sighed. Once again, the weathercock seemed to have its head pointed directly away from them. And that was the thing about weathercocks. Where they turned and when they turned were subject to the vagaries of nature, and there were no clues to tell one what to expect next.

CHAPTER TEN

Henri's quiet knock on Jeanne's sitting room door that afternoon was a welcome distraction. Had she known what was to come, she might not have been so grateful for the interruption. "Monsieur Corder requests to see you, madame. I bade him wait in the entrance hall as Raoul is currently occupying the study, working on his ledgers."

Befuddled about where and how to record John's generous donations in the west, she thought. Aloud, she said, "Exactly as I would have wished, Henri. Thank you. Tell Monsieur Corder I'll only be a moment." She finished the flower petal she'd been working on then tucked the end of the thread under half a dozen stitches on the back side of her embroidery. This was going to be awkward, but she had no choice but to make the best of it.

She found Corder appearing rather nervous as he waited near the door – almost as if he was afraid to be seen there. "Ah, monsieur." She avoided using his name. "I was just on my way to the cathedral. Will you walk with me?"

"With pleasure, madame." Once outside, his anxiety disappeared. "Thank you, my lady, for your discretion."

Not another word passed between them until they were settled on a bench at the back of one of the side aisles, well away from anyone who might come in to pray. Jeanne waited patiently for Corder to reveal what was on his mind.

"I understand, madame, why your husband couldn't risk making time to speak with me while his ally was in residence. And yet, no one could have failed to notice his departure this morning in the company of King Philip's men." He paused, presumably hoping she might comment. But there was nothing for her to say. "A departure, I might add, without providing any answer to my lord's generous offer of support."

Careful, Jeanne. You can't make a commitment. But neither can you shut the door on Edward's offer. "We were as surprised as anyone by the king's summons. But we decided we could learn more about Philip's mood and disposition – perhaps even what his plans are for his ongoing conflict with your lord – by answering the summons straightaway than by delaying. Would not that information – coming directly from the source, as it would – be of enormous value to your lord?"

"I can't dispute that, madame, but your husband's prevarication has left me in a difficult position. Having heard nothing from me these several weeks, my lord will be growing restive for news. And beyond that, I've already far exceeded the bounds of my excuse for being here in the first place. So I must leave on the morrow, with or without your answer."

"I must respect your judgment, monsieur, but in this matter, I cannot speak for my husband."

"That is indeed a disappointment."

"I can, however, offer you this. Your lord should not interpret the lack of acceptance so far as a refusal. Merely as a reflection of the treacherous path the duke is trying to navigate between protecting his inheritance and not inviting interference from the French Crown. You may give your lord my assurances that the duke will send his response as soon as he returns from Paris."

"Perhaps that is something." Corder rose from the bench. "So I shall take my leave. May God go with you, Duchess. And with your husband."

"And may He watch over your journey, monsieur, and the fortunes of your lord."

Jeanne waited a long time before returning to the castle. There was little she could do now but wait. Wait and hope she had kept the door open enough that they could walk through it if fate conspired against them.

FROM THE WRITINGS OF JEANNE DE FLANDRE, DUCHESS OF BRITTANY AND COUNTESS OF MONTFORT
FOUND AMONG HER BELONGINGS AT THE TIME OF HER DEATH

Tickhill, South Yorkshire, 1348

Waiting takes a toll. Especially when one must wait at a distance with nothing to occupy the time except imagining what might be happening in that far-away place where your loved one's future is in the hands of others. And in our case, it wasn't only John's future, but our son's as well. The little boy I'd already begun to think of as the future Duke of Brittany.

He was still too young to comprehend even that his father was an important man. But I'd begun telling him stories of his uncle and his grandfather and the exploits of the Breton rulers all the way back to Duchess Constance who was such a fierce defender of her lands and titles.

Perota chided me for it. "You're just putting ideas in his head," she'd say. But that was precisely my intent. I wanted him never to remember a day when he didn't know his place in the world and the patrimony he'd inherited. When he didn't have the expectation of succeeding his father and of having a son follow in his own footsteps. When he wasn't confident he would be Duke of Brittany and Earl of Richmond and Count of Montfort and nephew of the Count of Flanders. This was his future. And with each story I told him, I vowed nothing would prevent me from seeing that future come to pass.

In the meantime, all I could do was wait. Wait and imagine every possible scenario that could be playing out in Paris. Wait and imagine and envision exactly how we should respond to each one. Wait and hope that right would prevail. Wait and worry that innuendo and jealousy might very well shape men's minds. Wait and put on a cheerful face so those around me would never suspect the turmoil inside.

CHAPTER ELEVEN

Nantes, September 1341

The sound coming through the open window of Jeanne's sitting room, where she was contemplating a letter to her brother, was unmistakably that of horseshoes on the cobblestones of the courtyard. She wasn't expecting visitors. Could it be that John was back so soon? *Dear God, please don't let it be bad news.*

The next sounds she heard were bootsteps rushing up the stairs. It had to be John. Henri would never allow anyone else up the staircase on their own. *Or – oh my God, heaven forfend – what if it's more of the king's men come for me and the children?*

When a droplet of ink fell from the quill to the paper, she realized her hands were shaking. Pulling the inkpot toward her lest she dribble ink all across the writing table, she carefully wiped the tip of the quill on the lip of the pot and laid it on the already spoiled paper. She clasped her hands together and pressed them into her lap, trying to get a grip on her anxiety as the bootsteps stopped outside her door.

Her relief when John stepped into the room caused her to leap from her chair and rush into his arms. But she could feel in his embrace that all was not well. "Let's sit," he said. "There's a lot you need to know." Taking his hand, Jeanne steeled herself for what was to come.

"I'm not supposed to be here, you see," he began. "I never thought to be saying such a thing, but I'm actually a fugitive."

"Why don't you start at the beginning," she suggested. "Did Philip not receive you?"

"Oh, he received me. From his manner, though, one might have thought it was against his will. And yet he was the one who'd ordered me to appear. I offered him my homage – even offered him Brittany's help in his conflict with the English. His only response was 'Now is not the time, Montfort.' And then he instructed me to remain at the Louvre and said I was not to leave Paris without his permission. I was clearly being treated more like a hostage than a guest.

"Two days later, I was summoned to be questioned by the *parlement*. Not just a small council, mind you, but the entire body. From the first question I knew it was to be a confrontation. Jeanne, they treated me like an upstart challenger – like I was a usurper rather than the lawful heir. They seemed quite willing to ignore the late duke's will. Appealing to French adherence to Salic Law fell on deaf ears. It was abundantly clear the pot had been poisoned.

"I kept to myself for the rest of that day, but I couldn't just wait around for what increasingly seemed inevitable – that Philip would refuse my homage, make me his prisoner, and grant the duchy to Blois. So for the next two nights, I walked the corridors, getting the guards accustomed to my restless wandering. On the third night – when they paid me no mind – I made my escape with only the clothes on my back and the coins in my purse."

"Thank God you're safe," said Jeanne. "And here," she added.

"There's much to be done. I'm dispatching couriers to all our garrisons. Every one of them to immediately assume a war footing. No matter what the *parlement* decides, I expect Charles de Blois to come against us. And if the decision also goes against us, he'll be coming with the entire French army in his train. Then, I want you to take the children and the treasury to Rennes."

"But why leave at all?"

"Remember how you insisted we take Nantes straightaway to establish our legitimacy? I have no doubt Charles will have the same goal. And he'll be after the treasury as well. If we're to survive, we can't let that happen."

Jeanne nodded. She knew he was right.

"Besides, the town officials here aren't to be trusted. It may seem we've won them over, but don't forget they made their homage contingent on Philip's approval. They'll turn in a heartbeat if they learn Philip is backing Blois. It'll be safer for you in Rennes. And I'll send Durant and a troop of Montfort loyalists to make sure that's the case."

"And you?"

"A man of honor has to defend what's rightfully his. If we succeed in defending Nantes, I'll send for you, of course, but you'd best be prepared for a long stay in Rennes. Or even to flee west if the worst should happen."

"I trust you'll be sending word to Hervé? At least *he's* with us."

"I will. But that's not all."

Jeanne didn't ask. She didn't need to. She could guess what was in his mind.

"If the *parlement* rules against us, I've decided to accept Edward's support. He wants my homage in return, but two can play that game. I'll give it to him. But only after an English army lands on Breton soil to fight for our cause."

"If Philip comes against us," Jeanne said quietly, "we have no other choice."

It seemed as if the world stopped inside that room as they sat in silence, neither wanting to give voice to the turmoil inside their head. At long last, John said, "I'm sorry, my dear."

Jeanne rushed to him, sitting in his lap and taking him in her arms. "You've nothing to be sorry for, my love. Quite the contrary. You should be proud of what you've done. And I know your brother would be proud of how you've carried out his wishes." He wrapped his arms around her and buried his head in her chest, both of them drawing strength from the embrace.

However much she might have wanted to, Jeanne knew they couldn't linger in each other's arms forever. When she sensed he had calmed, she kissed his forehead and he raised his lips to her for a lover's kiss. "If I'm to move the household," she whispered, "there are things I must do."

He released her slowly. "And I must write messages to the garrison commanders to send with the couriers."

"There's ink and paper just there." She indicated her writing table. "You needn't leave here to do that. No need to get the servants gossiping until they see the messengers leave."

"Thank you, my dear."

Jeanne found the steward in the kitchen, embroiled in a quiet but intense debate with the cook over the menu for the evening meal, the one insisting it must be grand to celebrate the master's return and the other protesting that her preparations were already too far along to make a change. Neither noticed their mistress's appearance in the room. They both stopped mid-sentence and turned in startled surprise when she announced, "I think I can solve your dilemma for you."

The cook dropped a curtsey and Henri's face flushed as he bowed his head, his embarrassment palpable. "Madame, please forgive me. I had no idea you—"

"There's nothing to forgive, Henri. But I *can* solve the question of this evening's meal. The duke is tired and wants nothing more than a simple supper in my sitting room. A bit of potage and some bread, if you can manage it, Cook. Tomorrow evening we can have that nice meal you propose, Henri. But for now, may I have a word?"

"Of course, madame. I'm at your service always."

They made their way to the small room just off the ewery that served as the steward's office, and Henri invited his mistress to take the only chair. "We have work to do, Henri, you and I," she began. "We're to move the household to Rennes."

Despite what must have been his complete astonishment, the steward managed to keep his expression as bland as always. "And when is this to happen, my lady? If I may ask."

"In the next few days."

Astonishment finally won out. His mouth opened then shut in silence as he struggled to find a response. "Madame, I ... Madame, this is a monumental task in so short a time. Am I permitted to know why?"

"Of course you are, Henri. The duke reports that things have become rather unsettled at court and that the king may now be paying some attention to the Countess of Penthièvre's complaints about the succession. It may yet be that nothing comes of it, but the duke and I both think it wise to be prepared. We needn't move the entire household – the duke will be staying here with his men. But the children and I will be going, and we'll need sufficient household staff to sustain us." She paused. "And you, Henri. I want you to come with us. There's no one else I trust to be in charge of things."

"It would be my honor, my lady."

"Good. I'll leave all the arrangements in your hands. We'll be taking all my traveling trunks."

"All of them, madame?" Henri was one of the few people who knew what some of those trunks contained.

"All of them, Henri. The ones that are already packed as well as two more that Aaliz will pack tomorrow."

• • • • •

The following morning, Jeanne woke to the sound of something shuffling on the floor and raised herself up in bed to find her husband dressed and walking toward the door. "John?"

He turned back. "I'm sorry, my dear. I tried not to wake you."

"Where are you going?"

"To have the letter of introduction prepared for my emissaries to Edward. You needn't get up." He reached for the door latch.

"John, wait!" There was no mistaking the urgency in her tone. By now, she was sitting on the edge of the bed and grabbing for her robe to cover her nightdress.

"What's wrong, Jeanne?"

"John, you must write that letter yourself. You can't have Raoul do it."

"Why else does a man have a secretary if not as a scribe?"

"John, you must do this *yourself*. Or if you don't want to, let me do it for you."

"Why? I don't understand." He'd returned to sit beside her on the bed.

"I don't trust him, John. I have no proof, but my gut tells me he may be in league with those who oppose us. I can't explain it. He may be no more than an incompetent fool. But my instinct says *we'd* be the fools if we let him become aware of what you're about to do." He said nothing. She knew her instincts usually carried weight with him, but they'd had differing views on de Chartres from the beginning. She put a hand on his arm. "Besides, it will hardly win you any favor with Edward to send him a letter in Raoul's atrocious handwriting."

He chuckled and patted her hand. "Now, that's something I can't argue with. Do you have more paper and ink in your sitting room?"

"As much as you need."

· · · · ·

For two days, the castle was a flurry of activity, preparing for the journey. On the morning of the third day, just as Jeanne was about to join Aaliz, Perota, and the children in the carriage, a courier galloped into the courtyard with a message for John. He tore open the page and read quickly. "The *parlement* reconvened at Conflans. They've issued an edict proclaiming Charles de Blois Duke of Brittany, and the army has been summoned to meet at Angers." His tone was flat.

"Everything you feared," said Jeanne.

"Everything and more. Philip has sequestered Montfort l'Amaury. He holds all my rights there for the present."

In that instant, the threat became real and the departure took on an urgency she hadn't felt before. She hugged her husband tightly. "Stay safe, my love."

"You should go," he replied. "I'll send for you when I can."

As their little procession made its way through the streets of Nantes and onto the road north to Rennes, Jeanne tried, for her son's sake, to make the journey seem like a great adventure. But she knew John's emissaries would sail on the afternoon tide, putting in motion things that had seemed unimaginable just four short months ago.

It was an enormous risk. But it seemed their only option.

FROM THE WRITINGS OF JEANNE DE FLANDRE, DUCHESS OF BRITTANY AND COUNTESS OF MONTFORT
FOUND AMONG HER BELONGINGS AT THE TIME OF HER DEATH

Tickhill, South Yorkshire, 1348

Though I never spoke the words, I knew, even at the time, that Philip could have branded John a traitor for his flight from Paris. There was no time to dwell on it then, but of late, with so much time on my hands, I've often wondered why he did not. Was Philip still of two minds about the succession? Had someone else, whispering in the king's ear, begun to dispel the rumor of John's homage to England? Or had Philip himself worked out that it was nonsense? Was he simply testing Charles de Blois? Testing his conviction about his rights to the duchy or his prowess in the field? After all, Charles was best known for his extreme piety. Did Philip choose not to accuse John of treason so that, if Charles failed, there could be a great show of forgive-and-forget and restoration of the rightful heir? Or was the king simply too lazy or distracted to be bothered?

I'll never know, of course. What I do know is that, once our emissaries sailed, the question of treason took on a very different meaning.

CHAPTER TWELVE

"I believe it is from the duke, madame." Henri proffered the message which had just been delivered, holding it in such a way that the seal was readily visible.

"At last!" Jeanne's relief brought a rare smile to Henri's countenance. He knew how worried his mistress had been, exiled, as it were, in Rennes while her husband prepared to face the might of the French army. "Thank you, Henri," she added, his cue to leave her to her reading.

It had been three weeks since they'd left Nantes and established their household in the large home just inside the walls of Rennes that was reserved for the ducal entourage. Jeanne was glad she'd brought Henri with her. It had taken him no time at all to have the household running as smoothly as if they'd lived there always. That was a comfort – and certainly made things better for the children. One thing she had insisted on. "Unpack only what's essential, Henri. And especially not my traveling trunks. Whenever we must move again – whether to return home or go elsewhere – I don't want to be hindered by the necessity for a long delay to pack."

"I believe we are of like mind in the matter, madame," he'd replied.

But the familiar household routine couldn't fully relieve her anxiety. John had promised to send news as often as he could. She chided herself for her impatience – he was undoubtedly beset with his own worries as he prepared their defenses. But it took all her self-rule to wait until the door closed behind the steward to break the seal and devour John's words.

Her first glance produced an audible sigh of relief. The missive was in John's own hand. Thank God he'd listened to her misgivings and not entrusted this to Raoul.

My dearest Jeanne,

There is much to tell you, but first I must inquire after your health and welfare and that of the children. You're in my thoughts every moment that isn't occupied by the necessity of preparing for a fight. And I know you're doing your own part to protect our son's future.

Hervé has arrived. He's a good advisor and I'm grateful for his loyalty, though I do miss having the benefit of your always wise counsel. Best of all, he brought with him two men he says are expert spies, and they've already brought us some useful insight into the French dispositions.

The army is gathering, as expected, outside Angers. They have their siege engines and artillery. The spies didn't really know how many men except that it seemed to be several thousand. They did discover there was a whole section of the camp made up of Genoese mercenaries. Hundreds, according to one spy. The other thought maybe a thousand or even two.

Philip has put his eldest son, the Duke of Normandy, in command. It seems, however, that the king doesn't fully trust his own son, as he's provided the duke with two minders in the form of the Seigneur de Noyers and the Duke of Burgundy. The gossip among the troops is that Philip's orders are that they're not to mount an assault on any town where it's not a foregone conclusion that the town will capitulate.

Jeanne paused in her reading. Could the gossip really be right? It might be. Tidbits of information inevitably leaked from command tents and word traveled fast among men living cheek by jowl in the cramped confines of an army encampment. If so, it was a puzzling strategy. Why send an army if not to force capitulation? Maybe it was just another example of Philip being Philip. Everyone knew he didn't like war. They also knew he was always hard-pressed to make up his mind. She turned her attention back to John's letter.

Charles de Blois is also with the army. Commanding the advance guard, according to Hervé's spies.

She paused again. Maybe the idea is to have him lead the charge to claim what he believes he's entitled to, but sending him out in front while the main force lags behind? She would have expected he and his men would be shoulder-to-shoulder with the Duke of Normandy.

One thing we can be confident of. Coming from Angers, their only plausible route into Brittany is by way of Champtoceaux. The garrison there is loyal and well-disciplined, so the French will not have an easy time of it.

I've dispatched a significant portion of our forces to reinforce the garrisons in the west. In particular, Brest must hold fast for the arrival of reinforcements.

In the meantime, stay strong, my dear. Though as I write those words, I rather suspect that's superfluous advice. But know that I'm doing everything in my power to ensure we can be together again, in our rightful roles, as soon as may be.

Your loving,
John

She folded the page and held it to her heart, as if, in doing so, she could impart her strength and will his success.

. . . . .

It was unusual for Durant to ask her to come to the barracks. That was his domain. So her apprehension rose with every step she took . . . and was in no way relieved by the sight that greeted her in the tiny room that the garrison commander used as an office. Durant's expression was grim. The unfamiliar man – hardly more than a boy, really – standing at his side looked rather the worse for wear. As he bowed to her, he rubbed his head, apparently trying to arrange his hair, but succeeded only in making himself look more disheveled. "You need to hear this, my lady," said Durant. "But I didn't want to alarm anyone else. Tell her, lad. Just like you told me."

"Aye, sir. So the French army, they've mounted a siege of Champtoceaux. And the duke, he decided the garrison needed help, so we all rode out of Nantes to do just that. But we never quite got to Champtoceaux. We just got as far as l'Humeau."

"Where's that?" Jeanne interrupted the young man.

"About three miles away, my lady. A farm, see. And the farm house and buildings had been turned into a sort of fortress, with soldiers and all, but there wasn't any banner flying, so the duke figured it was our own men and we rode in to join them. But it weren't. Was the French. So we had a big fight on our hands straightaway." He paused.

"Go on, lad. Tell the duchess everything."

"Well, we fought hard, my lady. And the duke, he was right in the thick of it."

Jeanne felt her breath catch and hoped neither of the men noticed it.

"He was as brave as ever I see a man, madame, and all the men, they took courage from him. But in the end, we were outnumbered and the duke decided we couldn't win there – that we'd be better off fighting from the fortifications in Nantes. So he gathered up the men and made a hasty retreat, and we had to leave Champtoceaux to fend for themselves. The duke and the rest, they'll be back in Nantes by now. But the duke, he ordered me to ride here, straight from the battle, fast as could be, to tell you and Captain Durant here what happened."

Inwardly, Jeanne sighed with relief. At least John was safe. Sometimes, surviving to fight another day, when the odds are more in your favor, was the smart tactical decision.

"Do you have any idea of the size of the French army, young man?" Jeanne asked.

"Not really, my lady. Like I said, they outnumbered us at l'Humeau. I guess there must be a whole lot more of them manning the siege."

John hadn't said, in his letter, exactly how much of his army he'd sent to the western garrisons, so neither she nor Durant had any idea how many men were left to defend Nantes. She could only hope it was enough. "Is there anything else we should know?" she asked the young messenger.

"Only this, my lady. And the duke said I was to say it to you in his exact words."

Now she was curious. "So what did he say?"

"He said, 'Tell the duchess I almost captured that scoundrel Charles. We had him cornered and somehow he managed to slither away. Next time, he won't be so lucky.'"

Jeanne smiled. *Oh, how I hope you're right, my love.* "Thank you, young man, for remembering that. Now, did the duke say if you were to stay here or return to Nantes?"

"He didn't say, my lady."

"Then you'll stay with us. Captain Durant will give you a place in his troop, right, Captain?"

"Of course, madame. See to your horse, lad, then find a bed upstairs and get some rest. See the sergeant in the morning for your duties."

Jeanne's happy demeanor disappeared as soon as the boy left. "Can they hold out in Nantes, Durant?"

"I really couldn't say, madame."

"John's letter said they think the French army numbers in the thousands. Do you think they might divide the force and attack here and Nantes simultaneously?"

Durant didn't answer straightaway. He walked to the door of the little room and looked around outside for eavesdroppers before closing it and returning to face Jeanne. "Permission to speak freely, my lady?"

"Until we're reunited with the duke, Captain Durant, I expect you to tell me nothing but the raw truth. No matter how unpleasant. And you mustn't concern yourself with what some might call my woman's sensibilities. We're going to have difficult decisions to make, you and I, and anything less than complete candor could lead us to make mistakes. Now, do you think the French might divide their forces?"

"It seems unlikely, madame. The king has a tendency to be reluctant to committing to a fight. And Charles de Blois is just trying to fulfill his wife's expectations that they would inherit the duchy. So I'm thinking they'll put all their effort into capturing your husband, thinking that once that happens, the rest of Brittany will fall in line with the new order and they can avoid a wider war."

It was Jeanne's turn to ponder their situation in silence for several moments. Her words, when she eventually spoke, were steeped in determination. "I've asked for candor from you, Durant, and you'll get no less from me. I think your assessment is likely right. But theirs is utterly wrong. John de Montfort is the rightful heir to Duke John and Duke Arthur, and our son is his rightful successor. The only thing they will accomplish by taking John prisoner is to light a fire in my breast to protect the rights of our son. They'll be surprised at the depth of their miscalculation."

A smile found its way to Durant's face. "You find something amusing, Captain?" she asked.

"Not at all, madame. When the duke ordered me to accompany you, he made a point of saying I would find you an adept commander. At the time, I wasn't sure what he meant. Now I know."

FROM THE WRITINGS OF JEANNE DE FLANDRE, DUCHESS OF BRITTANY AND COUNTESS OF MONTFORT
FOUND AMONG HER BELONGINGS AT THE TIME OF HER DEATH

Tickhill, South Yorkshire, 1348

I'll never forget the moment we heard that Champtoceaux had fallen. It was the feast day of Saint Jude Thaddeus, which fell on a Sunday that year so we had just returned from mass when the messenger arrived. The priest's words, reminding us of Saint Jude's exhortation to the faithful to persevere even in the face of what might seem the most desperate and difficult of times, still rang in my ears.

When I heard the news, I felt a curious frisson – as if those words had been meant for me. Looking back, it's easy to imagine that I knew somewhere deep in my soul that the fate of both my Johns – husband and son – would soon be in my hands. But at the time, I dismissed it as silliness.

There were far more pressing concerns. Champtoceaux was a setback, to be sure, but if Nantes fell, that would be a serious blow. Did John and Hervé have enough men to hold Nantes? Would the Nantais stay loyal or switch their allegiance? And where were the English?

CHAPTER THIRTEEN

Palace of Westminster, mid-November 1341

Walter de Mauny had come to dread Thursdays. Thursday was the day, every week, that the king expected an accounting of progress on his Breton campaign.

Edward had reached an agreement with Montfort's representatives in September and the Council had signed off on the plan. When de Mauny was given joint command of the venture, responsible for the land forces, he was honored – and in truth, he still felt that way. But with his counterpart, Robert Morley, perpetually moving from one port to another trying to requisition and reposition ships for the expedition, it had fallen to Walter to handle the Thursday meetings on his own. The king's grandfather had been famous for his volcanic temper. And though the grandson tended toward a more even temperament, when Edward felt his current enterprise was being stymied at every turn, he could unleash a dozen different ways to take the Lord's name in vain in a single breath, leaving every man in the room fearful lest that royal wrath be directed at him personally. And with each week that passed, de Mauny could see the king's impatience growing.

The problem was the ships. As soon as they'd been released from the previous requisition, the owners had put them straight back to work carrying trade goods. And it being the height of the Gascon wine trading season, every available ship was making the trip to Bordeaux. Walter didn't blame the ship owners – they made far greater profits from trade than from ferrying soldiers. So the only way Morley could requisition them was to be in a port when they docked. And even then, many of the owners would send them back to sea under cover of darkness to make just one more lucrative run before being pressed back into the king's service.

Last Thursday, Edward had made himself crystal clear. "Next time you're here, de Mauny, your words had better be the ones I want to hear else you and Morley will both find yourselves wishing you'd carried out my instructions. This isn't a big expedition. Get it underway!"

Luck was with them and they now had eighty-seven ships and were ready to launch the venture as soon as the king gave the word. But even with that news, Walter felt his gut churn with trepidation as he was shown into the presence chamber.

Not without reason, it seemed. Edward was in a grumpy mood. "So what's it going to be today, de Mauny? More trouble with ships? I've had nothing but bad news this morning, so why should yours be any different?"

"Actually, Sire, I can finally report that we have the ships sorted. Morley would be here with me, but he felt it best to stay in Portsmouth to keep the ship owners in line. We can sail when you give the order."

Edward threw his head back in laughter. "Now isn't that just the crowning glory of the morning!"

"Sire?"

Lifting a page from among the papers on the table in front of him, the king shook it briefly in the air then let it fall back to the table. "The latest from France. The worst of this morning's bad news. I won't trouble you with the details. Suffice it to say, the expedition is delayed. And before you ask, no, I don't know when it will be resumed." De Mauny stood silent, unsure what Edward expected from him. "Send your men home and release your ships. You're free to go. If things change, I'll send for you."

"As you wish, Sire." De Mauny bowed low before turning to exit. His morning had just become as bad as Edward's. Morley was going to be livid. The soldiers were going to be disgruntled. Thursday had now become firmly entrenched in his mind as absolutely the worst day of the week.

· · · · ·

Rennes, mid-November 1341

Jeanne got the news at the same time as everyone else in Rennes. It was the Feast Day of Saint Martin de Tours, which fell on a Sunday that year. At the end of the Mass, before anyone had risen to leave, the mayor rushed forward and climbed into the pulpit. "Citizens of Rennes, I have news that concerns us all. A message that arrived just this morning, just as I was preparing to come here for the service. The town of Nantes has surrendered to the army of France. Charles de Blois has entered the town and proclaimed himself Duke of Brittany. I know little else except that there was no great battle, no great loss of life."

The murmuring that had begun in the congregation the moment he uttered the word "surrendered" was now growing to a roar, its volume amplified by the natural acoustics of the cathedral – a roar that required some effort to silence. "Please!" the mayor shouted, waving his arms frantically. "Please, my friends . . . my fellow Rennais! Please . . . if you'll just listen, I have more to say." Slowly, the noise abated.

"There's no reason for panic. We're safe here. Our walls are strong. Our garrison well armed. Our duchess – the lawful duchess – is in our midst. Our larders and storehouses are full, and we will keep them thus." The mayor paused, looking out across the assembled citizenry. A few heads began to nod. Slowly, others followed suit. Then, almost as a benediction, he added, "And we will all send our prayers that God may continue to smile on us and keep us safe from harm." As he descended from the pulpit, people slowly began to rise and make their way down the aisle.

Jeanne could barely take in what she'd just heard. Nantes should have been easy to defend. They should have been able to withstand a siege for months on end – not mere days. What had gone wrong? Where was John? Something must be terribly amiss that he hadn't been able to send word to her. In a daze, she made her way down the aisle and out into the street. Aaliz usually accompanied her to mass, but today Jeanne had insisted on going alone, and now she was grateful for the chance to walk back to her lodgings with only her thoughts for companions. Despite those thoughts being interrupted frequently by citizens pausing in the street to wish her well, she managed to be gracious to everyone who greeted her along the way. *I'll need their goodwill in the coming days more than ever,* she reminded herself.

Henri met her at the entry to her house. "The mayor requests a moment of your time, madame."

Hardly what she wanted to do next, but she couldn't refuse. "Of course, Henri."

"I asked him to wait in the dining hall, as there was already a fire lit there."

She entered the room to find the table laid for her midday meal and the mayor warming himself in front of the fire. "*Monsieur le maire,* what can I do for you?"

He doffed his cap and bowed. "Ah, my lady, nothing at all. It's what I can do for you. I come to offer my apology for the very public way I broke the news to you this morning. I foolishly assumed you would have been privately informed as was I. But I could see from your distress that you were hearing it for the first time."

Did I really let my guard down that much? Jeanne wondered. *Is that why so many people who would normally have passed in silence paused to wish me well?*

"I also wish to offer my assurances, my lady," the mayor continued. "Rennes did homage to your husband the duke, and we remain loyal. The actions of a usurper do not deter us from the pledges we made."

"Your assurances are gratefully accepted, monsieur. Your apology as well. I myself would have expected a private message, but events often overtake one's intentions, do they not? I'm sure we would both understand why things occurred this way if we knew more about how those events unfolded. But as we do not, we'll take what we do know and move forward."

"Indeed, madame."

"Allow me to commend you for the way you reassured the town. The duke could not have said it better. And now, as you're here, I invite you to share my midday meal."

The mayor bowed again. "With respect, my lady, I must decline. My wife expects me for our own meal and will, even now, be wondering what's taking me so long."

Jeanne smiled. "Of course."

When the steward returned after seeing the mayor out, Jeanne announced, "I think I'd prefer to take my meal in the work room, Henri. Please tell the servants I appreciate their efforts, but I'm not in the mood for something formal at the moment."

"We've all heard the news, madame. No one will begrudge you some time to reflect in private."

At the top of the stairs, she crossed the corridor into what she called her work room – a combination sitting room and office. A cozy place that was bright on sunny days and easily warmed by the fire on chilly ones. Slowly, her racing mind settled. The mayor was right. She and the children were safe here for now. Thank God for John's prescience in sending them away. She needed more information, and she had some time in which to gather it. In the interim, it was up to her to keep everyone's spirits up. Not just here in her household, but in the town as well. She knew, though, that some of the townspeople tended to waver in their support and that others might be swayed, so she needed to exercise some care.

One thing she dared not do was speculate on John's fate. But there were plenty of others happy to do that for her. The rumors began the very next day. Charles had captured John and was holding him in a cell in the ducal castle. The French had executed Montfort in the cathedral square. John was being taken to Paris to stand trial for treason. The Duke of Normandy was holding her husband hostage for ransom. Montfort had turned tail and sneaked away in the night, leaving the Nantais to fend for themselves.

That last one actually sparked a bit of hope. She knew from John's last letter that he had a substantial force in the west. Had he perhaps gotten word that the English had landed at last, and he and Hervé had gone to meet them?

Oddly, there had been no mention of Hervé at all, either in the mayor's news or in the gossip. Where was he in all this?

As November faded, so did the gossip about John's fate. Things were oddly silent – a strange state, to Jeanne's way of thinking, for an armed conflict. Had John negotiated some sort of truce? Was Philip vacillating again about supporting Charles?

But with the onset of the Advent season, the rumors resumed. From the comfort of the ducal castle in Nantes, Charles had been writing letters, promising God-only-knew what to try to persuade the noble families to switch sides. And in a few cases, he was succeeding.

As December progressed and the weather grew colder, Jeanne began to sense another kind of chill in the town. She'd been making it a habit to be seen by the townspeople, going to the market when the weather was nice, accompanying Henri when he visited the butcher and the wine merchant, and even taking her young son with her to Mass. Most people wished her God's good day, but recently, she'd noticed a few who turned away as she approached.

When the news arrived, just two days before Christmas, that Saint-Aubin-du-Cormier had capitulated to Charles without any resistance, she realized the fate of the Montfort claim was in her hands . . . and it was time to act. Thus it was that, three days before the New Year, she had reached a decision.

"A gentlemen to see you, my lady," Henri announced at the door of the work room where Jeanne was seated at her writing table trying to frame a letter to Edward of England urging him to delay not a moment longer in sending his promised support. "Amaury de Clisson," Henri added when his mistress looked up from her task. "He brings news of the duke."

"Then don't bid him wait a moment longer."

"He hasn't, my dear." De Clisson stepped into the room as Henri bowed and made his exit. De Clisson cut an imposing figure. He'd been a champion in the lists on numerous occasions and had the bearing to prove it. Tall and of a muscular build, he exuded the confidence of a man who knew he could prevail in a fight. But none of this intimidated Jeanne. In fact, it was those very characteristics that made him such a valuable ally.

"Amaury," she leapt from her seat and rushed to greet the visitor, offering her hand, which he graciously kissed. "You're the most welcome sight I've had in weeks." She led him to the chairs in front of the hearth where a recently tended fire kept the December chill at bay. "We heard Nantes had fallen and Charles had begun retaking our garrisons, but I've had no news of John. Needless to say, I've been terribly apprehensive."

"Understandably so." De Clisson stood in front of the fire, warming his hands. "I can put your mind at rest on one point. When I left, John was very much alive."

"So you've seen him? Spoken with him? And left where?"

De Clisson turned to face her but remained standing, soaking up the warmth. "Paris. He was still a free man when we spoke, but I rather doubt he remains so. The Duke of Normandy convinced him to go to Paris for talks with Philip. As soon as I heard the news, I made straight for Paris to discover what was afoot."

"But you're a known Montfortist, Amaury. How did you manage? And how did you manage to get near him?"

He chuckled. "Comes in handy, sometimes, to have a strong resemblance to one's brother. It's well known that Olivier's a close ally of Charles de Blois. All I had to do was make sure we were never in the same place at the same time, and I was allowed to come and go as I pleased." Stepping away from the hearth, he reached into his pocket and produced a folded page, which he handed to Jeanne before taking the chair opposite her. "John gave me this for you. It explains a lot. But I've no doubt you'll have questions after you read it."

She wasted no time breaking the seal and unfolding the missive, so eager had she been for even the smallest bit of news.

My dearest Jeanne,

If you are reading this, then Amaury is with you and that is for the best. His loyalty to us is unshakeable, and you can rely on him without question both for his advice and for any undertaking you might require. It may be some time before I am able to rejoin you, as it is most likely that by now, Philip has once again made me his prisoner. But I'm getting ahead of myself and there's much you should know.

You already know what happened at L'Humeau, so I shall pick up the tale from there. The French pursued us back to Nantes, even as they continued to besiege Champtoceaux, which fell soon after. Nantes should have been easy to defend. We'd have had no problems being resupplied by river. In fact, I believe we could easily have outlasted a siege for so long that the French army would've eventually given up and gone home.

If it weren't for the perfidious Nantais. That bastard Allaire was quick to remind us as soon as we returned that their support had been conditional on the king's recognition and that the king had just done otherwise. In truth, it's not fair to lay all the blame at Allaire's feet. He's not entirely unreasonable. But that wine merchant with the crooked nose was his usual insistent self as the French began establishing their camp outside the Porte Saint Pierre and along the Rivière d'Erdre. To the mayor's credit, he insisted everyone give their attention as Hervé and I explained how the town was ideally situated to resist. I also hinted that relief was on its way.

Jeanne paused in her reading. If only Edward weren't taking so long to fulfill his promise. Was he turning out to be as unreliable as the Nantais?

It didn't help that the French launched attacks on some of the outlying castles and brought their prisoners back to execute them in front of the town walls to show those inside they meant business. Nevertheless, we secured the Nantes officials' agreement to help defend the town on the condition that, if some sort of relief hadn't arrived within a month, we would leave the city and pursue our cause outside the walls. I was certain that would be sufficient time, certain that the reinforcements we'd negotiated would arrive by then.

To convince the townspeople we meant business and were not just hiding behind their walls, we launched raids against the French – raids that cost us more men than either Hervé or I would have liked. But our shows of courage seemed to hearten the ordinary folk and even some of the officials, though crook-nose refused to acknowledge our achievements and even once called me Pretender to my face.

I continued to be hopeful until the night we set out to capture the food wagons on their way to replenish the camp. The train was better defended than we'd anticipated, with even the wagoners armed to the teeth, and we began to take heavy casualties. Seeing some of the townsmen in our midst being slaughtered, the mercenaries turned tail and ran, led by Hervé, if you can credit that. They left me no choice but to call off the raid and follow them back inside the walls.

It pains me, now, to say that I completely lost my temper with Hervé. He tried to persuade me to see his point of view, but my disappointment at not being able to deal a manifest blow to the French forces fueled my anger and I refused to listen. The next morning, he and his men left in search of Charles de Blois to offer his allegiance and his services.

Once again Jeanne paused in her reading. *Oh, my dear, dear John,* she thought to herself. *How could you have made such a sad mistake? He was your strongest ally.* But then she brought herself up short. There was no way to know, sitting here in the safety of Rennes, what the strain on a man's emotions might be like in the midst of such a pitched fight to see your best friend turn tail and run for safety. She turned her eyes back to the letter.

Quarreling with Hervé was a mistake I have lived to regret and for which I must now beg your forgiveness. The following morning, Allaire called a meeting not only of the town officials but of all the merchants and guildsmen. It didn't take them long to agree on the ultimatum they delivered to me. Either I immediately undertake negotiations with the French for the surrender of the town or they would take matters into their own hands.

By then, my dear, I had little choice. I presented myself to the Duke of Normandy. Despite the disadvantages of my position, I was able to secure some considerations. In return for the surrender of all our garrisons in Brittany, Normandy granted me a safe conduct to Paris, in his company, and the promise that he would secure for me negotiations with his father, by which I hoped to reach some sort of compromise.

Before I surrendered, I ordered Kerveil to leave with as many men as he could smuggle out and make his way to Hennebont to reinforce the garrison there. The people there are intensely loyal and deserving of as much protection as I could provide them.

I must tell you also, Jeanne, that Raoul deserted us the moment we returned from L'Humeau. I spied him leaving the castle and scurrying across to the Convent of the Jacobins, all the while looking furtively around to see if anyone was watching. No way to know if he was in league with our opponents as you suspected or just an abject coward. Either way, his departure relieved me of the worry he might be eavesdropping when I was unaware.

But back to my account of events. We languished in Normandy's camp for the rest of the month. It broke my heart to see Charles ride into Nantes and receive the same reception and celebrations that had been ours just a few short months ago. I'm grateful you weren't there to witness it. We finally departed for Paris in early December.

Philip didn't receive me straightaway, but I remained at liberty, with the safe conduct in my possession while Normandy persuaded his father of my willingness to negotiate. During that time, Amaury found an opportunity to make his presence known to me. We had to be extremely circumspect in our meetings lest someone realize that he was not, in fact, Olivier. But he's privy to everything that transpired and can answer all your questions.

When Philip finally summoned me, his demeanor quite surprised me. Far from being vindictive or imperious, he seemed in the mood to strike a deal. And his offer was not ungenerous. Extensive lands in France, from which the income would be quite substantial. And of course, restoration of our Montfort lands. All in return for ceding my claim to Brittany. He also promised that, should Jeanne de Penthièvre die childless, Brittany would revert to Montfort hands.

I have agonized over the decision and even sought Amaury's advice. What I really craved, my dearest Jeanne, was your advice, your opinion, your insight. But that was not to be. In the end, I remembered my deathbed promise to my brother to see that his legacy was preserved and his wishes carried out. And so, my dear, I have come to the painful conclusion that accepting Philip's offer would dishonor not only my half-brother but our father as well . . . and, in truth, the people of Brittany.

All of which means that, by the time you read this, I will no doubt be Philip's prisoner once again. And this time, effecting an escape would be highly unlikely. In fact, I won't even consider it, for I'll do nothing to jeopardize the possibility of regaining the title and securing our son's rightful inheritance.

It also means that, for now, our cause is in your hands. There is no one I trust more. And so I exhort you to trust your instincts and to act on them. No matter what happens, know that I will never gainsay any decision you make nor any engagement you undertake on our behalf.

Know also how very dear you are to me and that I shall pray each day that it will not be long before we are reunited. Until then, I entrust to you the legacy I've sworn to uphold and the protection of our children.

Your loving

John

She folded the page and held it in her lap. So many questions, but really only one. "And he's in Philip's prison now?"

"Held in the Louvre," de Clisson replied. "I confirmed it before coming here. But held as a proper noble prisoner, not as a common villain. So long as he does nothing to provoke the king, it's unlikely that will change."

Jeanne could feel the moisture gathering in her eyes. To avoid succumbing, she crossed the room and stepped into the corridor, calling to her maid.

Aalix scurried from her mistress's bedchamber next door. "*Oui, madame?*" Her usual way of asking what was wanted.

"Find Henri and send him to me, please."

"*Oui, madame.*" Aalix rushed down the stairs.

Blinking several times quickly then wiping her eyes, Jeanne turned back into the room and crossed to the hearth to stoke the fire. In no time at all, Henri was at the door. "You sent for me, madame?"

She replaced the poker in its holder and turned around. "Lord de Clisson will be staying with us for now, Henri. Take him to the nicest room, please, and see to whatever he needs. Then once you've refreshed yourself, Amaury, return to me here. And Henri, find Durant and join us . . . both of you."

"As you wish, madame. My lord?" The steward stood aside for de Clisson to precede him into the corridor.

When the door was closed behind them, Jeanne sank into her chair, held John's letter to her heart, and let the tears spill freely down her cheeks.

· · · · ·

By the time the three men had returned, not only had Jeanne regained her composure but her demeanor had changed completely. Anyone seeing her for the first time that day would find but a single word suitable to describe her . . . resolute.

While de Clisson made straight for the chairs in front of the hearth and took a seat, Durant and Henri stood respectfully aside. "Come. Sit." Jeanne beckoned to them. "What we're about to do, the four of us must do together." Obviously discomfited in this unfamiliar situation, the two men reluctantly took the remaining chairs.

"Now, what you two don't know," she addressed her words to her steward and her captain, "is that I've had news from the duke. A letter in his own hand, thanks to Lord de Clisson. The news we'd feared rather than what we'd hoped for. He's once again been detained by the king and there are no prospects for his release, so it now falls to us to repulse those who challenge the rightful succession.

"And I've decided that we cannot do it from here. You've both heard the rumors – seen the shift in mood of many of the Rennais. Our support here is no longer as solid as it once was, despite what the mayor continues to claim. Charles will soon turn his sights on Rennes or Vannes, and that will open wide the division of loyalties that's now simmering below the surface here, fueled by the gossip.

"Durant, am I right that the garrison here isn't strong enough – even if everyone was loyal – to withstand an assault by the French army?"

"Not for long, my lady. And the town's not well situated to endure a protracted siege."

"I thought as much. Not only that, the fact that I'm here makes it an even more attractive target than Vannes. But I will *not* give Jeanne de Penthièvre the satisfaction of calling herself Duchess of Brittany in my presence or of demanding my submission. So we must leave here at once."

The furrows in Henri's brow had grown deeper with every word she spoke, his distress now pinching his entire face. "Henri, you look troubled," said Jeanne.

"It's not for me to question, madame."

She softened her tone. "Your deference is much to be admired, Henri, but what I need most now is your competence and your clear thinking. So if something's on your mind, the best service you can give me is to speak up. It will in no way reflect poorly on you."

"Then . . ." He hesitated before testing her words. "What concerns me, madame, is where we can go. Where is a place that's safer? And, of course, how soon do you wish to leave?"

"My thought is that we should go to Hennebont. It has a strong fortress and easy access to the sea should things go horribly wrong and we were forced to flee. And the duke has said more than once that the people there are intensely loyal to us. As to when . . . as soon as you and Durant can be ready."

De Clisson had been silent throughout her recitation but now spoke up. "An excellent choice, my dear. For all the reasons you cited. The people in that area are fiercely Breton, with no love for the French. And they have no ties at all to Penthièvre."

"And I can confirm the strength of the fortress," Durant chimed in. "Saw it with my own eyes during the western campaign with Lord Hervé and the duke."

"Good," said Jeanne. "We're agreed. The best way to undertake an enterprise. So now, Henri, in addition to being responsible for the household, I need you to become my paymaster. The soldiers must be paid – the ones with us, those in the garrison at Brest, and those with Malestroit at Saint-Renan. Nothing will change a soldier's loyalty faster than not being paid. Durant can advise you how much you'll need. Take all that and whatever you'll need to run the household in coinage with us."

"For how long, madame?" Henri spoke up this time without waiting to be asked.

"Half a year at least," she replied.

"Perhaps you should plan for a bit longer," de Clisson suggested.

"I shall heed your advice, my lord."

"The rest of the treasury," Jeanne resumed, "the plate, the jewels, and the rest of the coinage must go to Brest – as far away from French hands as possible."

"Why not just take it all with us?" asked Durant.

"To confound Charles," she replied. "If I'm in one place and the treasury in another, then he has to make a decision about which to try to capture first. Either that, or divide his forces." What she didn't tell them at this juncture was the scheme she was still turning over in her mind. Thankfully, her explanation seemed to satisfy everyone's curiosity.

"Amaury, I must ask you for a great favor."

"If it's within my power, my dear."

"Take the treasury to Brest. See that it's secure there. Make sure whoever you leave in charge is completely trustworthy and their loyalty is without question. Then join me in Hennebont. I may have another mission for you then."

Despite remaining seated, de Clisson made a great show of bowing his head to Jeanne. "As you wish . . ." He paused for effect. "Duchess."

CHAPTER FOURTEEN

Dunstable, England, February 1342

When the stranger unhorsed yet another opponent, Queen Philippa touched her husband's arm. "Do we know who the newcomer is?"

"I'm told he's a Breton nobleman. Remarkably skilled, don't you think?"

"I do indeed. Any idea what brings him here?"

"No. But I intend to find out."

Amaury de Clisson had spent the Channel crossing trying to devise the best approach to carry out his mission. A frontal assault might not succeed. What he needed was a way to attract Edward's interest. And when he heard about the tournament at Dunstable, it seemed he might have found the solution.

His skill in the lists was widely heralded in Brittany. In his younger years, he'd often gone undefeated in tournament after tournament. Even after he stepped away from actively competing, he tried to keep his skills fresh, though there'd been few opportunities to use them in the past year or so.

Arriving at Dunstable as the contestants were gathering, he set about assessing his chances. According to the squires, King Edward quite enjoyed seeing a challenger to his knights ... provided the challenger wasn't a Scotsman. So Amaury acquired some armor and added his name to the roster of competitors.

By the end of the first day of the tournament, everyone was talking about the Breton who, so far, remained among the top contenders. De Clisson smiled to himself and kept to himself. Being elusive was part of his plan.

By midday on the second day – still among the leaders – he knew it was time to change tactics. Besting all of Edward's knights would hardly get him the kind of attention he wanted. So he waited until he was paired with the strongest competitor – being unhorsed by a man of questionable skill wouldn't serve his purposes either – and allowed the man's lance to deal him a glancing blow, ensuring that he and his horse parted ways in a manner that was least likely to result in serious injury. When he yielded, the applause continued even after the victor had ridden off the field, and Amaury managed to steal a glance toward the royal platform to see Edward and his queen applauding with the rest. He affected an awkward bow, then made his way off the field on foot.

That evening, he'd just returned to his room at the inn after joining a bit of the celebratory revels when he was startled by insistent knocking on his door. He opened it to find a man in royal livery bearing a message, which he thrust into Amaury's hand before turning on his heel and leaving without a word. The seal bore the lion passant guardant of the English king. Amaury opened the missive carefully.

His grace King Edward invites you to attend him at his lodgings in Dunstable Priory on the morrow, an hour before midday.

No signature, but the seal said all that was necessary. Amaury had his audience. Now it was up to him to make the most of it.

• • • • •

At the appointed hour, de Clisson stood in the entry hall of a rather grand house on the grounds of the priory. The length of the hall and its elaborate vaulted ceiling with brightly painted bosses reminded him of a cathedral. *Perhaps that shouldn't be a surprise*, he reflected. *It's quite likely the house was erected by the same craftsmen who built the priory church.* Much to his surprise, he wasn't kept waiting. The liveried servant who'd ushered him in returned almost immediately with a curt, "Come this way."

The English king received him in a south-facing room warmed both by sunlight through its numerous windows and a roaring fire in the hearth. Tapestries on the walls depicted both hunting scenes and religious themes, a peculiar contrast in a single room, de Clisson thought. *Perhaps not so peculiar, though, for a secular house within the grounds of a religious compound.*

He doffed his cap and bowed. "Your Grace. I'm honored by the invitation."

"I quite wanted to meet the man who gave my knights some lessons in the art of jousting," said Edward. "That was an extraordinary performance. I'm told you hail from Brittany."

"Your praise is most generous, Sire. Amaury de Clisson, vassal of the Duke of Brittany. It's been my good fortune to hone my skill in the duke's past tournaments."

"Which leads me to wonder why you might choose to test your prowess here."

"Your Grace is no doubt aware of the conflict that currently divides the loyalties of the Breton nobility. As a result, there have been no tournaments for these many months."

Edward stroked his chin. That was hardly sufficient motivation for crossing the sea. Why was this man really here? "And where do your *own* loyalties lie, de Clisson?"

"I am Breton to the core, Sire. They could lie with no other than the rightful duke – the man named by our late, well-loved Duke John as his successor."

"You speak of John de Montfort."

"Who now, alas, languishes as a prisoner of the French king."

"So we were informed," said Edward.

Understanding dawned for Amaury. Perhaps this was why the promised English support Jeanne had spoken of never materialized. Was Edward going to be reluctant to do anything so long as Montfort was imprisoned? If so, his mission here had just become far more difficult. Nevertheless, the king showed no inclination toward throwing him out. Time to reveal another card. "For the moment, it's my privilege to serve the duchess, who acts on behalf of her young son, now formally designated head of the family until such time as his father is once again a free man."

"Indeed." Edward rose, leaving his guest scrambling to get to his feet. "Please ... take your seat." The king made his way to a sideboard where a bejeweled pitcher stood surrounded by mazers with silver-gilt rims and feet to match. "May I offer you something to quench your thirst? 'Tis but small ale, but I find it quite suitable to the purpose."

Far from throwing Amaury out, Edward was extending hospitality. Did this mean he was also ready to extend a listening ear? "I'd be most grateful, Sire."

The king filled two mazers and returned to his seat, proffering one of the vessels to his guest, before taking a drink from his own. "If you're in the duchess's confidence, then perhaps she's spoken of engagements the duke undertook while he was still a free man."

"She has, Your Grace." Amaury took a long swallow of his own small ale, using the time to make up his mind what to say next. The wrong thing could confound all he'd accomplished so far ... perhaps even upend his entire mission. But making progress required taking some risk. "She's also spoken of her disappointment that those engagements came to naught."

"You may be surprised to learn, de Clisson, that I share her disappointment. Sometimes events move things in ways we would not otherwise choose. But then, as time moves on, it can once again become possible to reconsider the original pursuit."

An invitation, if Amaury had ever heard one, to reveal his true mission. Still, he needed to tread carefully. The duchess was the supplicant in these negotiations, yet she wasn't without power. The chests from the ducal treasury that he'd brought with him and lodged for safekeeping with a London banker might prove as tempting to Edward as she hoped. "Then you should know, Sire, that the duchess would be glad of the opportunity to renew the arrangement."

Once again, Edward rose from his chair, but this time he gestured straightway for Amaury to remain seated. Walking to the hearth, he poked the fire then added another piece of wood before turning to face his guest. "I'm certain the duchess is not unaware of the costs associated with such engagements. Even now, I'm committed to help Hainault and Brabant prevent French encroachment as well as to defending my own holdings in Gascony. And the troublesome Scots continue to make a nuisance of themselves in the north. There's a limit to how much I can tax my own people to raise the money required for these pursuits."

"As you suggest, Sire, my lady understands full well that such pursuits don't occur solely by the grace of God. She is quite willing to participate in funding the effort to suppress the challenge to her husband's rightful – indeed, lawful in both France and Brittany – claim to the duchy."

Edward didn't reply – simply nodded his head, his expression bland and revealing nothing. Amaury knew the king wanted something more. He also knew things might not go well if Edward was forced to ask for what he wanted. "To that end, Your Grace, she has sent with me proof of her good faith – treasure that is at this moment secure with a London banker, awaiting the progress of our talks."

Amaury could see his words had hit the mark. The bland expression transformed itself into a half-smile. The king's next words were of encouragement. "Your duchess seems quite astute – far wiser in the ways of the world than most women. Has she also invested you with the authority to negotiate on her behalf?"

"The duchess has made her objectives crystal clear to me and, having done so, given me broad powers, Sire, to conclude an agreement without further consultation."

Edward's smile broadened. "Then it seems, sir, that we may have much to discuss. Come to me three days hence in the afternoon at Westminster Palace. For now, you're free to go."

"It would be my pleasure, Your Grace." Amaury rose and bowed his head in acknowledgment.

Making his way to the door, he stopped at the sound of Edward's voice. "And it wouldn't go amiss, de Clisson, for you to bring with you some evidence of your duchess's good faith."

Amaury turned. "Also my pleasure, Your Grace."

It was all de Clisson could do to maintain a formal demeanor as he was led through the house to the exit. But once on the street and headed for a tavern in search of a midday meal, he couldn't suppress a giddy grin. That meeting had exceeded even his wildest expectations. Now he just had to find a way to hurry the negotiations toward an agreement so Jeanne would get the help she needed before the French could overwhelm her.

. . . . .

That evening, as he shared a private meal with his wife, Edward, too, was almost giddy. "It seems my Breton strategy isn't dead after all," he announced the moment the servants had left the room.

Philippa was pleased to see him in a good mood. He'd been rather morose following the recent campaign to suppress yet another Scottish uprising. "Your meeting with the jouster from Brittany?" she asked.

"More than just a jouster, though I have to admit he was quite impressive. An emissary from Montfort's duchess. She wants to renew our arrangement. And this time, she's offering to pay for the expedition."

"The situation must be rather dire."

"All the more reason to think my strategy might succeed."

Sometimes, Philippa knew, her role was to remind her husband of things that could go awry. "But if she's in that much need of your help, then doesn't that mean you'd be in a fight with the French army straightaway? Even before you could lay claim to any useful territory?"

"Perhaps. But think, my dear. If Philip has to pour men into Brittany, he has to take them from somewhere. It would almost certainly relieve some of the pressure in Gascony."

"And what about the Truce of Esplechin? That doesn't expire until late June. Would you violate that?"

"If I have to. Think about it, Philippa. Brittany is the prize. Why keep slogging things out with Philip skirmish after skirmish, truce after truce in the Low Countries with absolutely no help from Emperor Ludwig when we have a far greater chance of achieving our ends by changing our strategy?"

"But if you break the truce, Philip will feel like he has free rein in Hainault and in Flanders as well."

"Not for very long. But it suits my strategy just fine for the short term. While he thinks he's getting the better of us there, we can get a foothold in Brittany. Once he realizes what I'm up to, he'll abandon the idea of expanding his holdings to the east."

"I rather doubt even *I* can convince my brother that's a good idea."

"Nor would I ask you to," said Edward. "In truth, dear, the more I contemplate this, the more I like it. And I'm confident if William were here, he'd approve as well. He was never fond of the Low Countries strategy anyway."

"Any progress on getting him home?" she asked.

"Barely. Philip's at least let him out of the Châtelet and allowed him to live on his own, but I'm told he can't take a step, even in his own lodgings, without French guards dogging his every move.

"For now, I just have to proceed without him. I've summoned the Council to Westminster. The Breton emissary as well. I want to see the treasure he claims to have in his possession. Then it will simply be a matter of how much money I can extract as part of the deal."

Philippa smiled. "Somehow I suspect you'll drive a hard bargain." She swallowed the last of the wine in her goblet and watched as Edward took another duck leg from the serving platter and wolfed it down. She knew his mind was made up and that the Breton money was the inducement he'd use to get the Council's consent.

That night, in her bedchamber, he took her with a ferocity she hadn't experienced in many months. There was no doubt in her mind he was imagining himself ploughing the fields of France.

CHAPTER FIFTEEN

Westminster Palace, 22 February 1342

Despite the honor of being summoned to serve the king once again, de Mauny was more than a little uneasy. Why in the name of Beelzebub's bastards did it have to be on a Thursday? *Don't be ridiculous, Walter,* he chided himself. *This is a completely new venture. Put the last fiasco out of your mind.* But somehow he couldn't quite shake the superstition. Then when the first words out of Edward's mouth were, "Good news, Sir Walter, the Breton expedition is back on," he groaned inwardly.

"How many men will I have?"

"I can give you two hundred men-at-arms and the same number of archers."

This Thursday was living up to de Mauny's worst imaginings. What was being offered was barely a token force in the face of the French army. Somehow, he managed to keep a grimace from his face and his tongue in check.

"You're in charge of the advance guard," the king continued. "To invest the western ports and support the duchess so she's not overrun before our main forces arrive. Northhampton and Artois will follow in April. I'll lead the rest of the army myself after the truce in the Low Countries expires."

De Mauny knew he couldn't just stand there, mute, but all he could manage for the moment was, "Yes, Your Grace." His mind was racing. He could predict with absolute certainty the first problem he would face. The same problem that had dogged him and Morley during the prior, aborted expedition. *If the king's so bent on fighting wars across the ocean, why in the name of Saint Swithun's bones doesn't he commission his own fleet?* Walter fumed to himself. Aloud, he said, "And do I need to find my own ships, Sire?"

"Not this time. I already have agents requisitioning ships for the entire campaign. The first sixty will be sent to Portsmouth for your use. Royal agents there will organize the ships and their provisioning. All you have to do is assemble your men and be ready by the middle of March."

All I have to do. Somehow I can't imagine it's going to be that easy. "Is there anything else, Your Grace? Anything more I should know before getting things underway?"

"Only that I'm counting on you, de Mauny. I *need* Brittany to bolster my claim to the French throne. So I need to be confident that when the rest of our forces arrive, they can land safely and not lose men even before they come in contact with the French." Then his manner changed – softened, as it were. "Look. I know your force is small. But the duchess's emissary assures me that the garrisons in those ports are deeply loyal to Montfort, so your job should primarily be to put Englishmen in charge. Recruit your men-at-arms with that in mind. To help disguise your efforts, I'm issuing letters of marque to a number of shipmasters to harass and pillage French ships in the Channel and off southern Gascony. That will be another distraction for Philip until our main forces can establish themselves in Brittany."

"Then I'll wish them happy hunting. If there's nothing else, Sire, perhaps I should get underway with my task."

"You're free to go, de Mauny. Make things ready for us."

Sir Walter left Westminster Palace as uneasy as when he'd arrived. He was going to need every bit of luck Fortuna could send his way. He had little confidence the royal agents would actually have sixty ships available in such a short time. Then again, it being barely the end of winter, maybe more ships were in port than would be the case in finer weather. If Northhampton and Artois were expected to sail at the beginning of April, the requisitioning would have to proceed at a much faster pace than usual. Not only that, de Mauny would need to get underway quickly in order to complete his mission before the larger fleet sailed. Acquiring the ships might not be his problem this time, but that wouldn't keep him from fretting over its getting done.

He already had in mind the men he wanted to put in charge of the Breton ports and was confident he could enlist them. Once they were with him, the rest of the plans could be laid. *But one thing I damn well won't do,* he told himself, *is land up in Portsmouth on a Thursday.*

CHAPTER SIXTEEN

Hennebont, April 1342

Waiting patiently for help from England was beginning to feel like a repetition of the events of the previous autumn. Was Edward going to renege on his agreement once again? What if he was holding out for greater enticements? If that was the case, she had nothing left to offer. The Plantagenet had driven a hard bargain. De Clisson had paid him five thousand *livres tournois* to finance the advance guard. Another sixty-eight thousand was due as soon as the first wave of the main army landed. Edward would then claim the rest of the ducal treasury when he himself arrived in the summer with the rest of the troops.

Jeanne had been disappointed that she'd have to empty her coffers to secure the support necessary to protect her son's future. But she also knew that once her husband was restored to his position as duke, they could soon replenish their wealth from the income of the duchy. They might even be able to force the forfeiture of Penthièvre as part of the settlement, depriving her rival of any rights in Brittany and securing that income as well for future dukes. The other Jeanne wouldn't suffer – as Charles's wife, she'd have more than enough money and prestige. It was a state of affairs to be wished for, but there were more pressing matters at hand in the moment.

They'd traveled from Rennes as unobtrusively as they could – no banners flying, no jupons sporting the ducal coat of arms – but it was inevitable that a richly decorated carriage accompanied by a cadre of armed men would garner attention wherever they passed. In the first two days, they encountered the occasional brigands, some claiming to be soldiers of Charles de Blois, but Durant and his men quickly put paid to whatever visions of glory they might have harbored. The farther west they went, the more they were met with little other than curiosity and the occasional cheer of encouragement.

Once in Hennebont, they discovered that Kerveil and his men had arrived several days earlier. "I only have three dozen men, my lady." Kerveil was apologetic. "'Twas all I could sneak out without the town officials getting wind of what we were doing."

"You've no reason to apologize, Kerveil," she told him. "You're here, and every man is valuable."

In truth, it wasn't the number of men he brought that mattered most to Jeanne. It was Kerveil himself. He was Breton from his name to his boot soles, and everyone knew he'd long been commander of the late duke's military forces. That he was casting his lot with the Montforts would reassure everyone in the west that their loyalties were not misplaced.

At the beginning of March, she'd agreed to a truce with Philip. The document had called it a surrender. But it also confirmed that she retained control of all her towns and garrisons. In effect, it was a temporary formalization of the status quo, and she understood that it was Philip's way of buying time. Just as it was hers. But now, with the end of the truce approaching, she was growing anxious about what was to come next.

Hennebont had welcomed her with enthusiasm. With her household settled in the little castle overlooking the Rivière Blavet, Jeanne spent much of her time among the townspeople. She frequently brought young John with her, especially on market days. The women in the stalls doted on him and loved spoiling him with sweet treats or little carved toys. And even though there was a small chapel inside the castle, she always attended Mass alongside the ordinary people at the church inside the town walls. The personal loyalty of these people would be invaluable when the inevitable confrontation with Charles de Blois's army occurred.

But creating a bond with the common people wasn't her only preparation. Once a week she met with the mayor and the town leaders, usually accompanied by Durant and Kerveil. She'd begun with praise for their defenses and discussions about the best ways to deploy both the garrison and her additional men-at-arms. By the fourth meeting, she came around to what she knew would be most important. "We're safe here for a time, *monsieur le maire*," she began, "but I think we all know that if the French take Rennes or Vannes, it won't be long before they turn their sights on us."

Everyone in the room nodded solemnly. "It's not a pleasant thought, my lady," said the mayor, "but one I fear we must reckon with."

She hadn't expected such readiness to face reality. "Then I have some ideas and, of course, encourage you to contribute your own. We're in a good position here, and if what's happened in the past is any guide, the French would rather wear us down than engage in an all-out fight. So we need to be prepared to withstand a siege. Which means we need to stockpile as much food as we can. Flour, oats, barley. Anything dried – lentils, beans. Every spare barrel you can lay your hands on should be used to capture rainwater. We should bring in as many chickens as we can make room for. Eggs will go a long way toward keeping people fed. Some pigs as well. Whatever dried meat we have left from the winter stores should be saved. Durant and Kerveil can organize hunts for fresh meat to eat now. Men from the town and men-at-arms together. I know it's early in the year, but we should take what we can."

"What about fish?" the mayor asked. "If we send a few fishing boats to the sea each week, their catch should be enough to have food now and to preserve some for when we might need it later."

"A superb idea, monsieur," said Jeanne. "Will you take charge of that?"

The mayor beamed. "With pleasure, my lady."

"The hunting and fishing will cost us nothing, but I know we'll have to buy the rest, and I'm prepared to contribute to the cost. See my steward for what's needed beyond what the town can do on its own." She knew Henri would be a stickler for accounting for every *denier* spent. She also knew he understood the stakes and wouldn't try to impose false economies when so many lives hung in the balance.

The rest of the time she spent with Durant and Kerveil planning their defensive strategy. They had to be prepared in the event English help didn't arrive in time. Mounted on her charger, she rode with them through the surrounding countryside, surveying the lay of the land and postulating how Charles might deploy his men. But even Durant, who'd known her for longer than anyone except her maid, Aaliz, was surprised by her next request. "I want some armor. Cuirass and backplate. With faulds. And spaulders. And I want a sword."

"My lady?" Durant couldn't help but gawp in disbelief.

"If I'm going to take the duke's place as head of his fighting forces, then I need to look the part. And protect myself from whatever weapons might come against me."

"I . . . I don't know if we have anything that would fit you."

"That shouldn't be a problem. The town has a blacksmith, no? If you can't find something, then have it made. Aaliz can give you a pattern that my dressmakers use."

Durant shook his head. This woman never ceased to surprise him. "Whatever you wish, madame."

She gave him a radiant smile. "You'll see, Durant. This will turn out to be a very, very good idea."

CHAPTER SEVENTEEN

For most people, April 15th was just another ordinary day, but for Jeanne and her captains, it marked the end of the truce. The end of their respite from the French threat. None of them voiced their thoughts. There was no need – each knew the others' without putting them into words.

Kerveil began sending out scouts every morning. Each day they returned with no sightings was another day the English had time to arrive. And each day with no sight of the English was another day added to the growing tension felt by the duchess and her lieutenants.

To avoid raising alarm in the town before it was really necessary, Jeanne kept to her habit of mingling with the townspeople. And with spring now in full swing, she often took both children with her, giving the women of the town a chance to fawn over her baby daughter even as they continued to spoil little John.

At the end of April, they got their first real news. It was the feast day of Saint Hugh the Great when a messenger reined his horse to a stop outside the castle gate and asked to see Captain Durant. Durant and Kerveil brought the young man straight to Jeanne's sitting room.

"I've seen you before," she said as the messenger doffed his cap and bowed.

"Aye, my lady, when I brought the news of L'Humeau to you in Rennes."

"He stayed behind with the garrison there," Durant explained. "To be my messenger when the need arose."

Jeanne's heart sank. She could guess the news even before the young man spoke. "Rennes has fallen, my lady," he said. "Charles de Blois took it about five days ago. But the army hasn't moved on. They're still establishing their control over Rennes."

"What's more interesting, madame," said Kerveil, "is the makeup of Blois's army. Tell her, lad."

"'Tweren't Frenchmen. Leastways, not many. Some wore the Blois badge. A few had emblems from some of the Frenchie Breton families. But most of them ... I couldn't understand a word they said. The garrison commander told me they were Spanish and Italian."

"So Philip isn't committing himself," said Durant. "He's leaving Charles on his own to take the duchy if he really wants it that bad."

"You mean, if his *wife* really wants it that bad." Jeanne's tone was caustic. Then she brightened. "Regardless, that makes it all the more important that we stop him here."

When the three men had departed, Jeanne rose and began pacing about the room. *Spanish and Italian mercenaries. That must mean he couldn't even raise enough men in the Breton marches to constitute an army. It also means the army has no interest in the conflict other than coin – no moral commitment to either France or Brittany. Unfortunately, I suspect Philip will sit up and take notice once the English arrive. If they ever do. What in God's name is taking so long?*

. . . . .

The feast of Saint Agnes of Poitiers came and went without any sighting of either Charles's army or the English. A growing uncertainty gnawed at Jeanne, making her more restive by the day. Had she wasted the five thousand *livres* already handed over to Edward? She still had most of her treasury. If Edward didn't live up to his part of the bargain, she had the wherewithal to hire her own mercenaries. But where would she find them? Could she bribe Charles's mercenaries to switch sides? Could she convince her brother in Flanders to send men? That seemed unlikely – he had problems of his own with the French.

Other worries troubled her mind as well. Would her own supporters become disillusioned? Would they come to think she was simply hiding like a coward in Hennebont rather than prosecuting their cause? And how long could Durant and Kerveil keep their men at peak readiness to fight before they, too, became weary and inattentive?

Then, on the eve of the feast of Saint Joanna, one of Kerveil's scouts – who'd been out for longer than usual – returned with reports of sightings of Charles's army. He'd ridden hard to bring back the news and was still somewhat out of breath as he repeated his report for Jeanne's benefit. "I didn't lay eyes on them myself, my lady, but there was talk in Locminé of an army camped at Ploërmel. I went on as far as Saint-Allouestre to see if I could learn anything more. The villagers there claimed to have heard there were as many as three thousand men."

"What did you make of those estimates?" Jeanne asked.

"Hard to say, madame. Might have been an exaggeration. You know how numbers like that get blown up with repeated telling of the tale. One thing I *can* say is that the villagers were pretty frightened of being in the army's path. Anyway, I didn't go no further. Decided Captain Kerveil would want to know soon as could be, so I raced back here, fast as I could."

"They've almost certainly reached Josselin by now, madame," said Kerveil.

"Likely they'll be here before the week is out," Durant added.

By some sort of perverse logic, Jeanne welcomed the news. At least now she would be able to set aside her concern for her people's state of mind and worry instead about her military options. And the absent English.

Durant's prediction was prescient. Just five days later, Charles's army had established its camp outside the walls of Hennebont. As soon as his banners had been spotted, the town closed its gates, locking the defenders safely within. At first, the army did nothing. On the second day, a man bearing a white flag delivered a message demanding immediate surrender. Jeanne sent him away without a reply.

The next day, over the loud objections of Durant, Kerveil, and even Henri, she donned her armor and climbed the steps to the ramparts. Hearing bootsteps on the stairs behind her, she turned to see Durant leading a dozen armed men. "You can come up, Durant, but no one else," she said. "I don't want anyone in that camp thinking we're doing anything other than surveying the situation. Soldiers will give the wrong impression."

Durant let out a huge sigh then ordered his men, "Wait below. But watch for my signal. If I see anything amiss, you're to run up and get the duchess to safety at once." Then he joined her atop the wall.

"It's quite a large camp," she observed. "How many men do you think they have?"

Jeanne watched as his commander's eye scanned the encampment and could imagine the calculations going on inside his head. So many tents. So many men to a tent. More men sleeping in the open. "The scout's information wasn't far wrong," he finally said. "Two thousand at the least. Perhaps more."

"Do we have anything in our favor, Durant? Besides these ramparts."

"Well, if most of those men are Spanish or Italian, I'd wager they're also mostly ship's crews pressed into service. Sailors aren't always soldiers by nature. A lot will depend on who's leading them."

"I've heard it said Charles is an able commander."

"Aye, I've heard that too. But what matters just as much is who the individual soldiers look to in the thick of things."

As they walked along the wall, away from the safety of the sentry tower, Durant grew increasingly agitated. "Don't you think you've exposed yourself enough, my lady?"

"I want the people inside the walls to see I'm not afraid, Durant. They're going to need all the courage I can give them. And I want the men in that camp to see my determination. They may outnumber us, but numbers don't always decide a battle."

FROM THE WRITINGS OF JEANNE DE FLANDRE, DUCHESS OF
BRITTANY AND COUNTESS OF MONTFORT
FOUND AMONG HER BELONGINGS AT THE TIME OF HER DEATH

Tickhill, South Yorkshire, 1348

I couldn't say it then. Not to Durant. Not even to myself. But now I can admit that the first time I walked those ramparts, I was truly afraid. One man with a crossbow who took it into his head to be a hero could have ended my life there and then.

But just as frightening was the vastness of the encampment to the north and east of us. How could we possibly prevail against such a force? Even if every man, woman, and child in the town joined in the fight, we were outnumbered by two, perhaps three to one.

We had the river at our backs, so we couldn't be surrounded. And of course, the river provided an escape should we be overwhelmed. But I couldn't think about escape – only about winning. Somehow I knew, deep in my soul, that our future – my son's future – depended on our thwarting Jeanne de Penthièvre's ambitions in that place, at that time.

So as Durant and I descended the steps back into the safety of the town, I cursed Edward Plantagenet for his false promises then made straight to the chapel and prayed to God and Saint Jude for our deliverance.

CHAPTER EIGHTEEN

Charles's army had been sitting outside the walls of Hennebont for five days and, other than the single message demanding surrender, had done absolutely nothing. "It's unnerving," Jeanne told her captains during their daily meeting in the garrison commander's little office.

"And that's precisely what they're trying to achieve," said Kerveil. "It's how they took Nantes. Inspiring enough fear in the town for the people to open the gates and capitulate."

"But the duke led raids into their ranks then," she countered. "Somehow, though, that doesn't seem like a good idea for us."

"It's not, madame," said Durant. "We can't afford to lose even one man. And especially not any of the townspeople. Nothing would demoralize these folk faster than to see their fathers and brothers fallen. Notwithstanding all the loyalty and goodwill you've built."

"So we treat it like a siege," said Jeanne.

"And watch for opportunities," added Durant. "Men just sitting in camp for days on end get bored. And sometimes they do something stupid."

"What if they have siege engines?" she asked.

"We've seen no evidence of that so far," said Kerveil. "We've got a good view of the whole camp from the towers. In the flat terrain of that meadow, catapults, trebuchets, ballistas ... those would be almost impossible to conceal. And if they were starting to assemble siege towers to get men over the walls, they'd most likely do that as close to the town as possible so they wouldn't have to tow them so far. We've seen no evidence of anything like that."

"That's not to say they couldn't bring them in, madame," added Durant, anticipating her next question. "But why? They control all the roads coming in—"

"And for all we know, they may have a force watching the river farther south," Kerveil interjected.

"So my guess is they're thinking all they have to do is starve us out," said Durant.

"And we've prepared for that. So, from this moment," she declared, "we go on siege footing. We treat the food and water we have as if it has to last for weeks on end."

"Do you want to call the people together to announce that?" asked Durant.

"No. I'd rather talk to them as they go about their business. Let them know I'm sharing their privation. But the one thing I won't do is starve the children. If the soldiers have to skip a meal now and then – if I have to skip a meal now and then – so be it. I won't have the children going hungry unless we're down to our last sack of flour."

The next day and the morning of the following day passed in utter calm. To Jeanne, it was an eerie calm. One could almost forget there were thousands of men just waiting for them to give in. But of course, she couldn't forget. She made her rounds, talking with the shopkeepers and the people in the streets, leaving the children with Perota while she talked about the realities of the situation.

As she crossed the market square shortly after midday, she heard Kerveil shouting from the ramparts. "Durant, get up here. Something's going on."

Despite not having her armor on, she rushed to the nearest stairs and scrambled up to the top of the wall to be met by Kerveil's angry, "You shouldn't be up here, my lady. It's too dangerous."

"If something's happening, Kerveil, I want to see for myself."

Just at that moment, Durant joined them at a run. "There." Kerveil pointed. "On the east side of the camp. Looks like they're getting organized for an assault. Mostly infantry, by the looks of it, but there's a small group on horseback."

As they watched, the men gathered in a ragged formation and started advancing toward the walls. "Get below, Duchess." Durant ordered, adding "Now!" when Jeanne hesitated. He followed her down the steps, making sure she didn't turn back, all the while shouting orders to his men to take their fighting positions.

Determined to be seen leading the fight, Jeanne hoisted her skirts and ran for the castle to fetch her armor. She'd only managed to get her cuirass and backplate in place when the sounds of something hammering the gate reached her ears. Abandoning the rest, she grabbed her sword and dashed back outside.

Soldiers and archers atop the ramparts were shouting to each other as they lobbed arrows and spears at the attackers. The noise at the gate grew louder. Was that because she was getting closer or because they'd brought up a more effective battering ram?

Halfway across the market square, she spied a young woman crouching beside a rain barrel screaming and crying and hugging a bucket to her chest. Obviously a kitchen maid from one of the finer houses who'd been sent to fetch water, the girl was terrified even though no fighting was happening inside the walls. Jeanne rushed over.

She tried to get the girl to her feet with no success. "We'll all be killed," the girl blubbered. "I can't get back home. I can't cross that square. I'll be killed if I do. We'll all be killed." Fear had consumed her, reducing her to a single thought.

Jeanne crouched down beside her. "Look at me. I'm here to help you. You won't be harmed, I promise. Now, if you'll just let me help you up, I'll take you home. Can you do that?"

A sudden blow made the gate shudder and the girl screamed.

Then Jeanne had an idea. She shook the girl's shoulders to get her attention. "You don't want to be killed, right?" The girl nodded through her tears. "Well, neither do I, so here's what we're going to do. We're going to take this bucket and fill it with rocks from the rubble pile where that house was pulled down last year, and we're going to climb to the top of the walls and lob those rocks at the attackers so they stop what they're doing and run away. Do you hear me?"

Again, the girl nodded. And this time, she snuffled back her tears and wiped her nose on her sleeve. "Good," said Jeanne. "Now give me your hand and I'll help you up. And while we get our rocks, we're going to shout to all our friends to fill baskets with rocks or anything they can find and come up on the walls to help us."

Through the noise of battle on the ramparts, Jeanne began waving her sword and shouting at the top of her lungs. "This is everyone's fight. Grab whatever you can find. Women, lift your skirts and fill them with rocks or wood or knives and climb the walls. Let's rain hell on the men who think to break us."

As dozens of women followed her instructions and Jeanne reached the top of the ramparts with the kitchen maid close behind, Durant turned to her with eyes as big as saucers. "Have you lost your mind?"

She grinned. "Perhaps. But I won't lose this fight." Then she raised the heavy rock she'd been carrying as high as she could and threw it down with all her strength at the man below, hitting him squarely on the head. He fell to the ground, knocked out cold . . . or maybe even dead.

Seeing what she'd done, the other women who'd reached the top of the walls began lobbing their own missiles. And now there was another sound that mingled with the shouts and battle cries from below, the occasional scream when a spear launched from the wall found a victim, and the rhythmic pounding on the gate – it was the squeal of delight every time one of the women's missiles found its target. When one of the women hurled a kitchen knife squarely into the back of an attacker, a great cheer went up from everyone on the walls, including the soldiers.

"What's that smell I get a whiff of now and then?" Jeanne asked Durant.

"A mix of blood and battle lust," he replied. "If you were down there, it would be inescapable."

Seeing the women's success with their rocks and chunks of wood, other people from the town began hauling more rubble up to the walls. Some joined in, while others took the empty buckets and baskets down to be refilled. Durant could only shake his head in a combination of dismay and admiration and pray that no one in the rabble below had a crossbow.

A slow stream of men coming up from the east side of the camp kept the defenders busy, but the rain of rubble from the top of the walls was becoming a distraction to those trying to breach the gates. Jeanne found herself celebrating not just every spear that found its mark but every rock that slammed into an arm, a back, or a head.

Kerveil, who'd been commanding from the other side of the gate, suddenly ran down the stairs on his side and came up to join Durant and the duchess. "Look there." He pointed toward the center of the camp, to what seemed to be the command tent. A well-organized cavalry formation was advancing from there toward the melée, led by a man wearing the Blois emblem.

"God help us," said Durant. "This rabble was just to soften us up for the main attack."

Kerveil shouted for the crossbowmen. He'd held them in abeyance, hoping not to waste bolts on mere infantry, but with cavalry on the way, he needed them to bring down the horses. They lined the ramparts, crossbows at the ready, as Kerveil held his signal until the horsemen drew closer.

But before they were in range, the formation veered to the right and came straight at the right flank of the attackers, riding them down and driving them back toward the camp. Discipline held in the Montfort ranks and not a single bolt was fired. Jeanne and her captains watched in amazement as the cavalry chased the rabble back into camp then returned to the command tent and dismounted.

"What just happened?" asked Jeanne.

Both men shook their heads. "Beats anything I've ever seen," said Kerveil.

"If I had to guess," Durant said, "that attack wasn't ordered. Just some hotheads who decided to take matters into their own hands and got trounced by their own commanders for their efforts."

While the captains stood their men down, Jeanne told the townspeople who'd watched the extraordinary scene, "Let's go home. The homes you protected. I've never been prouder of anyone in all my life."

That night, with a half moon high in the sky, the garrison commander opened the gate enough for his men to clean up from the afternoon's battle. They retrieved all the weapons – every spear that had been thrown, whether lying on the ground or embedded in a corpse, every arrow, every enemy weapon that had been dropped in the headlong dash to get away from the pursuing cavalry. Two battle axes retrieved from the heavy wood of the gates had done no harm. They dragged in what the attackers had used as battering rams – one, little more than a large piece of firewood, the other from the top of a small tree with a few limbs left on as handholds. Then, realizing how effective the rocks and rubble had been, they collected all they could find and made a new pile closer to the walls.

Finally, they dragged the corpses twenty or so yards away – as close as they dared go to the enemy camp. The hope was that the enemy would collect their dead. But if they didn't, the rotting corpses would at least be far enough away that their foul humors wouldn't infect the town.

The next day, the defenders watched as scores and scores of men departed from the east side of the camp. Mercenaries fed up with being denied a fight? Soldiers ordered to another place to try to take another town or garrison? There was no way to know. All they could be sure of was that by the end of the day, the encampment was visibly smaller. But they were still outnumbered.

CHAPTER NINETEEN

Toward dusk on the second day after what Jeanne had begun to think of as the first test of her resolve, she went up to the ramparts, as had become her wont, to survey the situation – to see and be seen. She could scarcely believe her eyes. The camp was almost completely deserted. Where had so many men gone? And why?

She dashed in search of Durant and found him in the garrison commander's office. "You've got to come see this," she announced.

"See what, my lady?"

"Just come. We may have our opportunity." She hurried out, leaving him to rush to catch her up. At the top of the wall, she spoke in almost a whisper, "Look. There's no one there."

Durant took his time scanning the camp before commenting. "And what do you think is the opportunity? It looks more like a trap to me. That many men can't have gone far. They just want to lure us out so we'll leave the gates open in case we need to get back in. Then they'll rush back, overwhelm us, and charge through the gates. Take the town with very little loss of life on their side."

"Most likely, you're right, but that's not what I have in mind."

"Then what, madame?"

"A raid. A few men – twenty or thirty – armed with torches. We set the whole camp ablaze. And then when they do come rushing back, they have to deal with the fires first, and we can make our escape."

Durant stroked his chin, something she'd seen him do before when he was mulling something over. Finally, he said, "It's not a bad idea. But you keep saying 'we.' Surely you're not thinking of going along yourself."

"Not at all, Durant. I intend to lead the raid."

A fish trying to breathe air couldn't have opened and shut its mouth more times than Durant did in the next moment. When he finally managed to form words, he couldn't put two together at the same time. "I . . . you . . . what . . ." Then he stopped and took a deep breath. "With all due respect, my lady, that is the most foolhardy notion I've ever heard. Your husband would be appalled."

She smiled. "Quite the contrary, Captain. I think he'd be absolutely delighted." Then, turning serious, she continued. "We need a bold gesture, Durant. Something to show the world the Montforts can't be intimidated. That we intend to defend what's rightfully ours. And not just to defend but to put any challenger on the back foot. So pick your men and get my charger ready. We raid as soon as I get my armor on."

"You're not going without me, madame." Durant's tone said he'd brook no argument.

Jeanne smiled again. "I wouldn't think of it, Captain."

While Aaliz helped the duchess into her armor, Perota was summoned from the nursery. Making small adjustments to her faulds, Jeanne instructed her servants. "You two are in charge of the children until I get back."

They both looked apprehensive – frightened in fact. "But when will that be, madame?" asked Aaliz.

"Later tonight, I hope," Jeanne answered. "But if we should have to flee for a bit, it might be a few days – no more. I'll be back. You can count on that."

"And you can count on us, my lady," Perota's tone was stoic. "Your babes will be safe here."

"I know they will. Captain Kerveil will be in charge while I'm gone, no matter how long that is. Follow his orders. Do whatever he says, alright?"

"Of course, madame." Aaliz now seemed a little more reassured.

Jeanne made for the door. "Wait," Aaliz called. "You forgot your sword."

"No swords tonight, Aaliz. I need my hands free for other things."

Durant and his men were mounted and waiting in the market square, each man holding a lighted torch. Kerveil held the reins to her charger and helped her mount. When she was settled in the saddle, her feet securely in the stirrups, he handed up her torch. "I don't like this any more than Durant does, my lady, but if you're determined to do it, by God's great crown, do it well. Burn the bastards out."

"You're in charge here, Kerveil. Now let us out and close the gates until you see us coming back."

"As you command, madame." Kerveil bowed and signaled to the men at the gate.

"Alright, men," she called out. "Ride fast and torch everything we can. Set the tents ablaze. Anything that will burn. If your torch goes out, relight it from one of the flames. We ride for all of Brittany." She squeezed her charger's ribs and led them through the open gate.

At a canter, they quickly closed the distance between the town walls and the camp. "The command tent is mine," Jeanne called out. As the others fanned out and began setting things afire, Jeanne made straight for the center of the camp, Durant at her side. Finding the largest tent, she touched her torch to a wall and the roof. When the canvas burst into flame, her charger reared in surprise but she was ready for that and quickly calmed him. Then she and Durant rode among what were most likely the commanders' tents, putting the torch to every one.

By now the entire center of the camp was blazing. Knowing that this fire would spread and would be the most difficult to reach to extinguish, she and Durant joined the rest of the men creating more conflagrations throughout the camp.

Then, through the smoke and shadows and the noise of the flames came the unmistakable sounds of the missing occupants returning. The raiders had left themselves an alley of retreat to get back to the town, and the duchess and her captain made straight for it, their men forming up behind them. But as they approached the edge of the camp, she realized their path had been cut off – a phalanx of soldiers had amassed between the camp and the town wall.

Wheeling her charger, she threw her torch down, setting the grass on fire. "Throw your torches onto mine," she shouted. "Make a wall of flame they have to get through to get to us. Then split up and ride for your lives to the west. We regroup in Quimperlé." She squeezed her horse's ribs hard and took off at the gallop with Durant hot on her heels.

They rode briefly north then swam their horses across the Blavet. Once on the right bank of the river, they asked the horses for a canter and didn't slow until they reached the bridge across the Scorff. In all that time, neither had spoken a word. "Let's give the horses a rest," said Durant as they approached the bridge. "I don't think we have any pursuit – not even by our own men."

They let the horses walk for a bit, then asked for a trot. The waning moon – what was left of it – was just rising as they neared Quimperlé. "Let's wait for the others outside the town," said Jeanne. "We can plan what to do next."

They found a little grove of trees off to the right side of the road beside a small pond where they could take cover in the trees if anyone approached who appeared to be a threat. After letting the horses drink, they sat on the ground, their backs to the tree trunks, and discussed their plans.

"We should make straight for Brest," said Durant. "It's a Montfort stronghold and your treasury is there."

"What you say may be logical, Durant, but my heart says otherwise. I can't leave my children behind."

"You've done that before, my lady, in Montfort, when the duke first inherited."

"Things were different then. My son wasn't the titular head of the family and my role wasn't to protect his interests. I really don't have a choice. What would the world say – my God, what would John say – if I abandoned my children and the people of Hennebont, who've put their trust in me, to whatever fate they might have at the hands of Charles's army?"

"De Blois will have men out looking for us. You know that, don't you?"

"He'll have men looking for a woman in armor riding a war horse and an armed man, similarly equipped, in her company. They won't be looking for a wealthy merchant's wife in mourning carrying her husband's body back to his family home for burial, accompanied by her manservant."

Durant threw his head back in laughter, bumping it against the tree trunk. "God's bones, woman, how do you think of these things?" Then, rubbing the back of his head, he added, "With all respect, of course, Duchess."

It was Jeanne's turn to laugh. "At last, Durant! The candor I need from you."

He shook his head from side to side. "Will you ever cease to surprise me?"

"I hope not."

"So tell me about this plan of yours."

"Alright, but I'm depending on you to point out any flaws it might have." She shifted on the ground to find a more comfortable position before continuing. "When the others arrive, we send all but one on to Brest to join the garrison there. The man who stays with us does all the work while we stay here so no one in the town sees us. We unsaddle the horses and he takes them into town, where he buys a wagon and the harness to hitch them up. He also buys a coffin if he can find one. If not, a large wooden box will do. Finally, he buys widow's weeds for me and a farmer's hat and black armband for you. Oh, yes, and some food for the journey.

"Then he brings it all back here. I change into the weeds – the veil will be useful to hide my face. We stow our armor, the horses' gear, and my clothes in the coffin and set off for the port of Lorient. Our story along the road is that of the wealthy merchant's wife. In Lorient, we'll hire a boat to take us on the incoming tide up to Hennebont and enter through the port gate, unseen by whoever remains in the camp we burned."

"That certainly sounds like it could confound anyone looking for an armed duchess. But you asked me to find flaws, and I see a few."

"Name them."

"The biggest one is, what do we do for money?"

Jeanne laughed softly and reached into a pocket under her faulds, pulling out a leather pouch. "Do you think I go anywhere these days without a purse, Durant? I have about forty *livres* in here. That should be enough for whatever we need." She tucked the pouch back into her pocket.

"Very well. First problem solved. So what's a man's excuse for buying women's clothing? Not to mention for buying an empty coffin."

"He's a farmer. His father died suddenly while out tending the fields. His mother's distraught and sent him into town to buy things. They need to take the dead man for proper burial."

"And why would a farmer need a new wagon? Why wouldn't he just bring one from the farm?"

"Their wagon has a broken axle that hasn't been repaired, and they can't wait that long to have the dead man buried. That's also why he's bringing the horses with him – they're draft horses from the farm."

"They don't look like draft horses."

"Well, plow horses then."

"Do you have an answer for everything?" he asked.

"So far."

Durant chuckled. "Then I have just one more question. Wouldn't a man from a farm near Quimperlé have been into town now and then and be recognizable to *someone*?"

"I'll grant you that's a risk. But I see little choice but to take it. If someone presses our man, maybe his excuse is that the farm is far enough away – say five miles or so – that they don't come into town unless something goes really badly for them."

"Or maybe it was always the alleged dead man who made the trips into town and this is the first time for his son."

"I don't know. That might require that the dead man have a name, and there's almost no chance of getting that right. We may be better off with the too-far-away story."

The rest of the raiding party drifted into their little camp in twos and threes throughout the following morning. Most had avoided the main road. A few had passed the night hiding in the woods along the way. But everyone had escaped. Durant chose a man named Binidig, who hailed from

Douarnenez and so was indisputably Breton, to stay behind, then sent the others on their way. "Avoid Quimperlé. I don't want anyone there able to say they've seen us or which way we went. Travel in smaller groups – ten at the most. But meet up outside Brest and present yourselves to Tanguy du Chastel. He's Montfort's captain there. Tell him I sent you as reinforcements. Understood?"

Throughout the afternoon, they dispersed in groups of five, six, or seven, having worked out which routes each would take and where they would rendezvous. Jeanne decided they'd wait until the following day to put her plan in action. "That might be easy for you to say," said Durant, "but I'm hungry."

"Then you'll be glad I'm the one you chose to stay behind." Binidig grinned, then rose from where he was sitting on a fallen log and walked over to his tethered horse. Returning with a cloth sack, he pulled out a bottle of wine, half a loaf of bread, and a chunk of cheese. "Didn't know what we'd be doing next or when we might find food, so we stopped in a village and traded the villagers some help fixing a broken wagon wheel for a bit of food. Isn't much for three people, I admit, but maybe enough so you don't starve before morning, sir."

"Give me that." Durant reached for the wine bottle and pulled out the cork that prevented the contents from spilling. He took a long swallow, then passed it to the duchess, who drank a bit more daintily, though still with marked thirst.

Using his dagger, Binidig carved the cheese and bread into rough thirds and spread everything on the sack. Hungry as they all were, they tried to eat slowly to make the meager meal last longer. Talking about what Binidig needed to do on the morrow gave them a reason to pause between mouthfuls. But the tidbits were gone long before anyone was sated.

Chapter Twenty

Binidig returned from Quimperlé shortly after midday. As he reined to a stop and set the wagon brake, both horses tossed their heads and pawed the ground. "That charger of yours, madame," said Binidig, "really hates the traces. Fought me every step of the way back." He jumped down from the wagon. "You'll have your hands full with him, sir." This addressed to Durant.

"Just give me some time to calm him," said Jeanne, walking to the horse and stroking his nose. "Perhaps I should have gone into town with you." The animal laid his big head over her shoulder as she stroked his jowls, scratched behind his ears, and cooed endearments to him.

"No, madame, it was better this way. They'd have picked up on your French accent straightaway and been really suspicious. As it was, no one questioned my story."

Durant had been examining the wagon. "Looks sound enough," he declared. "Should get us where we need to go."

"Couldn't get a proper coffin though," said Binidig. "Just that plain burial box."

"It'll suffice," said Jeanne. "Maybe my dead husband just won't have been quite so wealthy." She stroked her charger's nose once more, and the big animal stood quietly even when she stepped away to examine their acquisitions. "See? He just needed some reassurance that he wasn't being harmed."

"The clothes are in the box," Binidig continued. "I got a peasant's jacket for you as well, sir. All the clothes are left-behinds from dead people. Was all I could get. The dressmaker offered to make you proper weeds, my lady, but I told her my ma wouldn't care. Hope that's alright."

"Quite alright, Binidig. It's just for a few days."

"Got feedbags and some oats for the horses too, sir. And a bucket for them to drink from. That and the food are all under that bit of canvas that came with the wagon. We had the devil's own time getting them in harness the first time. I figure you won't want to unharness them until you get where you're going."

"Good thinking, Binidig," Durant climbed into the bed of the wagon to inspect what was there. Opening the box, he retrieved the clothing and passed the weeds down to Jeanne, who held it up to her body and pronounced it suitable for purpose.

"But it laces up the back," she added, "so I'll need your help to get it on properly, Captain."

Durant hemmed and hawed and turned bright red. "Are you sure that's a good idea, my lady?"

"A far better idea than having it fall off every time I climb into or out of the wagon, don't you think? If it makes you feel better, Durant, I can order you to do it."

Durant jumped down from the wagon and began removing his own armor. "Well, since you put it that way, Duchess, I guess I have little choice."

Jeanne took the dress and disappeared into the little grove of trees. Several minutes later, she called out, "Alright, Captain, time for you to execute your orders."

Donning his new jacket and cap, Durant took his time making his way into the grove, still uncomfortable with what he might see. He found the duchess standing with her back to him, her hands on her waist holding the garment in place. "Lace it up as tightly as you can, Durant. The last person who wore it was rather more plump, so we need to take up a bit of the slack."

When he'd finished, she turned around and pulled the veil down over her face. "What do you think?"

"I think we may just get away with this."

"Then let's get all our armor and my clothes hidden away in the box and be on our way."

When they emerged from the trees, Binidig let out a low whistle. "You look a proper widow, madame. No one would suspect otherwise."

She bobbed a little curtsey. "Why, thank you, Binidig. I couldn't have done it without you."

Having stowed everything in the box, Durant returned to the front of the wagon. "Shall we be on our way, my lady?"

"I can't think of any reason not to. We certainly don't want to attract attention here."

"Then I suppose it's time for you to be on your way as well, lad," Durant told Binidig. "Go catch up with one of the other groups." He paused, then added, "And thank you. The duchess is right. We couldn't have done this without your help."

"It was actually rather a lot of fun, sir. But I've been thinking all this morning. What if I stay with you? I could ride out ahead, like a scout. Stay about an hour ahead of you, and if I see anything that looks worrisome, I'd circle back to warn you. Then we could decide what to do about it."

Durant furrowed his brow in thought and eventually looked up at Jeanne, who'd climbed into the wagon. "What do you think, madame? It might be extra protection."

"I wish I'd thought of it myself, gentlemen."

"Then, on your way, Binidig," said Durant as he, too, climbed into the wagon and picked up the reins. "We'll wait here a bit for you to get a start."

"No need, sir," Binidig replied, mounting his horse. "We'd like a nice canter for a bit, and you'll have trouble getting any more than a walk from those two. When dusk starts falling, I'll circle back and camp with you for the night." And with that, he urged his horse to a canter as Durant clucked to his war-horses-turned-draft-horses, and they slowly made up their minds to get on with this new job.

They reached Lorient in late afternoon on the following day. Binidig had been right. The horses were unwilling even to trot, but at the walk, they were calm enough. The journey had been utterly ordinary. Anyone they met on the road politely removed their caps and bowed their heads to the grieving widow, but no one asked questions.

They took rooms at a little inn near the port. A far cry from Jeanne's usual accommodation when traveling, but as it was the only thing available ... Still, she told her companions she'd be sleeping on the floor rather than risk getting lice – or worse – from the bedding and admonished them to do likewise.

Binidig got about the business of finding a boat to take them up the river. The horses were the problem. Plenty of boatmen were willing to take people, dead or alive, but none seemed inclined to deal with what the horses might leave behind when they disembarked. That night, they talked about whether they might have to sell the horses. "I'll not leave them behind." Jeanne was adamant. "Not after everything they've done for us. Offer the boatmen more money if you have to, Binidig. Otherwise, we'll just have to go elsewhere to find transport."

The following morning, Binidig went out again. Jeanne and Durant had just finished a midday meal of watery potage and small ale at the inn when he returned with a huge smile on his face. "That looks like good news," said Durant.

"It is, sir. We have our boatman."

"I'm afraid to ask what that cost," said Durant.

"Well, at first, he said he wouldn't do it for less than fifteen livres, but then I had a thought. And he agreed to a trade. Our passage – horses and all – in exchange for the wagon. We were going to have to sell it anyway, and this way, it's one less thing we have to bother with."

"Very resourceful, Binidig," said Jeanne. "And to think, Durant – you were of a mind to send him to Brest." The smile on her face told the captain her chiding was all in jest.

"We missed this morning's tide and he doesn't want to be on the river after dark, so we're stuck in this place for one more night. We're to be at the dock when the church bells sound Terce tomorrow."

Knowing they'd need time to unharness the horses, the trio arrived at the dock well before the appointed hour – even before the boatman. "Maybe it would be easier if they had their noses in their feedbags," Binidig suggested. "We've got some oats left."

The idea proved to be just the thing. Neither animal paid the least bit of attention as Binidig and Durant went about the business of freeing them from the rigging. Jeanne held Binidig's horse then also took the reins of her charger while the men finished unharnessing Durant's mount. Suddenly realizing they were no longer confined in the traces, both war horses looked up from their feedbags and gave a great shake all over, as if removing water from their coats. Jeanne laughed.

And just at that moment, the boatman arrived. "God's bollocks." His tone was grumpy. "You fed them. Now there's no chance of getting to Hennebont without horse dung all over my deck. That better be a damn fine wagon."

"It's quite sound," said Binidig. "Just like I told you. And we've thrown in the harness to boot. You'll make good profit for your troubles."

"Hmph." He stepped onto the boat. "Alright. Get 'em aboard. The tide don't wait."

Once the horses were tied to the railing and the funeral box was on board, the boatman grabbed a chain and padlock from inside his own storage box and stepped back onto the dock. He chained one wagon wheel to a ring normally used for tying up a boat then stood and let out a shrill whistle. A rather scruffy lad of some fourteen or fifteen years came running from an alleyway brandishing an old broadsword. "You sit there, son." The boatman pointed to the wagon seat. "And don't you dare let anyone lay a finger on this wagon or the harness. They try, you give 'em a right thrashing with that thing. You got that?"

"Aye, Pa."

"And you best be here when I get back. You hear?"

"Aye, Pa."

"Anything happens to my wagon, it comes out of your hide." And with that, he loosed the mooring rope, jumped back onto the deck, and began to raise the sail. "You, there. Widow."

Jeanne turned toward the sound of his voice. "Me?"

"You. Get away from that horse. I won't be having you going overboard if he turns skittish."

"If you don't want him to turn skittish, sir . . ." Jeanne was ever so polite. ". . . then it's best I stay with him."

The boatman opened his mouth to object, but Durant pre-empted him. "She's right. I've seen it before. He can be cranky as anything, and the minute she strokes him and talks to him, he calms right down."

"On your head be it then," said the boatman. "I won't be going in the water after her." He let the sail catch the wind and steered the boat out into the estuary.

Just over an hour later, the dock at Hennebont was in sight. As he brought the boat alongside and luffed the sail, the boatman said, "Well, here you are. Don't know why you'd want to come here though. We hear tell the place is under siege. Mayhap you won't be able to get out . . . if they let you in."

"You let us worry about that," said Durant, untying his horse as Jeanne and Binidig did the same. They led the horses onto the dock as the boatman hoisted the burial box off the boat.

"What you burying with that guy? Stones?"

"You let us worry about that too. But thank you for the transport."

Just at that moment, Jeanne's charger lifted his tail and made a deposit on the dock. "Have a look, sir," she said. "I think you'll find your deck as clean as when we boarded."

The boatman grunted, untied his mooring rope, and pushed away from the dock without another word. That suited the trio just fine. They didn't need witnesses to whatever happened next.

In truth, this was the riskiest bit of the ruse. If whoever was in the sentry tower decided to shower them with arrows, they'd be sitting ducks. They stood watching the boat disappear upstream. "Boatman said he planned to go with the tide and see if he could pick up passengers or a cargo to take back south when the tide turns," said Binidig.

Long after they could no longer see the sail, they stood on the dock in silence. Durant was beginning to wonder if this sentry tower was even manned. If it wasn't, they could be waiting here for hours – days even.

Which meant he'd have to figure out another way to get in, and at the moment, he had no idea what that might be.

But why wasn't it manned? Had the town surrendered? Had Charles de Blois taken revenge for the burning of his camp by storming the town and killing wantonly? Just as Durant was heading down the path of worst-case scenarios, a voice came from up in the tower. "You there on the dock – state your business."

Jeanne removed her veil and the men their caps. "Fetch Captain Kerveil," Durant called up. "Tell him the raiders have returned."

A head popped out the window long enough to exclaim "Holy mother of God!" and then disappeared. It wasn't long before they heard the sounds of the heavy bar being lifted from its brackets, and then the gates opened to reveal Kerveil and the garrison commander. "God preserve us," said Kerveil, an enormous smile on his face. "It *is* you. Durant. Duchess. How in the name of all that's holy did you wind up here?"

"It's a long story, Kerveil," said Durant, "that I'll happily tell once we get cleaned up and into our own clothes."

"And the burial box?" Kerveil asked. "What's in that?" And then his face turned somber. "Or should I be asking 'who'?"

"Our armor, Captain," Jeanne replied. "We lost not a single man in the raid."

Kerveil gestured to the commander and they began putting the enormous bar back in place. Once he was satisfied that everything was secure, he turned his attention back to the new arrivals. "Well, then, looks like all we have to do is figure out how to get these horses up the stairs."

"Oh, I think they'll follow us anywhere so long as they don't have do it in the traces," said Jeanne. Durant and Binidig laughed. Kerveil just looked confused. Jeanne gave her charger's reins a gentle tug as she started up the stairs, and he followed without hesitation.

Kerveil shook his head in amazement and admiration. "You are one remarkable woman, Duchess." Durant and Binidig followed, their mounts equally compliant.

At the top of the short flight, they emerged into the streets of the town where people were going about their everyday business. Suddenly, someone recognized her and shouted, "Jeanne de la Flamme!" Others picked up the chant and soon she was mobbed by joyous townspeople eager to welcome her home and salute her as a heroine.

Jeanne knew in the moment that her instinct to return here had been right. Though this celebration was utterly unexpected, she made the most of it, taking her time on the way to the castle, clapping the men on the shoulder, hugging the women, doing little dances with the children. If she'd ever wondered how loyal these people might be, she no longer had any doubt. They would do whatever she asked, give whatever they could, follow wherever she led.

Today, she would revel in the adulation. Tomorrow, she would have to come to grips with the reality of what they faced. A reality that increasingly looked as if they would face it alone.

CHAPTER TWENTY-ONE

She didn't have to wait for the morning – she got her first taste of reality that very evening. When she walked into her bedchamber after greeting the crowds, Aaliz hugged her as if she'd been gone a year and not a mere five days. "Thank God and all the saints you're safe, madame. Safe and home again. We saw the flames and . . . oh, madame, I was so afraid for you. We didn't know if you were captured or if you'd gotten caught in the fire or . . . or even if . . ." She couldn't finish.

Gently, Jeanne extricated herself from her maid's embrace. "All's well, Aaliz. I'm here now."

"I'll call Perota to bring the children," said Aaliz. "We tried not to let them see how worried we were."

"Not just yet, dear. I'd like to have a bath first and get into my own clothes. Then I'll go to them." Aaliz's shoulders slumped and her smile disappeared. "What is it, dear?" asked Jeanne. "What's wrong?"

"I . . . I can't make you a bath, my lady. Captain Kerveil's orders. Until we get some rain to replenish the water barrels, no one's to waste water on bathing. I'm sorry, madame."

Jeanne sighed and looked down at her attire before returning her gaze to Aaliz. "I won't let you get in trouble, Aaliz, but I simply *must* have a bath. I've been wearing a dead woman's clothes for four days and I spent two nights in a dockside inn where I'm not sure they'd *ever* changed the bedding."

Aaliz gasped, her eyes wide with horror at what her mistress had described.

"Oh, I slept on the floor. I'm not sure it was much cleaner, but at least I could see it wasn't crawling with lice and mites. In any event, I'm going to be selfish this evening. You can make it a very shallow bath, but I can't bear the thought of donning my own clothes without getting rid of whatever might be on my person."

"*Oui, madame*. Whatever you say, madame. I'll be back straightaway."

Jeanne thought her maid actually looked relieved that she'd insisted on getting clean. "Before you go, just unlace the back of this, will you? Then I can shed everything while you're gone. And, Aaliz?"

"*Oui, madame?*"

"Burn all these clothes. God knows what's in them."

"*Oui, madame.*"

Aaliz had taken Jeanne at her word. The tub contained barely enough water for her to clean herself, but the bath had the effect not only of removing any remnants of the journey but also of refreshing her spirit to cope with their plight.

The next surprise came when Aaliz brought her supper. A small bowl filled only halfway with potage, a half slice of bread, and a goblet only half-filled with wine. The potage was much thinner than usual and contained only lentils with a few bits of onion. The expression on Aaliz's face said she was worried her mistress might complain. When Jeanne merely thanked her and began slowly eating the meal, Aaliz blurted out, "It's half rations for everyone, madame. Captain Kerveil's orders. So the cook makes the potage like always then waters it down so it'll last twice as long."

"No need to fret, Aaliz. I understand we all need to do our part to be sure our food lasts until the soldiers give up and go on their way."

What Jeanne understood was that their situation must be more uncertain than ever. For Kerveil to order half rations meant he believed they were in for a long siege. She got her answers the following morning when he asked her to join him and Durant on the ramparts.

The sight that greeted her was in part expected and in part a complete surprise. The damage caused by the fires was still much in evidence. Nothing had really been cleaned up – just shoved to the sides of the camp to make way for moving what was left closer to the town. The surprise was that the camp was far smaller than before.

"De Blois left two days after your raid, my lady," Kerveil explained. "As soon as they'd reconfigured the camp. As you can see, he took most of his army with him. What's left, I judge to be about seven hundred men. And from those banners . . ." He pointed to two tents in what was now the center of the smaller camp. ". . . I'd say it's mostly Spanish and some Rohan loyalists who support de Blois."

"What do you make of it, Captain?" Jeanne asked, though she could already guess what his answer would be.

"They intend to just sit there and starve us out, madame. It doesn't take a huge force to do that, and de Blois no doubt decided his own efforts were better spent subduing other garrisons."

"And that's why you've ordered half rations."

"That and the fact that our water supply is getting *very* low. It takes water to cook."

"Have you noticed, Kerveil, that the way half-rations are being created is by watering down the potage?"

Kerveil gave a sad little shake of his head. "God's truth, madame, I'd noticed the potage was thinner, but I just thought it was because they were using fewer lentils."

"I'm told what they're doing is just making regular potage and adding water to thin it down so one pot lasts longer."

"Shows you what I know about cooking. So how do we fix it?"

"Talk to my cook. Maybe it's as simple as putting water on half rations . . . or less, if we have to. Maybe less water means they have to use fewer lentils for potage or make smaller loaves of bread. People will sort it out."

"Don't chide yourself, Kerveil," said Durant. "Not sure *I'd* have worked it out either."

"What we all should do," said Jeanne, "is pray for rain. But while we're doing that, what do we do about them?" She inclined her head toward the camp.

Neither man said a word for quite some time. So long, in fact, that Jeanne was quickly coming to the conclusion that they had absolutely no notion of what to do. Finally, as if sensing her discomfort, Durant broke the silence. "I think we should ignore them. Pretend they're not there. Go on about our lives inside the walls for as long as we can hold out. And pray they get bored and give up before we exhaust our supplies. Without de Blois there to constantly remind them what they're doing this for, we have at least an even chance that our resolve will outlast theirs."

"Kerveil?" Jeanne asked. She wanted them all to be in agreement on the course they chose. If they weren't, there was no way they could inspire the townspeople.

"Durant speaks sense, madame. Even with their smaller forces, we're still outnumbered, so it would be foolhardy to try to attack them. With *you* back here, our people have no doubt what they're suffering these hardships for, so they won't give up easily."

"Nor will I, gentlemen. So we have two things now to pray for. Rain . . . and the arrival of the English."

FROM THE WRITINGS OF JEANNE DE FLANDRE, DUCHESS OF BRITTANY AND COUNTESS OF MONTFORT
FOUND AMONG HER BELONGINGS AT THE TIME OF HER DEATH

Tickhill, South Yorkshire, 1348

The rain came. The English didn't. By that time, neither surprised me.

*What **was** a surprise was just how much a physical siege becomes a siege of one's mind. My sense of purpose never wavered. The Montfort cause – my son's future – was in my hands. But it became increasingly difficult to envision how to achieve my ends. Perhaps that's because when one is forced to confront survival head-on, little else matters.*

*So I turned my attention to the one thing I **could** do – bolster the spirits of the people in whose world I'd chosen to make my stand. People whose fates were inextricably tied to mine. People who hadn't been asked for permission to use their town as my stronghold but who, nevertheless, gave their loyalty and their hearts to the woman who might not be able to save them.*

CHAPTER TWENTY-TWO

At Mass the following day, the priest did his best to divert his flock from their deprivations, offering thanks to God for the departure of so many soldiers, for the duchess's safe return, for the two new lives that had come into the world in the past week, for the robust health of everyone in the town, and for the love of their neighbors that would carry them through a rough patch in their lives. But, knowing what was on everyone's mind, he ended the service with a fervent plea to the heavens to bless his flock with much-needed rain.

His ardor must have impressed the deity or Mother Nature or the winds of fortune or whoever controls the clouds because Jeanne woke the next morning to raindrops on her windows. Not just a light patter, but the pelting of serious rainfall. Dressing quickly, she went to the castle entrance to watch out the open door . . . and found the townspeople out in the streets, celebrating in the pouring rain, utterly unconcerned that they were getting wet to the skin. Their joy was so palpable, she couldn't resist joining them. Children splashed in puddles, their parents laughing at their antics. Adults danced. Men and women stood with cupped hands, catching the rain and drinking their fill. But most important of all, the barrels filled, minute by minute, inch by inch . . . and everyone brought out buckets and cooking pots and bath tubs and pitchers and anything to capture the precious water that would keep them alive.

By the end of the day, when the rain had slowed to a gentle drizzle, every barrel, every horse trough, every container in the town was filled to the brim.

And on the morrow, with the return of sunny blue skies, there was a new sense of determination not to waste a single drop of the salvation they'd been given. Kitchen maids fetching water took extra care not to slosh their buckets lest some of the precious contents spill on the ground. The men in the garrison watered the horses from buckets rather than letting them drink their fill from the troughs. No one forgot to keep the lids on the rain barrels to prevent evaporation in the summer sun.

Though the water crisis had been avoided, all the news was not good. On the morning after the great rain, Henri came to Jeanne's sitting room carrying a ledger and wearing a rather grim expression. "I think, my lady," he began, "that we should consider how long we might be under siege."

"Show me, Henri." She joined him at the writing table where he'd placed the ledger for her to read.

"We were able to capture more water yesterday than we had before, madame. But that's because we had more empty barrels from the stores that have been depleted. The horses have eaten the oats more quickly than I would have imagined, having no experience as a stable master. I think perhaps we need to restrict them to hay and save the oats that are left to make porridge."

"Have you suggested this to the captains or the garrison commander?" Jeanne asked.

"I've been reluctant to do so, madame, as I know so little about feeding horses."

"Do it straightaway, Henri. When horses are working hard – on long journeys or especially in a fight – they need lots of nourishment. But just waiting out a siege, they can get by on much less. The captains won't argue with you."

"Thank you, madame. I'll do that straightaway."

Then another thought occurred to Jeanne. "Do we have enough hay?"

"Knowing so little about horses, madame, it's hard for me to say."

"Well, the captains will know. And they'll know how to ration the horses' food so that they're not excessively weakened. Now, what about our stores for people? It's been ... what? ... a dozen days since we closed the gates?

"Precisely a dozen," Henri replied. "And while we're not yet in danger of starvation, what we have left . . ."

"Let's have a look."

The steward stood behind her chair, pointing to various entries in the ledger. "The smoked fish is almost all gone. I don't know why, but that's what people wanted first. We're down to a single barrel of flour, a barrel of lentils, and half a barrel each of oats and barley. The chickens are still laying well, but if we have to start reducing their feed, that may not last. We'll need to slaughter the pig this week. Part of the problem, you see, my lady, is that we have nothing from the gardens to fill out the meals. The fields are outside the walls, so whatever is ripening is going to feed the men in that encampment."

He paused to let his mistress study his accounts then added, "The problem, my lady, is not knowing how long all this has to last."

"It has to last until the English arrive, Henri."

"Until what?" Henri's usual unflappable demeanor dissolved into complete astonishment.

"Until the English arrive," she repeated. "I didn't tell you before because it's a rather risky strategy. But now, I think it's time you know. I've made an agreement with the English king. He will support our cause, help us to defeat Charles de Blois and secure the duke's release from prison."

"Surely he'll want something in return."

"Indeed he does. Money to fund his fight with King Philip. And John's homage for lands the dukes of Brittany have long held in England." She hadn't told anyone – not even Durant – the real nature of the homage Edward demanded.

"And when are the English to arrive? If I may ask, madame."

"I wish I had the answer, Henri. They should have been here long since. Lord de Clisson tells me the English king is notorious for having trouble requisitioning enough ships to transport his armies, so I've given them the benefit of the doubt so far."

Silence reigned for several moments, Jeanne giving her steward time to take in what he'd just heard. Eventually, it was Henri who spoke. "Would I be correct, madame, in thinking that you may now be worried lest they not come at all?"

How lucky she was to have this man in her service! His insight and his capacity to maintain equanimity regardless of what fell from the sky helped her maintain her own calm and clear thinking. "I'd be foolish not to worry, Henri. But de Clisson has been steadfast in his confidence of the English king's intentions, so there must be something else in play – something we have no knowledge of, shut inside these walls. And for that reason, I won't give up. But it means I can't tell you how long we need to hold out."

"Then we should assume the longest and pray for an early relief, even if that means we have to become more strict with rationing food."

"I quite agree, Henri. But the burden of telling people about the rationing is *my* job, not yours. I'll talk with the townspeople and help them see that I'm sharing their sacrifice. But, Henri?"

"*Oui, madame?*"

"Only you, Durant, and Kerveil are privy to this knowledge. And it absolutely *must* stay that way. If it got out, the gossip would be uncontrollable ... and would sink our cause faster than the flames tore through the enemy camp."

"You have my word of honor, my lady. No one will hear it from my lips."

"If I had any doubt of that, Henri, I would never have revealed the secret. So I leave the management of our stores to your judgment. Just tell me in advance what privations are coming so I can keep the people prepared."

CHAPTER TWENTY-THREE

Over the next two weeks, spirits flagged as the depletion of the supplies became inescapable. When the priest celebrated Mass on the feast day of Saint Libert, he no longer attempted to uplift people's spirits. Instead, he preached of the trials of Job and of his patient and pious acceptance of the will of God. When, in his final prayer, he invoked the help of Saint Jude to deliver Hennebont from the clutches of the army outside its gates, Jeanne was appalled, despite the fact that she herself had sent a few prayers to that very saint when she was at her lowest. The last thing her loyal people needed was to have their priest suggest they were suffering for a lost cause.

When Henri presented his ledger to the duchess the next day, the story it told was one she'd never thought to see. All the flour had been distributed, all the dried meat and lentils consumed. There were no onions left. Some oats and a bit of barley remained. "I'm sorry to say, it won't last the week," said the steward. "We've no choice but to start eating the chickens, madame. But they're not laying much anyway, since we had to stop feeding them."

"What about the water?" she asked.

"We'll not go thirsty, madame. The showers we had last week didn't fill the barrels completely, but they replenished them well enough for now."

"And if help doesn't come soon?" Jeanne tried to keep the despair out of her voice, but it was no use.

"Then we'll have no choice, my lady, but to start eating the horses."

Jeanne buried her head in her hands. What had she brought these people to? How could any cause be worth all this suffering? Should she give up the fight? Not for the first time she chided herself for her thoughtlessness. How could she have failed to bring more supplies when they returned from the raid? There had been more than enough room on that boat for several barrels of food.

But self-recrimination wouldn't solve the problems of the present nor give anyone the will to persevere. So she squared her shoulders and looked her steward straight in the eye. "If it comes to that, Henri, then it will be my own charger that's sacrificed first."

"A noble gesture, my lady, that would not go unnoticed. But for myself, I prefer to pray that help arrives before then."

"As would I. Do what you must, Henri, to keep us alive."

•   •   •   •   •

Each morning, Jeanne climbed the ramparts to survey the besiegers' camp. Nothing changed. Much as she prayed to one day find it abandoned, that prayer always fell on deaf ears. Much as she longed to see another opportunity she could exploit as they had with the fires, nothing presented itself.

Each noonday, she climbed to the highest window in the castle tower to look down the river toward the sea, hoping to spot great sea-going ships coming to their rescue. But never did she see anything other than small boats plying the river – north with the flood tide, south as it ebbed.

Each afternoon, following these two great disappointments, she would to go her children and pretend that nothing was wrong. She would tell them stories, play games with them, promise them how wonderful their lives were going to be as they grew up.

And in the evening, with only a goblet of water to tide her over to her few morsels of food the next day, she would kneel at her window, look into the stars, and have an imaginary conversation with John, hoping that somehow, across the heavens, he could inspire her to know what to do next.

On Friday, just as she finished her meager midday ration of a small piece of chicken and a goblet of water, Henri knocked on her door to announce, "The mayor has come, my lady. He wishes to speak with you."

"Bring him up, Henri."

The man who walked into her sitting room showed every sign of the toll the siege had taken on the people of Hennebont. What were obviously his best clothes hung loosely on his frame. His cheeks were pale. And the sparkle in his eyes that she remembered from when he welcomed her arrival with such delight had been reduced to dull resignation.

"Please, *monsieur le maire* . . ." She gestured toward a chair near where she sat. ". . . please sit with me and tell me what brings you here."

"I . . . you see, my lady." He was obviously reluctant to broach the reason for his visit.

"There's no need for concern, monsieur. I truly want to know what's on your mind."

"Well, you see, my lady, we don't think we can go on. We love you. We know you've shared in our sacrifices. We do still believe your husband is the rightful duke. But we know there's no more food. And we know there's no sign of that army giving up and leaving. And most of all, my lady, we don't want our children to starve to death.

"So I've come on behalf of the town to ask you, with the greatest respect and the utmost reluctance, to either surrender or leave. We have boats on the river. You and your children could sneak out the same way you sneaked back in, and then we could open the gates and let that army take over the town and share their food with us. We'd have to pretend to switch our loyalty, just to stay alive, but in our hearts, I assure you, we'd always be with you, and we'd welcome you back with open arms once your husband is back in his rightful place as our duke."

The effort of getting all that out seemed to exhaust him. He sighed deeply and slumped in the chair.

"Monsieur, I know what it must cost you to ask this. And I hope you can believe that I'm as heartbroken as you are over the suffering your people have endured. It's not what I wished . . . not what I intended when we came here. I'm grateful beyond measure for your love and for the fact that you've shared my plight. Whatever I do, I want to be certain you and all the people here will be safe. So I need to think and pray about how to ensure that. Will you give me one day? I promise you . . . before the sun sets tomorrow, you'll have my decision. And if that decision is to leave in secret, we'll do so by the light of the moon tomorrow night."

A sad little smile came to the mayor's face. "I knew you would understand, my lady. You have your day. And no matter what happens, may God's blessings be on you." He rose to leave.

"God's good day to you, *monsieur le maire*. And may you have many, many good days to follow."

Jeanne spent most of that night staring at the stars, alternately asking God and John for guidance. She'd meant it when she told the mayor she wanted to choose the course of action that put the town at the least risk. Long after midnight, she finally retired to bed, but her sleep was fitful, her mind unwilling to completely abandon her worries.

Aaliz woke her with a cheerful reminder that it was the feast day of Saint Peter. "That's bound to be a good omen, madame," she declared. But Jeanne didn't see how even Christ's Rock could alter their fate.

She followed her rituals with a deep gloom overshadowing her movements and her thoughts. That nothing had changed in the army camp was no surprise and no comfort. She decided to forego even the meager midday meal that might be offered to her. Not that it was some grand sacrificial gesture. Merely that she had no appetite. And was no closer to a decision than when she'd put her head on the pillow the night before. Whatever she was going to do, though, she had to make up her mind. Durant, Kerveil, and Henri would need time to prepare.

In one last gesture to her broken sense of normality, she climbed the tower at noon and gazed out to sea. And did a double-take and rubbed her eyes and gazed again. And then started down the stairs shouting at the top of her lungs. "Durant! Kerveil! Come quickly! Get up here now! Kerveil! Durant!"

She reached the ground floor just as the two captains ran in, out of breath from their sprint from the barracks. "What the devil?" Durant asked.

Jeanne laughed out loud. She couldn't remember when she'd felt so joyous. "Oh, my dear Durant, that candor that I relish! But it's not the devil. Come see for yourself." She turned and dashed up the steps, leaving the captains to follow in her wake. Even before they made the landing, she was pointing out the window, an enormous smile on her face. "Look there. In the estuary and heading up the river."

Durant stepped to the window. "A fleet of ships. But whose? It could be de Blois has decided to come at us from the opposite direction."

"The banners, Durant." Jeanne clapped her hands like a child getting a new toy. "Look at the banners they're flying. The lion of England."

By then Kerveil had reached the window to see for himself. "By God, Durant, she's right."

Durant took another look. "Holy Mother of God. They've come at last."

Kerveil studied the river. "The tide's in flood. With all that sail, the first ones will be here in less than an hour. We'd better get men down there to get the gate open and the dock ready. That's a lot of ships to unload."

"I just hope it means a lot of men," said Durant.

"On your way then," Jeanne admonished them as they took another look through the window, seeming to want convincing that they weren't imagining things. "I'll be down in time to greet the flagship."

She took one final look out the window to reassure herself the ships were still advancing toward Hennebont then scurried down the stairs and up to her bedchamber. "My best gown, Aaliz, and the jewelry that goes with it."

Aaliz looked puzzled. "Madame?"

"Quickly, now."

"But why?"

"Because I have to receive our savior."

"Our savior, madame?"

"I'll tell you while I dress. Now, please. I need to hurry."

While Jeanne wriggled out of the plain gown she'd donned that morning, Aaliz retrieved a beautiful dark-green velvet one with wide, flowing sleeves from the clothes chest. Lifting it over her mistress's head, she asked again, "What savior, madame?"

"The savior whose ships are even now coming up the river bringing fighting men and food and the help we've been longing for." Once the gown was in place, it was painfully obvious that it didn't hang right. The mayor wasn't the only one who'd lost weight as food became scarce. "Can you make it fit better, Aaliz?"

"You just stand there, madame." Aaliz retrieved her sewing box, pulled out needle and thread, and began sewing tucks in the back of Jeanne's gown. "I'll have to cut these stitches to get you out of the dress later, but you'll look nice for this savior." A few moments later, she was done. "There. Now let's get your jewels."

From the duchess's jewel chest, she brought out a diamond and emerald necklace and fastened it around Jeanne's neck. "The duchess's coronet, madame?"

"I think that might be a bit too much, Aaliz. This is perfect. I have to get down to the dock, so would you do me a favor?"

"*Oui, madame.*"

"Help Perota get the children cleaned up and into their best clothes. John in particular. The head of the Montfort family should look the part when I present him."

"*Oui, madame,*" Aaliz called after Jeanne as she dashed out.

At the bottom of the stairs, Henri was waiting. "The house is in an uproar, my lady. No one knows what all the excitement is about, but there's no lack of interest."

"They're here, Henri. At last."

Henri's face lit up like she'd never seen before. "They, madame? You mean?"

"I do indeed, Henri. But let's keep things between us until people start to see the new arrivals entering the town. It's my greatest hope they bring enough food that the whole town will eat better tonight than we have in weeks."

"Mine as well, my lady. I presume we should prepare to entertain this evening?"

"Not on a grand scale. But maybe – just maybe – there might be wine for you to serve. For now, just make sure we have suitable quarters here in the castle for whoever's in charge."

She arrived on the dock just as the captain of the lead ship was heaving to. Half a dozen crewmen leapt over the railings onto the dock to catch the great ropes tossed over the side and tie them to the moorings while the anchor was dropped. A second ship dropped anchor in the middle of the river, and a third took the other mooring at the dock. The rest of the fleet anchored in the river to await their turn to unload.

Standing at the railing of the flagship was a man of somewhat more than average height wearing what Jeanne would learn was the uniform of the household knights of the king of England. As soon as the gangway was in place, he strode down it and made straight for Jeanne, offering her a sharp little bow of the head before kissing her extended hand. "Jeanne de Montfort, I presume?" he asked.

"I am." Jeanne gave him her most radiant smile.

"And I am Sir Walter de Mauny, in the service of His Grace Edward, King of England and of France, here as the advance guard of my king's forces."

"You arrive not a moment too soon, Sir Walter."

"So it's true then. We've heard rumors that this place has been under siege for some weeks."

"Indeed we have. And it's my fond hope that you can help us break it. But a greater hope is that you bring food for the people here, who would be facing starvation without it."

"Put your mind at rest, my lady. We have stores aplenty and my shipmasters have orders to unload them straightaway."

Jeanne took his arm and led him to where Kerveil and Durant stood watching. "My military commanders, Sir Walter. Captain Kerveil and Captain Durant. Their men will assist with unloading and distributing the food and with getting your men and arms into the town. They'll join us for a small supper this evening, and we can discuss how to break the siege." The military men offered each other polite bows. "Now, if you'll come with me," Jeanne continued, "my steward should have your quarters ready by the time we arrive."

When they reached the top of the stairs and Jeanne turned toward the castle entrance, de Mauny paused in his tracks. "If it's not too much trouble, my lady, I'd like to see the opposition camp . . . get a firsthand look at what we're up against."

"Of course, Sir Walter, but let's look from inside the sentry tower at the main gate. I don't want to take the chance someone there might notice an unfamiliar figure on the ramparts and realize our situation inside the walls has changed."

"I like your thinking, madame." He offered her his arm.

That evening, over a veritable feast – a full bowl of fish and barley potage and a goblet of wine – Jeanne, de Mauny, Durant, and Kerveil took stock of the situation. De Mauny's ships had delivered a huge catch of fresh fish, barrels upon barrels of flour and grain along with a few sacks of onions and six wheels of English cheese. Jeanne herself had supervised the opening of the first barrel of flour, walking among the queues of people urging quiet so as not to alert the besiegers that help had arrived. For the first time in more than a month, people were allowed to help themselves to as much flour as they wanted. And yet no one took more than what they needed for a day or two. Whether it was habit from the weeks of rationing or simply the recognition that there was more to be had wasn't apparent. Regardless, everyone knew that by noon on the morrow, the smell of baking bread would once again permeate the town.

"And that's why I want to act quickly, gentlemen," Jeanne told them as she tilted her bowl to get the very last drops of potage into her spoon. "Before they get a whiff of cooking aromas or any other clue things might have changed."

"How many men do you have, Kerveil?" de Mauny asked.

"Just shy of a hundred, if you don't include any of the men of the town."

"We had thirty more," Durant added, "but we were caught behind enemy lines following a raid, so I sent them to Brest to reinforce the garrison there."

"Then how is it you're still here?" de Mauny asked. Durant recounted the story of the raid and the subterfuge Jeanne had devised to get them back inside the walls.

"What a tale, Captain!" de Mauny exclaimed. "And what a bold move."

"The duchess gets the credit – both for envisioning it and leading it. Truth be told, I thought she'd taken leave of her senses, but it turned out to be a brilliant move that ended by reducing the size of the siege army by more than half."

"And another bold move is what I have in mind now." Jeanne brought everyone's attention back to the present. "How many men-at-arms do you bring, Sir Walter?"

"Only thirty-four, I'm afraid. Just enough to replace those you sent to Brest."

If falling faces made a sound, it would have been heard three times over around the table in that moment. Never had Jeanne been so disappointed in her life. This was what the Plantagenet called support for her cause? If it was, she'd vastly overpaid. She almost didn't hear what de Mauny said next.

"But I also have two hundred archers. Mounted archers, which means I also bring their horses so they can move quickly to wherever they're needed on a battlefield."

"That still leaves us outnumbered by almost two to one." Kerveil sounded almost despondent.

"Have you ever seen an English longbowman in action, Captain?" asked de Mauny.

"Nay."

"Nor I," Durant added.

"Then you wouldn't know they're each as deadly as two or three men-at-arms. If what you need is maximum killing from afar, they can loose as many as a dozen arrows a minute and from a distance of two hundred yards or more. If what you want is accuracy, get them within seventy-five yards of target and they rarely miss. Put them on a parapet, and they rain death on anyone advancing toward those walls – man or beast. Give me archers over hand-to-hand fighting any day."

This time, the sound around the table was that of three jaws dropping. Jeanne's face broke into a huge smile. "If they're as good as you say, Sir Walter, then we stand an excellent chance of driving away the besiegers. Especially since we'll have surprise on our side."

They stayed there in the dining hall until midnight, making and refining their plans. Jeanne barely slept that night, but this time it wasn't from despair but from sheer excitement over what the morrow would bring.

Shortly after daybreak, Durant, Kerveil, and de Mauny gathered all the fighting men and laid out the plan of attack, and preparations got underway.

Keeping to her usual routine so that all would look mind-numbingly normal to anyone paying attention, Jeanne climbed to the ramparts to survey the scene. What she saw was no different from any of the previous twenty days. Hundreds of men lazily getting a start to another day of boredom. Good. No one yet suspected anything was afoot.

She descended the steps into a group of a hundred or so men opening crates filled with arrows. What caught her attention was just how different these men looked from the knights and men-at-arms in her husband's army. They were all taller than average, and their shoulders and arms were heavily muscled – out of proportion to the rest of their bodies. Fascinated by what she'd heard the previous evening and what was happening right in front of her, she stopped to watch.

With remarkable speed, they took arrows from the crates, examined the fletchings – occasionally straightening a crumpled feather – and loaded them into cloth sacks designed to keep the fletchings from getting tangled together. The sacks were made so they could be slung over a man's shoulder. They were soon joined by several young lads who took over the loading of the sacks while the archers examined and strung their bows – which were the same length as the height of the archers – and drew them to test the draw weight and stringing.

Curious, Jeanne approached the archer nearest her. "May I have a look?"

He handed her the weapon, which was considerably heavier than she'd expected. She ran her hand along the smooth surface of the wood. "Made from the finest Welsh yew and English ash, madame," he pronounced. She was surprised he spoke French.

The bow was much too long for her height, but she couldn't resist the temptation to try it out. Holding it off the ground, which was awkward in and of itself, she attempted to mimic what she'd just observed. And was unable to pull the string even an inch.

The archer offered her a kindly smile. "Takes years of training, madame, to draw an eighty-pound bow. No one does it on the first try."

She handed the weapon back to him. "What does that mean? Eighty-pound bow. It wasn't that heavy in my hand."

"Draw weight, madame. Drawing the bow is like pulling an eighty-pound rock straight backward from your nose to your ear. Then, when you release the arrow, it has all that force behind it."

"And the arrows," she said. "I noticed you were putting some in one sack and some in another."

"Different kinds, madame. I'll carry one sack on each shoulder. Bodkins for piercing armor. Curved broadheads to bring down the horses."

Clearly, she had a lot to learn about archers. But now it was time to go reassure her children and be sure Henri knew what to do if things went awry.

A quarter hour before midday, she was back at the main gate wearing her armor. This time, Durant had insisted she watch from the safety of the sentry tower and she'd reluctantly agreed. Their entire force was amassed just inside the gate, but off to the sides so they wouldn't be visible to anyone peering in through the open gates from a distance. Durant commanded the left, Kerveil the right. Both groups would be led by cavalry, followed by the men-at-arms.   De Mauny was in command of the archers, who were amassed beside the steps leading to the ramparts on either side of the gate. The young lads were huddled next to the walls beside the crates of arrows, their job, Jeanne had learned, being to take fresh sacks of arrows up to the archers and return with the empty ones to refill. So much depended on the archers. She sent up a little prayer that de Mauny was right about their skill.

Despite their curiosity, the townspeople had retreated inside their homes. Jeanne was grateful she hadn't had to coerce them to do so. The plan was for all the fighting to take place outside the walls, but battles rarely unfolded exactly according to plan.

Even the horses seemed to understand the portent of what was about to happen. Not a nicker, not a headshake, not a single stomp of a single hoof. No man whispered to his comrade. No one coughed.

At long last, the church bells began to toll the noon hour. The sound of the heavy iron bar being lifted from its brackets on either side of the gate was drowned by the sound of the bells. Slowly, the massive gates swung inward.

No one moved. They barely breathed. Everything now depended on what those in the camp did. The waiting seemed to last two lifetimes. But at length, just as Jeanne had predicted, curiosity got the better of the commanders outside. From the window of the tower, she watched as the formation was organized and the slow advance began.

Watching from the shadow of one of the huge gates, de Mauny let the enemy advance until they were about sixty yards from the wall before he gave the signal. The archers scrambled to the top of the walls and began loosing their missiles. In less than a minute, they'd felled every horse in the front rank creating havoc as those behind tried to leap or dodge the fallen animals to keep moving forward. The next round of horses were down almost as quickly and the archers went to work on the unhorsed knights who tried to approach the walls.

Then de Mauny gave another signal and the archers switched tactics. Those on the right side began loosing arrows into the enemy's rear to suppress any attempt to relieve their falling comrades. The ones on the left concentrated on bring down as many targets as possible within the advancing formation.

Jeanne gasped at the sight of the constant volley of arrows wreaking its own havoc in the rear. The barrage of missiles, claiming victim after victim, soon had its effect. Unable to find any shelter, men began deserting the battlefield, unwilling to wait for the arrow meant for them. One by one, the archers on the right were replaced by fresh men, ensuring the rain of death continued nonstop. And the trickle of desertions became a river.

At the front of what was once a formation but had become a disorganized rabble, orders to retreat initially fell on deaf ears but soon were being obeyed.

Now it was the cavalry's turn. Durant and Kerveil each charged through the gate, their mounted warriors in pursuit. Their jobs were to flank the retreating forces and drive them back toward the archers, a tactic that worked briefly until every man in the opposition decided to take matters into his own hands and flee for his life. The cavalry pursued as the enemy raced away, but pulled up short before getting into the range of the archers who were still suppressing the rear.

Both captains led their men back through the gates in triumph. The enemy camp was a shambles. Once the retreating soldiers were out of range, de Mauny called a halt and the archers descended, to be replaced by the men

Durant and Kerveil had assigned to be on watch. The great gates were closed and the townspeople flooded into the streets to celebrate.

Jeanne was overjoyed, overawed, overwhelmed ... grateful for their success, but acutely aware it belonged not to her fighters, but to the archers.

When morning came and the watchmen reported the enemy encampment abandoned, she mounted her charger for one more foray into the realm of those who would've condemned an entire town to starvation. But this time she wore no armor and took the townspeople with her. They deserved to see firsthand that their tormentors were well and truly gone. And they deserved to be the ones to claim whatever had been left behind.

What had once been a more or less orderly army camp was now littered with corpses – equine and human – most pierced with English arrows, but some obviously trampled or crushed in the melée. Durant, Kerveil, and the garrison commander set their men to collecting the weapons left behind. Dozens of archers went about the business of retrieving every arrow that wasn't broken. Even those they pulled from the bodies of their victims could be cleaned and reused so long as the fletchings hadn't been damaged beyond repair.

The townspeople were more interested in the things it took to keep an army alive. Three vast tents near the back of the camp housed a treasure trove. Half a dozen barrels of ale. Salted fish and dried meat. Oats. But all the women rushed to a smaller tent where they found baskets of strawberries and currants, *petits pois* and *haricots verts*, spring onions, courgettes, lettuce ... the summer harvest of what they'd planted in the spring that had been denied them for weeks. Jeanne's instinct was to grab some of the beans for her own table, but she managed to stifle the impulse, instead calling for wagons to be brought from the town to collect the bounty. "We'll take it all to the market square," she announced, "so everyone can get some. And tonight, we'll tap a barrel of ale—"

"Or two or three," the mayor chimed in from the tent entrance.

Jeanne laughed. "Or two or three if that's what it takes to quench our thirst. God knows you're entitled to celebrate."

In addition to the food, they salvaged cooking pots and utensils, a box of horseshoes, some blacksmith's tools, saddles and bridles from the fallen horses ... anything that could be used or sold. *A fitting recompense,* thought Jeanne, *for what these people have endured.*

The meal Jeanne presided over that evening had all the trappings of a ducal banquet. Henri had outdone himself from the laying of the table to even finding some summer wildflowers to create a small bouquet. Cook had managed to snare some of the *haricots verts* that Jeanne loved so much, and de Mauny contributed multiple pitchers of wine from his personal stores on board his flagship. Combined with perfectly prepared fish that wasn't in a potage, strawberries and English cheese after the main course, and Henri's impeccable service, it was as close to a proper banquet as she'd had since leaving Nantes.

When Henri left after filling the goblets once again to enjoy with the strawberries and cheese, Jeanne finally asked the question she'd been holding back since first greeting de Mauny on the dock. "Now that we've dispensed with the threat, Sir Walter, I have to satisfy my curiosity. Why was your arrival delayed so long? Our agreement with King Edward was made in February and yet it's now the end of June."

"I admit our departure was delayed, madame. But my mission has been to secure safe harbors to land the main English forces. When I arrived in Brest, I was met by your emissary – de Clisson, I believe?"

"That's right," she replied.

"His news was most disturbing. Though Brest itself was still firmly loyal to you, madame, there was another Breton noble working hard to disrupt that. Hervé de Léon, who I'm given to understand was once your husband's closest ally. He was going to great lengths – writing letters, paying personal visits, exhorting everyone of his acquaintance to change sides. And some were paying attention to his arguments. Had that continued, we might have lost Brest. De Clisson thought we might have lost all of Finistère, which would have been a disaster for your cause.

"To secure Brest, I had to put an end to de Léon's campaign. Which meant I had to find and capture him. He's now spending his days in a cell in the Brest garrison, in the custody of the administrator I installed in the port before moving on."

"Just deserts for a turncoat," growled Durant.

"It's his wife I feel sorry for," said Jeanne. "She's related to both sides of this conflict."

"Don't feel too sorry for her, madame," said de Mauny. "She'll know where her loyalties should lie when I take her husband to England as hostage for her good behavior."

When they'd finished the last of de Mauny's wine, Jeanne suggested they walk to the market square, where they found most of the town in full celebration. The town's musicians had brought out their instruments and were playing a farandole. Jeanne and her captains eagerly joined the dancers, and she grabbed de Mauny's hand. "Join the celebration, Sir Walter."

"I'm no dancer, madame."

"You don't have to be. Just follow the person in front of you." She laughed and pulled him into the line.

"You know, madame," he said as he stepped awkwardly between her and Kerveil, "I see why these people would do anything for you. Watching you in the fields today and now, here, no one could doubt your care for them."

They stayed for half an hour before returning to the castle. It was important for the townspeople to have their own fun, without having to think about a duchess in their midst.

Tonight was for celebration. Tomorrow the soldiers would undertake the grim task of collecting the corpses and the remains of the camp and setting it all on fire. The smell of burning flesh would fill everyone's nostrils for a day, but when the flames subsided, all that would be left was a few piles of bone and ash, and nature would go to work reclaiming the land. The people of Hennebont were already reclaiming their lives.

FROM THE WRITINGS OF JEANNE DE FLANDRE, DUCHESS OF BRITTANY AND COUNTESS OF MONTFORT
FOUND AMONG HER BELONGINGS AT THE TIME OF HER DEATH

Tickhill, South Yorkshire, 1348

I knew that, as soon as the refugees from the siege camp returned home and told their stories, everyone who mattered would know I had support. And their accounts of the archers would prove from whence it came. Those whose hearts were with France would say I had made a pact with the devil.

No devil to my way of thinking. More a deliverer. Having seen how the English archers – with their bows no ordinary man could draw – could completely change the course of a battle, I knew my money was well spent. With such an advantage on our side, it was almost a foregone conclusion that we would prevail quickly once the rest of the English forces arrived. Or so I thought in the moment.

*Sir Walter had left his men-at-arms and archers with us. But even with the forces under Malestroit's command at Saint-Renan – and assuming, of course, that we could join up with them, which was certainly **not** a foregone conclusion – our numbers were insufficient to take on Charles directly. Our only option was a defensive posture, protecting what we still held until more reinforcements arrived.*

In mid-July, the garrison at Auray – which had been under siege since Charles had taken the bulk of his army away from Hennebont – deserted, slipping through enemy lines into the nearby woodlands under cover of darkness rather than having to eat their own horses to survive. De Blois walked in and invested the town, undeterred, then turned his attention to Vannes. Within a week, they, too, had accepted Charles's terms of surrender.

When we learned that the citizens of Guémené-sur-Scorff had forced their commander to capitulate, there was no mistaking Charles's intent. Rather than risk being surrounded, we abandoned Hennebont for the safety of Brest. And still there was no sign of the English reinforcements despite de Mauny's promise that a thousand more men-at-arms and a thousand more mounted archers would arrive soon after his departure.

In no time at all, word reached us that Charles was once again on the march, this time toward Brest. At Durant and Kerveil's urging, I summoned Malestroit to bring his forces into the fortress. If we had to face the French army on our own, we'd need every man we had. Though the archers gave us something of an edge, they would no longer be a surprise. And as my captains kept reminding me, once they'd used all their arrows, the only advantage they brought to a fight was their considerable strength in wielding a conventional weapon. So deciding when and how to deploy them would be crucial.

I can't pretend that the sight of Charles's advance guard beginning to establish a camp outside Brest didn't send a frisson of fear down my spine. It was so reminiscent of what had happened at Hennebont that anyone seeing both would have been mad not to have had a visceral reaction.

Four days later, we were heartened to see ships on the horizon ... only to have our hopes dashed when they drew closer and it became obvious they were Genoese galleys. It was the middle of August, and we were trapped between Philip's Genoese mercenaries and Charles's army.

CHAPTER TWENTY-FOUR

Unwilling to sit around fretting about their situation, Jeanne sent for Durant, Kerveil, and Malestroit to consider whether there might be any way out of their dilemma short of enduring another siege. Charles's camp was fully established but as yet had demonstrated no intent to attack.

"My first thought was using the archers against the galleys," said Durant.

"How would that help?" Jeanne asked. "We might kill some seamen, but could we possibly kill enough to incapacitate all fourteen of them?"

"I was thinking of fire arrows. Set as many ships as possible ablaze and that might leave us with an escape route. When I spoke to the head archer, he said it wasn't a bad idea, but the galleys were staying just out of range. Too many arrows would fall short. He also reminded me that any arrow used against the galleys wouldn't be recoverable, so we'd be depleting their supply for a dubious outcome." Durant paused. "It was a thought, but it didn't turn out to be a practical one."

"I can guess what your next question is going to be, madame." Kerveil's smile belied the gravity of their situation.

"So can I," chuckled Durant.

Malestroit just looked puzzled. "She wants to know if the tactics we used in Hennebont might work again here," Kerveil clarified for his compatriot. "And the answer, my lady, is an emphatic no."

Jeanne opened her mouth to speak, but Kerveil held up his hand to forestall her. "Even if the situation looks similar, the differences are vast. Yes, we have more men than we did then, but so do they. By quite a lot. They know we're nowhere near starvation. They know we have the English archers. We have no element of surprise on our side."

"When I was talking with the head archer," Durant picked up that thread, "I asked if they could suppress this army as they did in Hennebont. He answered a somewhat tentative yes ..." Jeanne's expression brightened. "... before adding 'if there were more of us.'"

"How many?" Jeanne asked. "I know longbowmen can't be trained in days or weeks. I just want to get his sense of what it would take."

"Twice as many was his first response. Then he said it would take at least five hundred more to keep them suppressed for any length of time. That kind of continuous, rapid firing tires even the strongest men quickly, so they have to spell each other often to sustain an attack."

"Not to mention," Kerveil chimed in, "that it would require a lot more arrows than we have."

"So all we can do is sit here." Jeanne sounded as near defeated as Durant had ever heard her.

"Wait and watch is not always a bad strategy, madame." Malestroit spoke for the first time. "Especially if your objective is to keep your losses to a minimum. We change the lookouts frequently, so no one gets bored or distracted. If they're preparing to make a move, we should spot some sort of activity. Then we'll know how to act."

"And perhaps reinforcements will arrive by the time we need them," said Durant.

She gave a sad little laugh. "Don't count on it, Captain."

And so they waited. Changing the sentries every hour kept fresh eyes on the enemy camp and the galleys anchored in the roads. The archers set up practice butts in the market square, drawing crowds to marvel at their marksmanship. Jeanne began laying plans with Tanguy du Chastel for rationing food to endure a siege. Durant, Kerveil, and Malestroit organized exercises for their men to keep their fighting skills sharp, but that wasn't easy within the confined space of the town. They also did their best to keep the horses fit by walking them through the streets so that no animal went more than two days without some exercise. It gave the impression of purposeful activity, but did nothing to take the minds of the duchess or her commanders off their dire straits.

As Wednesday rolled into Thursday and Friday and finally Sunday, Jeanne went to Mass as she always did. She listened as the priest sent up prayers to Saint Helena, whose feast day it was, then sent her own to Saint Jude. Though she tried to hide her despondency from others, her cause was feeling more and more like a futile one and the faith she'd placed in her pact with the Plantagenet, more and more like wishful thinking.

She emerged from the church to a flurry of activity in the square outside the castle and Henri waving frantically. "Madame! Madame! Come quickly." She quickened her pace as he rushed to join her. "Hurry, madame. Captain Durant says you must come to the south tower straightaway. He said you mustn't delay."

The south tower being the farthest possible point from the castle entrance and the urgency in Henri's voice being something she rarely heard, once she was inside where the townspeople couldn't see her, she lifted her skirts and ran the entire distance, slowing only to negotiate the somewhat treacherous steps to the top. She found all three of her commanders staring out the window and pointing. It was an eerie echo of her own performance when she'd spotted the ships arriving at Hennebont. Did she dare hope?

Suddenly aware of her presence, Durant turned and beckoned. "Duchess! Come here. You won't believe your eyes."

There, just exiting the channel into the roads, were two ships flying the banners of England. And behind them in the channel and the open ocean, as far as the eye could see, a fleet the size of which she'd never seen before. "There must be scores of them!" she exclaimed.

"Hundreds, more like," said Kerveil.

They watched, mesmerized, as the flagship veered right, leading those in its wake behind the Genoese galleys. It was like a slow dance. The large English ships were far less maneuverable than the galleys, but the channel was completely blocked by the incoming fleet and the commander's decision to encircle them from the south left them no escape. Three managed to get away into the Élorn river, but the others had no option but the Penfeld, with its marshes surrounding what quickly became a narrow stream. As the

English pressed them north, the galleys foundered in the mud, leaving the seamen and mercenaries no option but to abandon ship and run for their lives. The lead ships put boats over the side manned by seamen with torches and in no time, all eleven galleys had been put to the flame.

And still the English ships kept coming. By the time the entire fleet had anchored in the roads, there were well over two hundred of them. "I lost count after that," said Kerveil.

"How many men must they have?" asked Jeanne.

Durant pointed toward the flagship, where a boat was again being lowered into the water. Half a dozen seamen scrambled down the rope ladder followed by a man dressed in noble finery and a plumed hat. A standard she hadn't seen before was raised at the bow. Three red stars on a silver diagonal bordered in gold, with three lions rampant on either side on a field of blue, surmounted by an earl's coronet. There could be no doubt of the man's proximity to the English throne. He took his seat in the stern, and the seamen began to row for the dock. "I think we're about to find out," said Durant.

With Malestroit leading the way and Jeanne calling out instructions, they hurried to the great hall. "Henri, find Tanguy and get him here straightaway. The English commander will be here any minute," she ordered as they slowed their pace to walk into the hall. "And have Perota bring my son."

Placing a low stool beside her own chair, Jeanne smoothed her skirts, checked her hair, and slowed her breathing. It would never do to receive King Edward's representative in a state of disarray. Tanguy arrived first. "Good. You gentlemen stand there, to my right." She was arranging the tableau she wanted to present.

Perota dashed in carrying the three-year-old John and set him on his feet beside his mother. "Sorry, madame. I had to clean him up a bit."

"For which I'm grateful, Perota. You may go." She took her son's hand in one of hers and patted the stool with the other. "We're about to meet a very important man, John," she told the boy. "And you get to meet him too. So I want you to sit here beside me and be nice and quiet until I tell you it's alright to get up. Can you do that for me?"

"*Oui, maman.* But when can I go back and play?"

"It won't be long. I promise."

He'd just taken his seat when Henri appeared in the doorway. "My lady duchess. Monsieur William de Bohun. The Earl of Northampton." He bowed and stepped aside to make way for the man they'd watched climb into the boat.

Jeanne smiled to herself. *At least I outrank him, being a duchess and he just an earl. Not by much if what I've heard about the English aristocracy is right and the king has only just begun to use ducal titles. But the reason he's here is to support me and my son, so I'll use whatever small advantage I have.*

Northampton removed his hat with a bit of a flourish. "Jeanne de Montfort, I presume."

She rose and extended her hand, eliciting the proper courtly kiss. "And this is my son John, the head of our family now that his father suffers confinement as Philip of Valois's prisoner."

"A fine lad he is indeed." Northampton was all graciousness. Jeanne resumed her seat as he continued. "I bring you greetings, lady, from His Most Noble Grace Edward, King of England and of France."

"And not a moment too soon, sir. Tell me, does Edward make it a habit to delay so long in fulfilling his part of agreements that he himself has signed? Twice now we've been on the brink of disaster while waiting for what we'd been promised months earlier."

Northampton didn't take the bait. "I can't deny there have been delays, but we're here now and have already demolished the force that was blockading your access to the sea."

Jeanne tempered her tone. "A most impressive display, monsieur. My commanders and I had the privilege of watching from the tower. An impressive fleet as well. Would I be correct in assuming this means you bring quite a substantial army?"

"Thirteen hundred fifty men, madame. Half men-at-arms, half archers." Jeanne struggled to keep disappointment from her expression as he added, "Robert of Artois is but a few days behind me with another eight hundred, and the king expects to sail in early September with more men still."

"That seems an enormous number of ships for so few men, if I may say so," said Jeanne.

"Perhaps the lady doesn't understand what it takes to fight a battle."

Jeanne bristled. *And just what does he think I did in Hennebont? Why do men always have to be so condescending?* Much as she wanted to berate him, she knew in this instance, it would be better to hold her tongue.

"We bring provisions to last for months," the earl continued, "crates upon crates of arrows and bowstrings and extra bows for the archers, weapons enough for every man in the field to lose his own ten times over without having to fight unarmed. Horses. Cooks and all their paraphernalia to feed an army. Blacksmiths to tend the horses and forge new weapons. When England fights, my lady, we do not do so unprepared."

Though it was late in coming, at least she now understood just what her money was buying. She also understood it would have taken that much and more to assemble such might on her own – if it could have been done at all. "That, monsieur, is the best news I've heard in weeks. Your quarters here in the castle should be ready by now, and I invite you to consider this your headquarters. If I know my steward, he already has a better than average meal being prepared for this evening. I trust you'd enjoy a change from ship's fare."

"I'm grateful for your hospitality, duchess, and will take advantage of it while my ships are being offloaded and my lieutenants get things organized. But my job here is to wage war, and I prefer to do that from a command post with my army, so you'll not see much of me once we get underway. For now, though, I'd like to see what you're facing on the other side of these walls to know how to make my plans."

"Of course." She rose and stepped to his side, her commanders following behind. Henri was waiting just outside the door. "Henri, would you please take John back to the nursery?"

"As you wish, madame."

From the top of the eastern walls of the town, they surveyed the French encampment. "Charles de Blois himself is in command," Jeanne informed the earl as he scanned the army arrayed before him.

"Who are those men scrambling into the camp?" Northampton asked.

"Our sentries reported this earlier," Tanguy supplied. "We're confident they're the Genoese mercenaries fleeing from the galleys."

"Good," Northampton declared. "I hope they're scared out of their wits and telling tales of the disaster that befell them with no warning. The more fear they spread the better."

The next day, Jeanne turned over the sixty-eight thousand livres that were the second installment in her bargain, and Northampton went to work.

FROM THE WRITINGS OF JEANNE DE FLANDRE, DUCHESS OF BRITTANY AND COUNTESS OF MONTFORT
FOUND AMONG HER BELONGINGS AT THE TIME OF HER DEATH

Tickhill, South Yorkshire, 1348

The Earl of Northampton got his wish. Whatever stories the Genoese told of the newly arrived reinforcements and the demise of the galleys, they were enough to upend the French strategy. In less than a week, the army was gone. Charles retreated with his main force to his wife's lands in Penthièvre. The Spanish and Italians who had made up the rest of the army were last seen boarding Spanish vessels in the Baie de Bourgneuf, south of Nantes.

Northampton wasted no time. With Brest no longer threatened, he set out for Morlaix to secure a landing spot on the north coast and save the English fleets from having to navigate the treacherous waters between the island of Ushant and the coast of Finistère. The intent was that Edward should disembark there with the rest of his army.

But Edward ... as usual ... was late. I'd long since given up expecting anything different.

CHAPTER TWENTY-FIVE

Palace of Westminster, late September 1342

"Pacing about won't solve the problem, Edward," said Montagu. "Pour yourself a glass of wine and join me." He gestured to the empty chairs near where he sat by the hearth in the king's privy chamber.

Montagu had been home for almost four months and was now deeply immersed in Edward's Breton strategy – and relishing the prospect of getting some of his own back against the French king who'd held him hostage for two years. He had the Duke of Luxembourg to thank for the fact that he was even alive to enjoy the experience. Someone had poured stories into the French queen's ear that the Earl of Salisbury was a vicious monster who killed women and children for sport, causing her to announce to her husband that she'd never be able to sleep until Salisbury was dead. Philip was on the verge of acceding to his wife's wishes when Luxembourg intervened, pointing out that the earl had far greater value as a hostage than as a corpse. But as Philip was notorious for not being able to make up his mind, Montagu spent each day of the next two years with the specter of execution hanging over his head. Even as negotiations proceeded . . . even when he was released from the Châtelet to live under guard in a private house . . . he was never certain of his fate until he finally set foot on English soil.

Edward had met him at Dover Castle, greeting his oldest friend with a brotherly embrace. "In the end, what did you have to promise him?" was Edward's first question.

"To never again fight on French soil."

"And do you intend to keep that promise?"

"Fortunately for me, he neglected to define 'French soil.' And since there's another claimant to the throne of France, I'm not even sure I made that promise to a king at all."

Edward had roared with laughter. "Is it any wonder we get along so well?"

Today they were discussing the Breton campaign and Edward's impatience to get his own part in the plan underway. At Montagu's words, Edward stopped in his tracks. "Why is it *always* the bloody ships?" It appeared he intended to resume his pacing, but he only went as far as the sideboard, where he followed his friend's instructions. Finally taking a seat, he went on with his rant. "I've got over three thousand men just sitting around waiting in Winchelsea and Sandwich because of those devil's-spawn shipmasters that deserted the fleet. And the Welsh contingent had to be diverted to join Gloucester in Sutton. Meanwhile, I'm paying all those idle men to sit around wasting time."

Though he understood Edward's frustration, Montagu also understood that what his friend really wanted was some sort of reassurance that the delays wouldn't sink his grand strategy. "It may not be as bad as you think, Edward."

"And what leads you to *that* conclusion?"

"The latest from my spies is that all the activity in Kent and Sussex has drawn Philip's attention. He's worried your intent might be to take Calais."

"Well, he's got that right," said Edward, still grumpy.

Montagu allowed himself a chuckle. "True. But not from the direction he thinks it's coming from. In any case, he's worried enough to pull significant forces away from de Blois in Brittany, giving Northampton far better odds for now. And when you land in Brest, all those men he's moved east will have to be moved back."

"You make a fair point, William."

"Then think of what's happening as a diversionary tactic, even if you hadn't intended it that way. The outcome is what matters, right?"

Edward took a long swallow of wine. "God's teeth, how I've missed your clear head these past two years!"

"Don't give me too much credit, Edward. You came up with this Breton strategy all on your own. And it's a good one. Gets you out of that quagmire in the Low Countries."

It was Edward's turn to chuckle. "The one you never liked." Now, more relaxed, he took a smaller sip of wine and set the goblet on the little table beside his chair. "Maybe if you'd been here, you could have helped extricate us from those entanglements faster, and we'd be farther along in Brittany."

"Oh, I'm not sure it would have made much difference. Besides, having Philip distracted on three fronts just made it harder for him to make up his mind where to take a stand. Now ..." Montagu rose and went to the sideboard to refill his own goblet. "... let's discuss my part of the campaign."

They spent the next hour updating their plans to align with the new expectation that Edward would finally set sail at the beginning of October. Edward's first objective, once he'd met with the Montfortists in Brest, would be to retake Vannes, leaving it to Northampton to keep Charles de Blois occupied in the north. With Vannes in English hands, western Brittany would be secured. Salisbury's job was to land in the northeast and advance rapidly across a wide swath of the duchy – a shock force intended to shatter the morale of the French and the Blois loyalists.

The plans were set. All that remained was for the last of the ships to be positioned and provisioned. Finally, on the feast day of Saint Francis of Assisi, Edward attended Mass at the church of Saint Clement, patron of mariners, then boarded his flagship in time to sail with the tide.

CHAPTER TWENTY-SIX

Brest, late October 1342

There can be little doubt that Edward Plantagenet thought it propitious that he finally set foot on Breton soil on the feast day of Saint Alfred the Great. As Alfred's vision had been for a united England, so Edward's was for England to gather all the lands of his ancestors to its bosom as a united empire. An empire that included his rightful inheritance as the grandson of Philip IV.

Jeanne waited with her son in the great hall of the castle, both dressed their best finery to receive the man who'd promised to help her secure the little boy's future. It had been eight months since they'd put their seals to the pact that was intended to put paid once and for all to Jeanne de Penthièvre's pretensions and Philip's support for her unsupportable claim. And now they were about to meet face to face for the first time. She held her son's hand, as much to steady herself for the momentous occasion as to keep the child from fidgeting. It seemed as if they'd been standing for hours, though it had been merely moments since Henri had advised her the English king was approaching the castle entrance and would soon arrive in the hall. Little John shifted from one foot to the other. "Why do we have to stand, *maman?*"

"Because the man we're about to receive is a king, and that's how we show our respect. Now remember, watch me, and when you see me curtsey, make your little bow just like we practiced. Can you do that?"

"*Oui, maman.*"

And then came the knock on the door and the words she'd been waiting months to hear. "His Most Excellent Grace Edward, King of England and of France." And there he was.

Jeanne stood there, transfixed. He was remarkably handsome. But why shouldn't he be? His maternal grandfather was known as Philippe le Bel. Taller than most men. As tall as the archers she'd seen, but without their exaggerated shoulders and arms. And why shouldn't he be? His other grandfather was known as Longshanks. And for all she'd heard about his occasional bursts of temper, his expression in the moment was warm and congenial.

She recovered in an instant and hoped no one had noticed her momentary lapse. "Your Grace." She curtsied and watched out of the corner of her eye as little John made his awkward bow. "Welcome to Brittany."

"A land I've long desired to see for myself, Duchess." He crossed to her and lifted her hand for a proper courtly kiss. "And this . . ." He crouched down to address the boy. ". . . must be the future duke. What's your name, lad?"

Uncertain what to do, the boy looked up to his mother. "You may answer," she said.

"I'm John, monsieur."

"Ah, just like your father. Did you know that I bear my father's name too?"

"*Non, monsieur.*"

"Well, I do." He stood and tousled the boy's hair. "That bodes well for your future. Wouldn't you agree, Duchess?"

"I do indeed, Your Grace. Would Your Grace care for some refreshment? Food or wine, perhaps?"

"In due course. But before that, may I be so bold as to ask if I may take some time to refresh myself and rest from the voyage. We've had the most frightful journey with the worst storms I've ever experienced."

"Not bold at all, Sire. We've prepared the duke's rooms for your use and if there's anything you require that's not already provided, your servants need only ask my steward. Then, once you've rested, perhaps you might join us for the evening repast. I doubt it will compare to what you're accustomed to in your own palaces, but we shall do our utmost to make it enjoyable."

He reached for her hand once again for another courtly kiss. "Until this evening, then, Duchess."

When the door closed behind him, she finally exhaled. That had gone well. No one had put a foot wrong. Even her young son had played his role to perfection. Tonight would still be for pleasantries. Tomorrow, they would get down to the serious business of restoring Montfort rule in the duchy.

·   ·   ·   ·   ·

Three mornings later, Henri appeared at the door to Jeanne's bedchamber just as her maid had finished arranging her hair. "Lord de Clisson wishes a word, madame. I showed him into your sitting room."

"Very well, Henri. I'll just be a moment."

She found de Clisson staring out the window, his back to the door. "Amaury. What a nice surprise!"

He spun around at the sound of her voice. "Ah, my dear Jeanne, do forgive me. I was distracted by all the men milling about the courtyard."

"Do let's sit." She took her usual chair as he crossed the room to join her. "Now, to what do I owe the pleasure of your company?"

"I'm afraid you're not going to find it so pleasant. Yesterday evening, one of Edward's pages paid me a visit. It seems the king is curious when you'll be turning over the rest of the treasury to complete your part of the agreement."

Her face fell. "Oh, Amaury, must we turn *everything* over? With all the delays, the just-in-the-nick-of-time rescues … surely we're due *some* consideration."

"I'm sympathetic, of course, but I doubt Edward will see it that way."

"Then perhaps he should see it this way. Had he made good on his promises – sent his forces in March and April – and in reasonable numbers … had he himself come in June … we would still hold Vannes. And Auray.

And he wouldn't be in the position now of having to retake them. We might even have prevented Charles from *getting* to Guingamp, much less digging his forces in there. Edward bears some responsibility in all this. Why should I pay full measure when *he* hasn't?"

"I can't argue with your reasoning, but tell me, Jeanne? Are you willing to take the risk that Edward would abandon us and leave you to your fate?"

"Do you really believe he's that venal?"

"What I believe is that he's spent huge sums to launch this campaign . . . with the expectation that you intended to help finance it. There's as much at stake for him as there is for you. So perhaps the way *you* should think about it is, what is your son's future worth?" He paused then added, "After all, that's been your touchstone from the start, has it not?"

Jeanne rose and crossed to the window. The courtyard was indeed alive with men. There hadn't been so much activity here in the castle since the first days after the Earl of Northampton's arrival. And Edward's force was even larger. Perhaps now, they really did have a chance. Now that Philip knew the English were here in force, there really was no turning back. She had made her bargain. For her son's sake, she had to see it through.

She returned to her chair, her jaw set. "For my son's future, Amaury. And to secure John's release. For that, I'll release the rest of my treasure."

"You can hold back what Henri needs to run the household for a few months until you can once again begin collecting rents. But no more. Shall I take charge of the transfer?"

"I'd be grateful, Amaury."

· · · · ·

By the end of November, Edward had retaken Ploërmel, Rédon, and Malestroit. Northampton had invaded the stronghold of the powerful Rohan family and burned their manor to the ground. He and Warwick then attacked Nantes and invested the northern portion of the town, terrorizing the Nantais. Salisbury arrived in mid-December as planned, burning Dinan and several other villages. By the end of the month, Breton notables were switching sides in increasing numbers.

Just as Jeanne was becoming convinced her money had been well-spent, Philip's newly assembled army arrived and retook much of the Montfortists' gains. "Two steps forward, two steps back," Jeanne complained to de Clisson.

"Perhaps not the full two back, my dear. The Rohans have been rendered irrelevant. The English hold their lands. With the exception of Penthièvre, we hold the west – far more securely than ever. And there's no indication that any of the nobles who've come to our cause have any intention of deserting us."

"Perhaps you're right," she sighed.

"You didn't really expect, did you, that Philip would fail to respond to a large English army running roughshod over what he considers French land?"

"I suppose not. But neither did I expect so many of our gains would be lost so easily."

"Patience, my dear. Edward knows what he's doing."

By the middle of January, word reached Brest that Philip had set up court in Rédon, about a day's ride from the English lines. An audacious move, meant, no doubt, to tell the world this was French soil. Jeanne's anxiety grew by the day. Every morning she summoned de Clisson, hoping for news, and every day, he brought nothing but disappointment. For everyone else's sake, she kept up appearances, but inside, she struggled to suppress the memories of the near-catastrophe in Hennebont. *Don't be ridiculous*, she'd chide herself when her spirits flagged. *Then, the enemy was camped just a few yards away and you were running out of food. Now, there's plenty to eat and five thousand men between you and any threat.*

For a full week, they heard nothing more. Then, at midday on the twenty-third, sentries at the main gate announced the sighting of a group of armed men in the distance. Tanguy du Chastel ordered the gates closed as a precaution. It wasn't long before the standards were identified. The lions of England accompanied by a coat of arms unfamiliar to anyone in Brest – but the earl's coronet surmounting the shield announced its bearer as yet another of Edward's trusted nobles.

What brings him back? Jeanne wondered. It would be another two hours before she'd find out.

Edward strode into her sitting room with the air of a man who'd just been declared a tournament champion. "Good news, Duchess. William here has negotiated a most favorable truce that I put my signature to just four days ago."

"Truce?" Jeanne couldn't believe her ears. He was conceding defeat?

"Indeed. One that leaves us in an excellent position to consolidate our gains and take the measure of Philip's resolve." He lowered himself into a nearby chair and took a long swallow from the goblet of wine that Henri proffered. "Gascon?"

"Your Grace has discerning taste." Henri bowed, refilled the goblet, and returned the pitcher to the sideboard. "Will there be anything else, my lady?"

"Not at the moment, Henri. You may leave us." She took a sip from her own goblet. "You were saying about the truce, Sire?" she asked.

"Ah, yes. I think you'll be pleased. We gave up none of our gains. Philip can't advance beyond his current position."

"The only news we've heard here is that Vannes is under siege. Is it under our control now?"

"That's the one thing we had to concede. But Philip didn't get it either. The pope is to administer it until we reach a permanent solution."

"But isn't the new pope Philip's man?"

"It's true he's been in Philip's favor for years, so I suspect Philip counts Vannes as a win for his side," said Edward's companion, the man the king had called William. "But we judged papal administration an acceptable compromise to get something we were *not* prepared to compromise on."

"My apologies, Duchess," Edward interrupted. "I've let my enthusiasm overtake my manners. Allow me to present my oldest and best friend, William Montagu, Earl of Salisbury."

"Welcome to Brittany, Lord Salisbury," said Jeanne.

"I've heard stories of your exploits, Duchess. I think it's my good fortune that we're on the same side."

"Go ahead and tell her, William," said Edward. "Let's not keep her on tenterhooks."

"What we refused to compromise on, madame, was your husband's release. By the terms of the truce, Philip must grant him his freedom and restore his Montfort lands."

"I'm sure that rankled," said Edward, "but William stood firm."

"And for that, I'm deeply grateful." It was all Jeanne could do to restrain herself from jumping up and embracing both men. Instead, she raised her goblet, "To John's release!" They joined her in the toast. "And how soon will he be with us?"

"That, we don't know," said Edward.

"Having won the concession," William added, "I could sense that pressing for a specific timing might very well end with Philip feeling backed into a corner and withdrawing his agreement. We had what we wanted. If he doesn't comply, we have cause to resume hostilities."

Jeanne couldn't avoid feeling a bit crestfallen. Philip would prevaricate – of that she was certain. But it wouldn't be in his interests to dishonor a truce he'd signed. To mask her feelings, she said, "Then I suppose our best hope is that he wants to get something he considers distasteful over and done with."

·   ·   ·   ·   ·

While Edward and Salisbury busied themselves with fortifying their holdings against the possibility of a breach of the truce, Jeanne settled in to wait for her husband's return. De Clisson visited once a week, bringing her news from his own informants. If the weather was fair, they'd walk about the town so they could talk away from prying ears. By the fourth week, Jeanne had noticed a pattern to his visits. "I'm beginning to think, Amaury," she remarked as they circled the *Place du Château* for the second time, "that you choose the day of your visits specifically for the sunshine."

"No one could ever accuse you, my dear Jeanne, of a lack of astuteness," he chuckled. "But what I don't seem to have any say in is just how cold such days might be. What say you to having our little chat inside the church?" Despite the sun's best efforts, a brisk northerly breeze had them shivering inside their heavy cloaks, hats, and gloves.

"It might not be much warmer, but at least it will be out of the wind."

The church was deserted, so they chose a spot where sunlight streaming through a high window offered a bit of warmth, though not enough to warrant shedding even their gloves. "I'm afraid there's still no news of when John might be released," de Clisson told her. "It seems your view that Philip would be in no hurry is proving correct. Beyond that, I have little else to report. Edward has men firmly in control of all our main garrisons, so Philip will have no doubt he intends to enforce the truce in Brittany. Once John is free and takes charge of our cause again, I'm optimistic that even more of the Breton nobles will rally to us."

"Do we know anything of the Countess of Penthièvre's whereabouts?"

"It's said she's with her husband, but I haven't asked my informants to confirm that."

"Interesting," Jeanne mused. "A tactical retreat since Philip limited her options for now?"

"In truth, she has little choice."

"She may be on a short rein for now, but that doesn't mean I have to trust her. Be on your guard, Amaury. Assume she will pounce, given any opportunity."

Realizing that the angle of the sun had shifted enough he was now standing outside its warmth, he edged sideways into the light. "You make that sound like an instruction, my dear."

"Perhaps it is. Edward and Salisbury are setting sail for England next week, and Edward is determined that the children and I come with him. I'm extremely reluctant, but he insists it's for our safety."

"And what does he cite as the risk if you stay?"

"That we'd be taken as hostages."

"Not by Philip, surely." De Clisson seemed incredulous.

"Edward's argument is that it wouldn't be by force but by other means. An olive branch, a peace offering, a gesture that would seem utterly innocuous . . . not even necessarily by Philip himself but possibly by one of his adherents . . . something so seemingly benign that it would lure me to a place where we could be prevented from leaving."

"Doesn't he realize you'd be on your guard?"

"I've told him as much . . . even made my case to Salisbury in the hope he might convince his friend. The earl's words were kind and he appeared sympathetic, but if he spoke on my behalf, it in no way changed the king's mind. Edward's position is that the ruse would be so subtle even *he* might not recognize it until it was too late."

"Please tell me you didn't laugh in his face when he said that." De Clisson sounded genuinely concerned that she might have done just that.

She laughed softly now. "Because you know me too well, Amaury. Tempting as it was, I couldn't bring myself to actually insult the man who'd breathed new life into our cause. But what he said next gave me pause. He said that if Philip could claim my son was under his control, our position would be badly damaged. Worse yet, if my son were taken out of my care, it would be harder to rally our supporters. Even worse still, if an excuse could be found to execute my son, then it would all be over."

Neither of them spoke. The sun had shifted further, leaving them both now outside its warming rays in the cold gloom of reality. At long last, de Clisson said, "He's trying to frighten you, you know."

"I know. But he's right about one thing. Until John is released, our son is the pawn in the countess's game. Everything I've done so far has been to preserve his future and his inheritance. I can't abandon that purpose, Amaury. So I can't put his life at risk when I have no way to know how great or small that risk might be."

"You'll go then?"

"Just until John is released. Call it *my* tactical retreat if you like."

De Clisson's smile seemed to offer both sympathy and encouragement. "I can't speak for John, of course, but I do believe he would understand your reasoning. So much so that, when he *is* released, I'll encourage him to join you in England to reunite the family. Perhaps you can even make a triumphant return."

"Much to be hoped for, Amaury. In the meantime, I'll need news of what's happening here if I'm to make the appropriate representations to Edward for his continued support. Promise you'll write to me. Not just the bare facts of what's happening but your thoughts about what it portends as well . . . even your musings about what might happen next."

"I shall take it as my duty, madame, to ensure you're the best-informed duchess-in-exile mankind has ever known." He doffed his hat long enough for a courtly bow before returning it quickly to his head to ward off the cold.

"Then, as I can't predict what day Edward will choose to sail or what day next week Mother Nature will choose to bless us with sunshine, I suppose we should say farewell for now."

"Until we meet again when you return, my dear." He gave her a brotherly kiss on the cheek before she turned and hurried away to avoid having the emotion of the moment overcome her.

FROM THE WRITINGS OF JEANNE DE FLANDRE, DUCHESS OF BRITTANY AND COUNTESS OF MONTFORT
FOUND AMONG HER BELONGINGS AT THE TIME OF HER DEATH

Tickhill, South Yorkshire, 1348

I must admit to having mixed feelings when Edward announced we would sail on the feast day of Sainte Honorine. I don't know if the saint meant anything to him, though she should have as she was well-loved in Normandy, the land of his ancestors. Having been reared in France, I was taught to revere her and was once taken to Conflans to worship at her relics.

And therein lay the source of my conundrum, Conflans also being the location where the edict was issued disinheriting my husband. But Honorine was the patron of boatmen, and though that literally meant those who ply the inland waterways, I convinced myself she might favor my entreaty to extend her protection for a few days to those who ply the seas.

Concerned there might be objections to my plans for some of the household to accompany us, I'd broached the subject with the Earl of Salisbury, who I was coming to regard as my champion in Edward's entourage. There was no doubt he had the king's ear. In the end, my worries proved unfounded. Henri took everything in hand, organizing the staff and the preparations with his usual efficiency.

My resolve almost broke when it came time to bid farewell to Durant and Kerveil. These two who had been with me through everything. Who had fought at my side. Who had endured the privations of the siege. Who had trusted me when others might have turned away. How could I ever repay them? I longed to take them with us. But their duty lay in Brittany. To be ready, when John was free, to pick up their swords once again for his honor. Try as I might, I couldn't prevent a few tears from escaping when I heard Durant's quiet "God go with you, Duchess" as we walked up the gangway and onto our ship.

It seems a lifetime ago now. When we boarded that ship, I had no idea of the headwinds we were sailing into.

CHAPTER TWENTY-SEVEN

It was to be Jeanne's first sea voyage – the first time on open water for any of her household, for that matter. They'd been assigned their own ship. It meant they weren't crowded in with men-at-arms, but Henri was miffed nonetheless. "You're a duchess, madame. And the king's invited guest. You should be on the flagship."

"Perhaps it's just as great an honor to have our own ship, Henri. In other circumstances, we might hoist the ducal banner and proclaim our presence to the world, but I think today, discretion may be the better choice. Besides ... I'm quite content to be here with my children."

"If that's what you wish, madame," Henri was not at all mollified, "but that doesn't mean it's proper protocol for your station."

As the crew released the moorings and the ship eased away from the dock, she bent and picked up young John, who'd been standing at her side holding her hand. "Look up there." She pointed. "See the sailors scrambling up into the rigging? And there ... look ... they're lowering one of the sails." The little boy clapped his hands in glee as the wind caught the small sail and the ship began to move back out into the roads where the rest of the fleet, already loaded, waited for them.

Then one-by-one, the great ships lowered more sail and began making their way toward the channel that led to the open sea. Theirs was second in line, just behind the flagship. *Perhaps that's more to Henri's liking,* thought Jeanne as she smiled at young John's fascination with the men in the rigging.

"Ye best get yerself and the kid out of the way, lady. We got work to do."
A gruff seaman who'd been shouting orders at the men aloft was now
shouting at her, though she had no idea what he was saying. The sailors, it
seemed, spoke only English. Jeanne spoke none. Nor did anyone in her
household. The seaman turned his attention back to the rigging, apparently
assuming she'd follow orders as obediently as the crew.

Not knowing what to do, she stayed where she was but made sure John
was secure in her arms. Glancing over his shoulder, the seaman caught sight
of her and spun on his heel. "I told ye . . . get out the way. Where ye be, ye
gonna get hurt. Worse, ye gonna get som'un else hurt, and I need every
whoreson I got fit and doin' his duty."

Jeanne shook her head in confusion. "*Qu'est-ce que vous voulez? Je ne
comprends pas.*"

He lowered his face toward her, and she could smell the foul breath of
rotting teeth. "Get yer bloody arse to the stern and keep it there!"

Jeanne heard bootsteps on the deck behind her and turned to see the
ship's captain approaching. "*Arrière,*" he said, pointing toward the stern.

"*Mon fils veut regarder les marins.*"

"*Arrière,*" he repeated. Was it the only word he knew? Stepping between
Jeanne and the gruff seaman, he nudged her shoulder, forcing her to walk in
the direction he'd come from. When he stopped and faced forward, he
touched her shoulder once again, then pointed to the deck between his
position and the port rail. "*Là.*" Apparently he knew two words.

She did as she was bid and watched as the land on either side of the
channel began to recede. Soon, they were on open water and under full sail.
The smooth motion of the ship gliding through the water was exhilarating.
But it was February and the wind was cold and John was beginning to
squirm in her arms. Time to join the others below.

Jeanne and her children along with Aaliz and Perota had been assigned
a small, walled-off compartment on the starboard side near the stern. Henri
and the rest of the household staff had similar compartments on each side,
amidships, one for the women one for the men, giving them some privacy
from the open sleeping and eating area for the crew. In Jeanne's
compartment, there was a tiny window for light in the daytime and one

narrow bed – sort of a mattress in an open box, of which one side was the hull and the other three were high enough to keep the occupant from falling out with the rolling of the ship. Two more thin mattresses on the floor provided pallets for Aaliz and Perota, who each slept with one of the children.

That night, the gentle rise and fall of the swells made the ship feel like a child's cradle rocking everyone to sleep. Jeanne woke at dawn to the sounds of the night watch rousting their companions from slumber. Wrapping her cloak tightly around her, she left the others sleeping and went on deck to be greeted by a sight unlike anything she'd ever seen. Nothing but water as far as the eye could see. And off the starboard bow, the most glorious sunrise imaginable. Brilliant reds, orange, purple, and gold painted the horizon. She stood by the rail, mesmerized, as the first sliver of the sun began to emerge above the line of the sea. With no trees or hills or buildings to impede the view, it looked as if the sun were climbing straight out of the water. The wind had shifted overnight and was now coming directly toward them as if propelled by the sunrise.

She caught a glimpse of Edward's flagship some distance ahead and looked aft to spot two more ships of their fleet following in their wake. Directing her gaze back toward the sunrise, she was startled when the gruff seaman who'd yelled at her yesterday stopped beside her as he made his way toward the bow. "We be in fer a big blow, fer certes. Mind me words, it'll be gales afore nightfall." Having no idea what he was talking about, Jeanne merely smiled and nodded a greeting and headed back below to see if the others had awakened.

Though she spent most of her time in the relative warmth of their little compartment, Jeanne ventured on deck from time to time for a brief respite from the confined space. As the day progressed, the wind began to rise, and by the time the sun reached its zenith, the clouds were closing in. By midafternoon, she had an inkling what the seaman had been trying to tell her earlier. The clouds were heavy, obscuring the sun. Sailors scrambled into the rigging to reef some of the sails. Last night's gentle swells rose higher, forcing her to hold tightly to the safety ropes that had been rigged on deck.

The captain's orders to the helmsman manning the whipstaff seemed to have a new sense of urgency. A storm was closing in.

It was dark before sunset. Jeanne, Aaliz, and Perota huddled together on the floor of their little cabin, trying to reassure the children, as the noise of the gale and the rain rose around them. Baby Jeanne clung to Perota, crying. Little John was trying to walk from Aaliz to Jeanne when the ship suddenly pitched in the opposite direction, throwing him backward. Aaliz caught him just before his head hit the floor. The swells seemed to be getting higher and higher.

Until then, the thunder had been just a distant rumble, but now it was all around them, adding to the roar of the wind, the incessant battering of the rain, and the creaking of the ship's timbers. The thunder grew louder and suddenly erupted in the loudest crack Jeanne had ever heard just as the ship crested a swell and fell into the trough below. Aaliz screamed as she and Perota slid across the floor, each clutching a child, toward where their mistress sat with her back pinned against the hull.

Both children were crying now. "*Maman*, are we going to die?" Little John asked through his sobs.

Despite her own terror, Jeanne sought to reassure her son. "No, my little one, we're going to pray." And pray she did . . . to God and the Virgin and every saint whose name she could remember.

And still the storm raged. All through the night. Baby Jeanne finally fell asleep, as babies do when exhaustion overtakes them. Little John curled up in his mother's lap and sucked both his thumbs, his way, from babyhood, of trying to comfort himself until he, too, eventually slept.

But the women didn't. The noise and the violent pitching of the ship and the overwhelming fear that any moment might be their last . . . that the ship would break apart and they'd meet their maker at the bottom of the sea . . . meant their minds wouldn't still and their eyes wouldn't close.

And yet . . . at some point they must have succumbed. Jeanne woke to find her son still asleep in her lap, baby Jeanne clutched in Perota's arms, her tiny hands holding fast to her nurse's clothing, and Aaliz and Perota snoring softly, their heads each resting on one of their mistress's shoulders. The storm must have abated a bit. She could still hear the sounds of wind and rain, but the pitching and rolling was less extreme, the thunder had stopped, and the ship was no longer groaning under the strain.

Her feet and legs tingled from having been in one position on the hard floor for so long. She desperately wanted to shift a bit to restore the circulation but knew that any movement on her part would wake the others. Her dilemma was solved when a seaman threw open the door, glanced around, and then shouted "They be good enough in here" to whoever it was that had ordered him to check. He slammed the door shut again as Aaliz and Perota stirred and rubbed their eyes. Baby Jeanne woke whimpering then realized she was in her nurse's grasp and began squirming to free herself. Young John stretched and crawled out of Jeanne's lap to sit on the floor beside her. "You prayed good, *maman*."

Jeanne wiggled her feet and lower legs, and as the feeling slowly returned, she managed to get to her feet. "I'm going on deck to see how bad it is," she announced. "Wait here."

"*Non, madame.*" Aaliz sounded genuinely alarmed. "Don't leave us."

"It's only for a few minutes, Aaliz. I'll be back before you know it."

Just as she stepped through the door into the open area, the ship rolled and she found herself running headlong toward the opposite side of the hull. Catching herself just in time, she discovered that making any forward progress on a rolling deck was akin to a toddler taking his first steps, struggling to keep his balance and grasping whatever was nearby to keep from falling.

When she emerged on the open deck, she was assaulted by the wind blowing sheets of rain in her face. She grabbed the nearest safety rope and took a few tentative steps, barely managing to stay upright on the slippery surface. She steadied herself, both hands on the safety rope and her feet wide apart, and looked around. All the sails had been furled. The ship was bobbing around in the angry grey sea, beset by wind and rain so intense she could barely see the prow.

A seaman caught sight of her. "God's bollocks, woman! Get yer bloody arse back down below afore ye go over the side!"

That got the attention of the captain, who was standing just ahead, a rope around his waist securing him to the nearby mast. He spun around and caught sight of her. "*En bas*!" he screamed at her to be heard over the wind. "*En bas*! *Vite*!"

She didn't need any further encouragement. Careful not to lose her footing, she made her way back to safety below deck, realizing too late how foolish she'd been. She was soaked and her teeth were chattering, though she wasn't sure whether that was from cold or from the realization of how lucky she was not to have been swept overboard. Half stepping, half tumbling into their little compartment, she tried to remove her cloak, but her hands were shaking too much to manage the fastenings.

Aaliz screamed. "Madame! What have you done?"

"Calm down, Aaliz. You'll frighten the children. I'm just wet."

"I told you not to go up there, madame." Aaliz had the cloak off in no time. "And look. The bottom of your gown is soaked too." Before Jeanne could protest, Aaliz had her gown off and was bundling her into the narrow bed and covering her with blankets.

"Is *maman* sick?" Young John sounded worried.

Seeing the boy's distress, Aaliz set her own aside. "No, no, baby, she's not sick. Just cold. We'll have her warm in no time."

"I'm cold too. Can I get under the blankets with her?"

Knowing he was more scared than cold, Jeanne said, "Why not?" and lifted one side of the blanket for Aaliz to tuck him in.

"How am I ever going to get that cloak dry?" Alice fretted with the soggy garment.

"As soon as the rain stops, you can take it up on deck and hang it in the sun," said Jeanne.

"And if the rain doesn't stop before we get to port?"

"Then I suppose I'll just have to wear a blanket to disembark, won't I?"

"Oh, madame, that would be scandalous!"

Sometime around what might have been midday, a seaman threw the door open and stepped inside with a bucket and a dipper. "Rainwater," he said. Realizing they didn't understand, he set the bucket down and motioned with his hands as if something were falling into the bucket. Then he took a drink from the dipper.

"Ah," said Perota. "*Eau de pluie*." She took the dipper from him and scooped up a drink for herself before giving some to baby Jeanne and passing the dipper to Aaliz.

Sometime later, another seaman appeared and handed them half a loaf of bread. Perota checked it carefully for stones before giving any to the children. It was starting to go stale but no one cared. The women let the children eat their fill before dividing what was left. It was odd how they hadn't even thought about food while the storm raged, but now, having had a bit to eat, they were suddenly hungry.

And that's when Jeanne realized something. "Have you noticed?" she asked the others.

"What, madame?"

"The ship's not rolling so much. And the wind's not so loud. Could it be the worst is over?" It had at least calmed enough they could sleep through the night.

The storm added three days to their voyage, the gales and heavy seas having pushed them back toward the mouth of the English Channel so they had to retrace their steps, as it were, once the ships had found each other and the fleet regrouped. By the time they put in at Sandwich, it was the end of the first full week of March.

CHAPTER TWENTY-EIGHT

Westminster, England, March 1343

"This will do quite nicely, madame," were Henri's first words when they walked through the front door of the house that Edward had given to Jeanne for the duration of her stay.

"And how can you tell that by just looking at the entrance hall?" she teased him.

"It has the air of a noble house, does it not? Beautiful floors, a fine staircase, of a size to receive multiple guests without crowding. Not far from the great palace. And I'm given to understand that the Earl of Salisbury and his family have their home but a short walk away."

"Well, I'm pleased it meets with your approval, Henri. But I think I'll just wander about and see for myself."

While Henri busied himself organizing the household, Jeanne explored the entire dwelling, looking into every room, even including the kitchen. The house was far from palatial, but her bedchamber had an adjoining dressing room, there was a large room on the second floor suitable for the nursery, and it had a small garden in the rear. By the time she returned to the room on the first floor that she'd chosen for her sitting room, a pleasant fire in the hearth had already broken the chill and she could comfortably remove her cloak and examine the small writing table where she found a properly sharpened quill, ink, and a drawer containing paper. "Henri was right," she announced to the walls and the furniture. "This will do quite nicely, indeed."

Within days, the place had begun to feel like her home. The only thing missing was John. But she knew Philip could not prevaricate forever. John would be free by the summer and they could return together to finish the job of reclaiming his inheritance.

If Henri had been displeased by the accommodations made for her on the sea voyage, he could've had no such qualms about her reception in London. Everyone who mattered wanted to have the Heroine of Hennebont in their midst. The grand banquets were in abeyance during Lent, but Queen Philippa invited Jeanne to join the group of women who gathered around her every Tuesday afternoon for needlework, music, and conversation. Jeanne had expected these noble ladies to be scandalized by her choice to wear armor and to lead the raid on Charles's camp, but they were abundantly curious. "What's armor like? Is it heavy? Does it feel stiff? Can you move about? Isn't it big and awkward? How did you find something to fit right? Doesn't it squash your bosom? Did the men-at-arms laugh? What's it like to ride a charger? How big was he? Do you sit astride like the men do? Didn't the priests chastise you for being so bold? What would your husband think if he knew? Were you frightened? Do you have your armor with you so we could see it?" Even the queen wanted to know all about her warhorse.

Toward the end of April, Edward and Philippa threw an elaborate celebration of the Truce of Malestroit. There was a tournament, in which the one of the king's great friends, the Earl of Arundel, triumphed. An archery exhibition. Evening entertainments with mummers, musicians, and dancing. And finally the great banquet at which Jeanne was given the honor of sitting at the king's table. The feast was more elaborate than anything she'd ever seen. Every dish presented to the king for his approval before being served to the guests. Lamb, venison, boar, pheasant, goose, fish, savory sauces, loaves upon loaves of paindemaine and freshly churned butter. The wine flowed freely.

In a brief moment of pique, Jeanne found herself thinking, *And I'll bet it's **my** money that's paying for all this.* But she quickly chided herself for ingratitude. *You made your bargain, Jeanne, and it's secured your son's future. Don't be petty.*

When it came time for the toasts, Edward rose from his seat. "What a celebration this has been! And there is more to come tonight. I'm told the musicians are tuning their instruments, and Philippa has instructed me that I must dance with every lady in the hall." He raised his glass to his wife while the audience laughed politely. Everyone knew that would be no hardship.

As the laughter subsided, he continued. "And now, to our tournament champion, the Earl of Arundel. I'm rather glad I wasn't riding in the lists with you this time, Richard."

Arundel grinned. "As am I . . . since that would have meant I'd have had to find a way to lose." More laughter.

Jeanne had seen Edward's camaraderie with Salisbury and now realized it extended to others he considered friends. Perhaps that would soon include John.

Edward raised his glass higher. "I give you Richard FitzAlan, Earl of Arundel." He paused while the audience echoed "Richard FitzAlan," then everyone drank the toast, including Arundel himself.

"Now," Edward resumed, "for the man who gave us a reason for this celebration. The man who negotiated the Truce of Malestroit. And, now that I think of it, this is the first time we've celebrated getting him out of Philip's clutches. But don't think that will get you two toasts, William. It was your own fault Philip grabbed you in the first place."

Montagu grinned. "Never going to let me live that down, are you?"

"Well, not yet, anyway." The broad smile on Edward's face said this was all in fun. He raised his glass again. "William Montagu, Earl of Salisbury." Then, before the audience could respond, he added, "And hostage of his own making."

The audience roared. *They've seen this banter before*, Jeanne thought. Someone at a table in the back of the room shouted "William Montagu" above the laughter and the rest of the room joined in and drank the toast. Montagu rose from his seat and made a ridiculously exaggerated bow to his sovereign, drawing yet another round of laughter, which this time included the king.

When the room was finally quiet, Edward signaled for glasses to be refilled, sending the servants scurrying. Once they'd all retaken their positions by the walls of the dining hall, he picked up his glass again. "And finally, to the woman without whose valor none of our gains in Brittany would have been possible. I give you the true Duchess of Brittany, *Jeanne de la Flamme.*" He raised his glass as the chorus of *Jeanne de la Flamme* echoed in her ears. The moniker had followed her all the way to the English court.

Her mind raced, trying to come up with a better response than a simple nod of her head, and then it came to her in a flash. Something she'd heard twice in Brittany. She rose from her seat and raised her own glass. "To Edward, King of England and of France."

Everyone in the room rose to their feet. "King Edward!"

He sat back down, a signal that everyone else was permitted to follow suit, and the room was once again filled with the noise of chairs and benches scraping across the floor.

The rest of the evening passed in something of a whirlwind for Jeanne. Edward made good on his promise to dance with every woman present, and she was surprised to discover he was quite a good dancer. Sometime after midnight, she finally arrived back at her home still enraptured by the wonder of it all. The whole English court had toasted her. One day, when her son was old enough to understand, she'd tell him the story of *Jeanne de la Flamme* and the night the king of England treated her like one of his friends.

CHAPTER TWENTY-NINE

As the weeks passed, Jeanne settled into her new life. It was easy to forget that, just a few days away, across a bit of water, a conflict in her name still simmered. Too easy sometimes. She remained in the queen's favor. Her children were frequently invited to spend the day in the royal nursery. Now and then, she was invited to dine with one or another of the members of the court. Now and then, she reciprocated.

But now and then, she also brought herself up short. This wasn't her real life – just a temporary interlude. It wasn't unlike the life she wanted to create for herself and her family, but it was in the wrong place at the wrong time and with the wrong people.

May came and went and, almost before she realized it, Midsummer's Day was nearly upon them. And that's when her first letter from de Clisson arrived. She was in the garden, cutting flowers to make a small bouquet for her sitting room, when Henri brought it. "I thought perhaps you might want to see this straightaway, madame, else I would have left it on your writing table."

She set down her basket of flowers, took one look at the seal, and gave the startled Henri a quick hug. "Oh, yes, Henri. Yes! And thank you."

The steward squared his shoulders and offered a little bow of his head. "My pleasure, madame." Without waiting for her acknowledgment, he retraced his steps into the house.

Jeanne barely noticed. Her flowers forgotten, she dashed for a nearby bench and tore into the letter.

My dear Duchess, my dearest Jeanne,

Before any other words grace this page, I must inscribe my most sincere sentiments of apology. I have been more than a little remiss in fulfilling my promise to write to you, yet I dare to hold out hope that you will be forgiving of my negligence.

There is news – both good and bad. Perhaps it's best to start with the bad so that this missive may conclude on a happier note.

In truth, it isn't bad news so much as no news. None whatsoever of when Philip will fulfill his part in the terms of the truce and release your husband from confinement in the Louvre. My informants report that the topic is not broached at court – not even in rumor or innuendo. Quite a curious state of affairs, in my experience, as gossip is the lifeblood of the court and no topic is off limits. I will, of course, remain diligent in pursuit of any information we can glean.

Perhaps Philip is simply being methodical in the order in which he executes his promises and has not yet reached that item on the list. He has, after all, withdrawn his forces from Brittany, given control of Vannes to the pope's agents, and disbanded the army that was poised to attack Casseneuil in Gascony.

Jeanne pursed her lips and rolled her eyes as she read those words, then dropped her hands to her lap and stared at the garden wall. *I know you're just trying to offer me some consolation, Amaury, but surely you don't actually believe that. Releasing a prisoner requires no more effort on Philip's part than putting his name to a piece of paper. Recalling and dispersing armies is a far more complex undertaking.* Her disbelief voiced, even if only in her own thoughts, she turned her eyes back to the page.

And now for the good news. As I said, the French army has retreated, leaving Charles de Blois alone with whatever men he may have in Guingamp. Even better news is that a growing number of Breton nobles are switching their loyalties, the most notable among them being my own brother, Olivier. There is no doubt it is his influence that has guided the choices of some very prominent men. Olivier and I have spoken at length about his own choice, and I am most heartened by his commitment to our cause. I will say no more in this letter than that he is following in your footsteps.

My informants tell me Philip is surprised by the continuing presence of the English here. One can't know what he expected, but for now, they seem to be providing a deterrent to his ambitions in the duchy.

In the main, the truce is holding. I say that with a bit of caution because de Blois has conducted one or two small raids from his headquarters in Guingamp. They amounted to nothing and were most likely intended only to remind people that he's still nominally the duke. What I find curious is his justification for his actions. It seems he considers himself exempt from the truce on the grounds that the truce only applies to adherents of King Philip and that he, Charles, is not an adherent of the French king.

Such a claim is ludicrous on its very face, as everyone knows that Charles is Philip's nephew and that neither has repudiated the other. Is this merely Charles, having been challenged by one of the English garrison commanders, coming up with a convenient excuse on the spur of the moment? Or might it be part of some grand subterfuge agreed between de Blois and the king to allow Philip to disregard the truce without appearing to do so?

Jeanne furrowed her brow in anger. *Oh, Amaury, I can't fault your logic, but the truth is far simpler. If you knew her as I do, you'd see this for what it is – another of the Countess of Penthièvre's schemes. Denied what she wants by law, she's happy to proclaim her undying loyalty to Philip if he'll support her claim. Now, stymied by the truce, she's just as happy to renounce him so she can keep fighting. She's clever, I'll admit, but I have Edward's ear and will make certain he knows what's **really** afoot.* Confident in her assessment of the situation, she resumed her reading.

Which brings me to my last point, which is to encourage your return. You've always been a beacon for the Montfortist cause and, until your husband is released, you remain so. But your light is harder to see at so great a distance. It's my contention that your presence here, among the many powerful men now on your side, would be the most effective deterrent possible to whatever ambition de Blois may yet harbor. I would also venture to suggest that any danger to yourself or your children is now much mitigated by the strength of your supporters.

You must make your own decision, of course, but I look forward to the day when we may see your ship sailing into a Breton port.

Your most loyal liege lord,

Amaury

She sat in the garden mulling de Clisson's plea. It had been almost four months since she left Brittany. And in that time, she'd garnered even more support for her claim. Support from men who could convince others. Support, even, from some who had a long-held affinity for France. Was this the opportunity she'd long dreamed of to rally the heart and soul of Brittany? If she didn't grasp it now, would it be lost forever? Was she the only one who could expose the countess's schemes for what they really were? Was her presence at the head of a strong faction what was required to secure John's release?

Only when the children came bounding into the garden, laughing and squealing, did she realize how long she'd been sitting there, lost in thought. Baby Jeanne, now two, couldn't keep up with her brother's pace on the ground, but she could far outpace him in merriment. They'd spent their day in the royal nursery. "*Maman*, look!" Young John waved a scrap of paper in the air.

Jeanne folded her letter and put it in her pocket. "What's that you have?"

"Look!" He thrust the scrap into her hands. Crudely written on it were three letters: A, B, and C. "Lionel's tutor showed me how."

Jeanne gave her son a hug. "I'm so proud of you! Maybe you can show me later how you do it?"

By then Baby Jeanne had doddered her way to where her mother sat. "Me, *maman*. Meeeeee." Jeanne picked up her daughter, gave her a hug, and kissed her belly, eliciting a squeal of delight. Then she rose, took John's hand, and crossed the garden to where Perota waited with her usual calm.

"Alright, dearies," said the nurse, "come with me. Let's go upstairs and get you something to eat." Perota tried to take the baby from Jeanne's arms, but the little girl squirmed to get down.

"I walk."

"Alright," said the nurse, "but you'll be begging me to carry you before we get to the top of the stairs."

"I walk."

Jeanne couldn't help but smile. Her daughter had clearly inherited her strong will.

By the time she finished her supper, Jeanne had made up her mind. She hadn't seen Edward since the evening of the grand banquet, but now it was time. At the queen's gathering the following day, when the other ladies began to depart, Jeanne lingered behind.

"Is there something on your mind, Jeanne?" Philippa asked.

"I was wondering, my lady. How would one go about requesting an audience with His Grace?"

"That depends on who one is. For someone like you, who's already known to the king, a simple request to the Lord Privy Seal is all that's required."

"Thank you, my lady."

"But I can save you some trouble. Edward is away at present – in Leeds – and may not be back for some time. If you like, I can send you word when he returns."

"That would be most kind, my lady. Thank you."

Her other option was Salisbury, who'd seemed sympathetic to her when they were all together in Brest. But it turned out he was with the king. She didn't know Warwick or Arundel well enough to approach either of them, and the odds were high that they were also with their sovereign. What about speaking to the queen? She'd heard that Edward valued her advice. But if she approached Philippa and was turned away, that would put paid to any opportunity she might have to speak with Edward. And she needed to make her case directly to him.

That left but one option – a letter. That night, she sat at her writing table and stared at the blank paper in front of her. She had to make her case succinctly but irrefutably. When she read her first attempt, it sounded whiney – the very thing she'd accused Jeanne de Penthièvre of and that she had no desire to imitate – so she touched the paper to the candle and consigned the flaming page to the hearth.

She wiped the tip of her quill clean, retrieved a fresh sheet of paper from the drawer, and sat for several moments, thinking, before beginning again.

To His Most Excellent Grace Edward III, King of England and of France Greetings

I am this day in receipt of news that our situation in Brittany has improved considerably. A number of prominent and influential barons have abandoned Charles de Blois and embraced the Montfort cause. This information comes from a thoroughly trustworthy source – Amaury de Clisson, whom you no doubt remember as the emissary who negotiated our agreement.

De Clisson also makes it clear that de Blois is flaunting the truce with raids on our garrisons. De Clisson believes most strongly that the head of the Montfort family is needed to solidify the loyalty of the nobles and dissuade de Blois from further action. While my husband remains in Philip's custody, I am the head of the Montfort family.

As time has passed and the truce is largely holding, it seems the risk to my safety and that of my son is diminished sufficiently to warrant my return. It is for these reasons that I am putting plans in place to return to my homeland and once again take up the reins of leadership. Should you wish to supplement my household with any of your own forces, it would be my pleasure to make this a joint effort.

From Westminster this 19th day of June
Jeanne de Montfort, Duchess of Brittany

She reread her words and smiled. Exactly the right tone. No whining. Simply making her case and stating her planned action. She would have Henri deliver it to the palace in the morning.

Within a week she had her reply. Someone must have sent a fast courier to Leeds, and Edward must have dashed off his reply straightaway. She might actually be home sooner than a letter could reach Amaury. She eagerly broke the seal on the missive.

> *To the Duchess of Brittany*
>
> *I have long since been aware of the Breton barons who are abandoning their support for de Blois. As for his attempts to continue fighting in violation of the truce, my administrators and garrison commanders are prepared to suppress his efforts. They are fully capable of doing so without your personal assistance.*
>
> *Your assessment of safety for you and your son is overly optimistic. De Blois's rogue behavior is precisely what makes the situation in Brittany dangerous for you.*
>
> *I beseech you most fervently to abandon forthwith any thought or plan of traveling to Brittany. It cannot be much longer until your husband is released.*
>
> *From Leeds, 23 June 1343*
>
> *Edward R*

"I should have just stolen away in the dark of night." Jeanne addressed the empty room She wandered to the window, which overlooked the little garden. Her children were playing some sort of game under Perota's watchful eye. It seemed to involve baby Jeanne trying to steal something from her brother, but whether that was the point of the game or whether he was being mean to his sister, she couldn't discern from this vantage point. Perota seemed unconcerned, so there must not be anything to worry about.

As she watched, she was suddenly struck by something in Edward's letter, so she returned to her writing table and read it once again. There. That sentence. *De Blois's rogue behavior is precisely what makes the situation in Brittany dangerous for you.*

She knew Charles didn't act entirely in his own self-interest. His wife was complicit in everything he did. Complicit at a minimum. How often the instigator? She was still childless. Did she know that Philip planned to restore the duchy to the house of Montfort if she died in that state? Was she really so unflinching in her pursuit of her own ambition that she would kidnap – even harm – an innocent child? Perhaps Edward was right.

Perhaps it wasn't Philip but Jeanne – and by extension, Charles – who was the real threat to her son.

She chided herself for not recognizing this sooner. It had always been *she* who thought ahead of all the possible consequences and helped John steer the right course. But then, she'd always been able to talk things over with him. And for a time, with Hervé de Léon. And later, with Durant and Kerveil. And with Amaury. Here, she was at such a great distance from her advisers that conversations required days or weeks rather than moments or hours. But that didn't relieve her of the responsibility for both her family and her cause.

So for now, she would stay put. Her reasoning was strong enough that Amaury would have no choice but to see the sense of it. But her reply to his missive must exhort him to keep her informed far more frequently of events in Brittany.

You're my lifeline, Amaury. My path to good decisions. I beg you, please don't fail me. And in return for your diligence, I shall exert as much pressure as I dare on Edward to be more insistent on John's release. We both know how urgent that is to prevent Charles and his wife from feeling they have a free hand in Brittany.

Know that my heart is with you and all who champion John's cause. It's my fervent hope that we will both be back with you before the end of summer.

From Westminster this 27th day of June

Jeanne

CHAPTER THIRTY

The summer wore on. Jeanne was puzzled by the elation among the English servants in her household when Saint Swithun's day dawned fair. Fair summer days were indeed a delight, but this day seemed no different to her than any other. Perota explained it when she brought the children to join their mother for the midday meal. "They say, madame, that if it rains on Saint Swithun's day, then it will rain for the next forty days without any letup. There seems to be some sort of legend about the saint's anger when his grave was moved."

July turned to August with still no sign of John being granted his freedom, leading Jeanne to feel a pressing urge to return home to lead her faction. She wrote to Edward once again, this time changing her tactics.

To His Most Excellent Grace Edward III, King of England and of France
Greetings
There can be no doubt you share my dismay over the continuing imprisonment of my husband, contrary to the terms of the Truce of Malestroit. As we have a shared concern, I seek your advice on my best course of action. I am prepared to return with my children to lead his supporters in their quest for his release.
From Westminster this 6th day of August
Jeanne

Once again, Edward's reply was swift and to the point.

Madame,

Your intentions may be sincere but they remain ill-advised. I am prepared to wait yet a few more weeks for Philip to act. You should be as well.

Edward R

She balled up the page and threw it across the room in frustration. How many weeks was a few? How much longer could the Montforts be absent from Brittany before their cause faded into oblivion?

As August faded into September, Jeanne was forced to take stock of her situation. She'd paid little attention to the signs around her, passing them off as the ordinary, occasional shiftings of daily life. But when her invitation to the Montagus to dine with her was declined for a second time – on both occasions "because we are engaged at court" – she could no longer avoid the reality. It had been weeks since she'd been invited to join one of the queen's gatherings – months since she'd been invited to dine with the court. Her children were still welcomed into the royal nursery, but now it was at most once a week whereas it had previously been every second or third day. Where she was once toasted as the Heroine of Hennebont, she was now something of an afterthought.

It was Aaliz who jolted her out of her malaise. "I told Perota to get her charges ready, madame," she announced as she was arranging Jeanne's hair. "There's a fair in Saint Paul's churchyard today, and I think we should take the children. They need an outing. And, forgive me, madame, so do you."

"Oh, I don't know, Aaliz. What if news of John arrives while we're away?"

"It won't disappear before we return. You've moped around the house for five days now, and that's not like you. Now ... they're waiting for us downstairs. Are you coming or are you going to cast a pall on their excitement?"

"Well, if you're determined to put it like that, what choice do I have?"

By the time they returned in late afternoon, Jeanne's spirits were revived. She wolfed down her supper and even managed to get a raised eyebrow from Henri when she asked for a second serving of berries and cream. She hadn't been this hungry since … she couldn't remember, but thought it might have been when she fasted on the feast day of Saint Louis. And with her renewed appetite for food came a renewed appetite for her mission.

That night, she wrote once again to Edward.

To His Most Excellent Grace Edward III, King of England and of France
Greetings
It's clear to me now that Philip's prevarication in releasing my husband is tantamount to a blearing of the tongue at you and at me over this provision of the truce – a provision so important, you once told me, that it was worth concessions on the status of Vannes. It's also clear that he intends to continue in this vein until such time as Bretons forget the house of Montfort and fall into line with his desires. This must not be allowed to happen.
Boldness is required. Thus I no longer have a choice other than to return to Brittany and carry the banner for our cause. If that puts my children at risk, then that is a burden I must bear. Cowering will not succeed where courage is required. So I will cower here no longer.
From Westminster this 26th day of September
Jeanne de Montfort, Duchess of Brittany

• • • • •

The storm clouds on Edward's face when he walked into her sitting room told Philippa he was in a temper, so she dismissed her companions and all the servants straightaway. "Now," she said when the door closed behind the last of them, "what is it that has you looking as if you're about to burst apart at the seams?"

"That *bloody woman*! When will she realize she's played her part, and it's time to step aside and let those who know the stakes take the reins?"

"I presume that woman bears the name of Montfort?" she phrased it as a question. "What's she done now?"

"Written another letter. Here … read this." He thrust the missive toward his wife.

When she finished reading, she returned it rather more gently than she'd received it. "Well, I must say, she doesn't suffer from lack of boldness."

"God's teeth, Philippa! You're not taking up for her, are you?"

"Of course not, my dear. Just making an observation. And hoping you might find it amusing." She made her way to the sideboard and filled a goblet with wine. "Here. It's your favorite Gascon." He took the goblet and downed the entire contents. "Oh, dear. You really are in a state." She refilled his goblet and poured one for herself. "Now, come sit with me and tell me what you intend to do."

He took another swallow of wine – a more normal one this time – and followed her to the chairs they usually occupied when they were alone here. "I'm tempted to just let her go back and get herself killed."

"You think that's what would happen?"

"God knows. De Blois won't hesitate to go after her. I could order Northampton and the others not to come to her defense."

"Now, Edward, does that really serve your larger plan in any useful way?"

By now, his rage was subsiding. "No. Just a tempting thought. But it wouldn't win me her husband's loyalty. And she's right about one thing. I need him out of Philip's clutches."

"You know she won't go without taking her children with her," said Philippa.

"And that's the other problem. De Blois has no heir. Montfort does. And with Montfort's heir wed to a suitable English noblewoman, our position in Brittany is even stronger. So I have to make sure nothing happens to the boy."

"Then you must convince her to stay here."

•   •   •   •   •

When October dawned and there was still no reply from Edward, Jeanne instructed Henri to make arrangements for their return to Brest. "It may take some days to discover where we can get passage, madame," he said.

"Do whatever is necessary, Henri. It's time to go home."

CHAPTER THIRTY-ONE

Two days later, Jeanne woke with a new feeling of purpose – with a sense that the day would somehow be propitious. The children would be spending the day in the royal nursery, which she took as a sign that Edward still looked with favor on her family, even if he couldn't be bothered to reply to her letter.

The insistent knocking on the front door shortly after the church bells tolled Terce came as a surprise. No one was expected – and certainly not this early in the day. Henri would deal with it, so she went back to helping Aaliz with the packing of her trunks. But it was only moments before Henri appeared at the door to her bedchamber, his manner as distressed as Jeanne had ever seen him. "What's wrong, Henri?" she asked.

"I . . . I think you'd best come, madame."

She followed him downstairs to the entrance hall where half a dozen men dressed in the king's livery stood on either side of the open front door. When she crossed the hall to look outside, the nearest two stepped in front of her, barring the way, but not before she'd caught sight of two large carriages, a wagon, and at least two dozen mounted men, also wearing the king's livery.

Puzzled and more than a little alarmed, she turned around, intending to question Henri, and was immediately addressed by one of the visitors. "You're to come with us, ma'am. The king now has need of this house and has arranged a new domicile for you and your household. As his sergeant-at-arms, I've come with my men to escort you there."

"But I've had no such communication from His Grace," she protested.

"Those are our instructions, ma'am. So if you'll have your servants gather your belongings, we'll load everything into the wagon and be on our way. The carriages are for you and your household staff."

"Whatever your instructions may be, you can't just barge in here and throw us out at a moment's notice." Now, Jeanne was indignant.

"You're not being thrown out, ma'am. You're simply moving to a new residence, and the king has instructed us to see you arrive there safely."

"Well, I can't go without my children. They're at the palace at present, so we must wait for their return."

"Ma'am, your children will be brought to you in duc course. His Grace and the queen are of the opinion that it will be best for the children if you've established your household in your new home before their lives are disrupted by the move. We're to be on the road by midday, so I suggest you busy yourself with preparations."

"And if I refuse?"

"That's not a choice you have, ma'am. His Grace was most explicit that we're to take you to your new home straightaway, this very day."

"And if I simply lock myself in my bedchamber and refuse to come out?"

"Ma'am, please don't make this difficult for yourself. I can compel you to come, but it will be much better for everyone if you do so of your own free will. Surely you don't want your servants to see you being carried forcibly to the carriage and locked in for the journey."

In that moment, Jeanne realized she was defeated. If Edward had ordered his men to use whatever means necessary to evict her from these premises, she knew her objections would fall on deaf ears. But if she had to go, she would go with her pride intact. She squared her shoulders and addressed her steward. "Well, Henri, it seems the King of England has spoken. If anyone can relocate a household on such short notice, it's you. And since the sergeant here has orders to carry out the king's will, I'm sure he'll put his men at your disposal for any task you may require." She turned and flashed a smile. "Won't you, sergeant?" Then, not waiting for him to reply, she added, "Of course you will."

As she passed Henri on her way to the staircase, she said, "Make them work, Henri. I'm not leaving here without everything we possess, including the children's clothes and toys. And if it takes every one of his men to make that happen, then so be it."

Back in her bedchamber, she told her maid, "You need to finish the packing quickly, Aaliz. Everything. We're leaving today. Henri can fill you in on what's happening. I have things to attend to."

She had no idea what those things might be other than that she needed a moment alone to think, so she went to her sitting room and shut the door. She'd held her anger in check for the benefit of the servants, but now she picked up a vase filled with flowers and hurled it into the hearth, smashing the vase into tiny pieces and splashing water all over the stones. *God's bones, how I wish it was Edward Plantagenet's head that vase had shattered against! At least it's his vase.*

Her immediate fury spent, she gazed at the flowers, now scattered hither and yon, soon to be sad and wilted for lack of water. Was that what her life was becoming? She felt tears welling in her eyes and stamped her feet to keep them at bay. *I will not give in to feeling sorry for myself. This is just a temporary setback. I'll play Edward's little game for now, but the moment John is free, things will change. He'll see.*

It was an hour past midday when they finally had everything loaded and the little procession was ready to depart. Before she stepped into her carriage, Jeanne challenged the sergeant-at-arms one more time. "And you give me your assurances that my children will follow us straightaway?"

"That is what I've been told, ma'am."

"That's not what I asked, sergeant. I'm not setting foot in that carriage until I have your word of honor that my children will come to join me in their new home at the earliest possible time."

"Then you have my word, ma'am."

She climbed into the carriage knowing full well that his word meant nothing since he was only Edward's lackey. But she had made her point and could do nothing more now than hope he would report what she'd said.

FROM THE WRITINGS OF JEANNE DE FLANDRE, DUCHESS OF BRITTANY AND COUNTESS OF MONTFORT
FOUND AMONG HER BELONGINGS AT THE TIME OF HER DEATH

Tickhill, South Yorkshire, 1348

When the suburbs of London receded and gave way to open countryside, I understood this was not a mere change of lodgings. In truth, I'd known it all along. One doesn't send a troop of armed men to escort a person's belongings across town.

The journey took most of five days, during which I had ample time to chastise myself for foolishness. How could I have failed to recognize that Edward's response to my last letter wouldn't necessarily take the form of a written reply?

When we at last arrived at our destination, I was utterly dismayed. It was a castle, yes, but well away from any seat of power or proximity to any other noble families. The constable, Sir William Frank, welcomed us with reassurances that all our needs would be provided for, which was just as well because, by that time, my resources were largely depleted. In truth, I was penniless. Though John still nominally held the Honor of Richmond, from which we should have had a substantial income, Edward had created his then-two-year-old son, John of Gaunt, Earl of Richmond in 1342, effectively giving Queen Philippa, as her son's regent, control of every penny derived from the estate. So I was entirely dependent on Edward for the maintenance of my household.

Henri was given free rein to run the household, but Sir William made it clear that he was personally in charge of my safety. I knew what that meant but chose not to dwell on it in the moment. The most important thing to be done was to prepare the nursery for the children. With that complete, I could assure Sir William that the children's welfare was fully provided for and that he should make it known that all was in readiness for them to join us.

With the benefit of hindsight, I can now see that journey as symbolic of the time leading up to it. Over the course of seven months, I had gone from being Edward's ally and friend to being, if not quite a prisoner, at least cast aside in isolation.

The weathercock had turned again. But this time, so slowly that I was unaware of the change until it was too late.

CHAPTER THIRTY-TWO

When they hadn't joined her at the end of two weeks, Jeanne began to grow concerned for her children's welfare. If Sir William had sent word straightway that their new home was ready to receive them, then surely sufficient time had passed for both the messenger's travel and the children's journey north. When she confronted Sir William about when she could expect them, he was vague in his reply. "That's not for me to say, my lady. We all take our actions at the king's pleasure and according to his wishes. So there must be a reason unknown to us here why they remain in London."

She fumed for two days. If Edward thought he could hold her children hostage for her behavior, he'd soon learn that a mother bear is not to be trifled with. She waited until Monday to put quill to paper.

To His Most Excellent Grace Edward III, King of England and of France Greetings

Your concern that my children should have a smooth transition to their new home merits a certain gratitude. Your sergeant-at-arms was quite explicit that this meant they would be sent to me as soon as that new home was ready to receive them.

Their nursery has long been ready and this household is functioning just as it did during our time in Westminster, a fact of which you must certainly be aware from Sir William Frank's message.

There being no further impediment to their welfare here, the time has come for you to provide an appropriate escort to send them and their nurse to me.

From Tickhill this 27th day of October

Jeanne de Montfort, Duchess of Brittany

On Saint Leonard's day, two letters arrived. Jeanne recognized de Clisson's seal on one of them. As the other was unfamiliar, she set it aside. Whatever a stranger had to say could wait until she learned the latest from Brittany. Her sitting room here was a far cry from the bright, cozy room she'd enjoyed so much in Westminster. This one had only a small window, so candles were a necessity at all times. She was grateful Henri insisted on beeswax – the smell of tallow would have made the room unbearable. And even though the window was small, the room always felt drafty. Maybe that was just because it was November. Or was it because her spirits were so low?

Settling into her usual chair close to the warmth of the fire, she opened Amaury's letter.

My dearest, dearest Jeanne,
I hope this letter reaches you straightaway, for the news is glorious.

She glanced at the date he'd written at the bottom. October 3rd. The day she'd been evicted from the house in Westminster and dragged off to this awful place. It had taken over a month for the letter to reach her. She started over from the beginning.

My dearest, dearest Jeanne,
*I hope this letter reaches you straightaway, for the news is glorious. Your husband, the true duke, is free! Philip released him just four days ago. I'm given to understand that, despite the terms of the truce, Philip has placed conditions on his release that prevent him from returning to Brittany straightaway. I don't know the details at the moment, but I simply could **not** wait another moment to give you the news.*

I only wish that my dear brother, Olivier, was alive to celebrate with us. I shall never forgive Philip for Olivier's execution. But this serves only to give me greater fervor than ever in fighting alongside John to throw de Blois and his French supporters out of Brittany.

It is my fondest hope that you will soon be reunited with your husband to join us all in that fight.
Amaury
3 October 1343

Jeanne sat there with the letter in her lap, her emotions a tangle of joy, dismay, and more that she couldn't articulate. She was elated, of course, that John had been released at last. She should have been running through the corridors shouting the good news, dashing into the nursery to grab her children in her arms and kiss their little faces and tell them their father would soon be here to add his kisses to hers. But there were no children to tell, no children to kiss. She should have been overcome with emotion, tears of joy streaming down her face as she twirled and danced before the fire. Instead, all she felt was numbness.

Numbness and a growing sense of anger at the man she'd once called friend. Did Edward already know, when he had her removed to this godforsaken place, that John was free or soon would be?

As she sat staring at the fire, caught up in the injustice of it all, another emotion began to creep in. Something she barely recognized, having never felt it in all her life. Helplessness. She rose to put another log on the fire, hoping its light and warmth would keep the demons at bay. Returning to her chair, she caught a glimpse of the other letter, which she'd all but forgotten. Might as well read it. She knew it wouldn't cheer her up, but maybe it would take her mind off her troubles.

My dear mistress,

This letter is being written for me by Master William Wakefield, who informs me that you have been asking after the children. We are at present living in most luxurious conditions at the Tower of London. Our room is adjacent to the royal apartments where I am told that His Grace and the queen will be staying during Advent.

Master Wakefield has provided all of us with new clothes – very fine ones indeed – and we are given the best food at every meal. Master Wakefield has not told me when we will be coming to join you, though I ask him every second or third day.

I hug and kiss the children for you every night and tell them how much you and their father love them, but that is not the same as you doing it yourself. I pray that we will be together again soon, as I know you do.

Please tell Aaliz that I miss her company and look forward to the time when we can talk and sew together while we watch the children play.
Perota

The numbness vanished as rage poured in. How *dare* they use Perota to try to quell her concern for her children?! If John knew, he would be furious. Well, he would know soon enough. As soon as she learned where he was, she'd write to him. But in the meantime, there was someone else who deserved a piece of her mind. She marched across the room in righteous indignation to the small writing table Henri had found for her. This time, she wouldn't mince words.

To Edward Plantagenet
I have this day received a letter from my children's nurse telling me that she has been unable to learn from one William Wakefield – whoever he may be – when she and her charges will be coming to Tickhill. Nor have I received a reply to my letter of 27th October. Children should be with their mother, a fact Queen Philippa will no doubt agree with. Please make arrangements to send mine to me straightaway.
Jeanne de Montfort
From Tickhill this 6th day of November

For three weeks she fretted and fumed, unable to devise a way to extricate her children from their current situation. If they were indeed living in the Tower, they were being given every advantage. Perota wouldn't lie about that. But Jeanne couldn't just have them kidnapped from a royal residence. Besides, who could she hire to kidnap them? Not to mention that she had nothing to hire anyone with.

On the first Sunday of Advent, Sir William arranged for everyone to attend Mass in the village church. Under the watchful eye of his men, of course, but at least it was an opportunity to see what lay outside the castle walls. Not that it cheered her much – the little village was made out of the same grey stone as the castle, and the cloudy December day did nothing to mitigate the greyness of her world.

When she returned to her sitting room following the midday meal, she decided her only recourse was to write to Edward once again. But this time, she should probably be more respectful.

To His Most Excellent Grace Edward III, King of England and of France
Greetings
Now that Advent is upon us, I find myself longing more than ever for the presence of my dear children. As we celebrate the coming of the Christ Child, so should we parents celebrate our own children and look forward to sharing the joys of Christmas with them. With their father now a free man, young John and baby Jeanne are no longer bereft of a male guardian. They should now be returned to their mother so that we may, in due course, rejoin him and be a family once again.
Knowing that Your Grace will have like sentiments, I shall anticipate their arrival here with the greatest of pleasure.
Jeanne de Montfort, Duchess of Brittany
From Tickhill this 30th day of November

Christmas came and went. The children did not. New Year's Day dawned with a brilliant sun in a cheery blue sky – an omen, said Aaliz, of good things to come. When the royal courier arrived at midday on Twelfth Night, Jeanne dared to hope her maid might be right.

Her hand shook when she took the letter from Henri. "Are you alright, madame?" he asked.

"Just anxious, Henri. I so desperately want this to be good news."

"As do I, madame. I shall leave you to find out."

She had to sit on her hands to stop the shaking before she could manage to open the letter. Even then, she could hear her heartbeat. As much as she wanted to know what was in the missive, so was she afraid to find out. At long last, she broke the seal and slowly unfolded the page.

To the Duchess of Brittany
His Grace requires me to inform you that you are to cease forthwith any and all correspondence regarding the housing, care, and welfare of your children. They enjoy the enviable position of being members of the queen's household and will be raised alongside the royal children, an upbringing that

will be far more advantageous to them than anything you could offer. This is his final word on the subject, and you would do well to heed it.

> *Robert de Offord, Lord Privy Seal*
> *From London, January 1st in the Year of Our Lord 1344*

Her scream echoed throughout the castle. In an instant, Aaliz and Henri were there trying to comfort her – trying to understand what was wrong. The only answer Jeanne could manage was loud sobbing and a waterfall of tears. She paced around the room like a caged animal then, overcome by rage, began throwing things into the fire. Henri picked up the letter and read, then whispered something to Aaliz, who grabbed her mistress in her arms and forced her to sit in her favorite chair.

Holding Jeanne's hand and stroking her hair, Aaliz spoke softly, doing her best to soothe. "Now, now, madame. We know what's happened. It's ever so sad. And oh so wrong. Let's get you to bed . . ." She led Jeanne, who offered no resistance, into her bedchamber. ". . . and I'll sit with you and you can cry all you want and tell me all about it." She removed her mistress's gown then turned back the bed coverings while Jeanne stood stock still, tears coursing down her cheeks.

When she got her mistress into the bed and propped on the pillows, Aaliz climbed in as well and held the grieving woman in her arms, rocking her gently. "I'm here, madame, and I won't leave you. You just cry out all your tears, no matter how many there are."

A soft knock on the door. "Come," Aaliz called out without raising her voice more than necessary.

Henri stepped in carrying a small glass filled with brown liquid and placed it on the table beside the bed. "Brandy," he said. "It will help her to sleep."

As he left the room, he turned to look back at his stricken mistress. Not even in the darkest days in Hennebont had he seen her completely broken. Then, she had something to fight for. Now, what she'd fought for had been cruelly taken from her. *It's our turn to lend her **our** strength*, he thought. *I just hope we have enough.*

FROM THE WRITINGS OF JEANNE DE FLANDRE, DUCHESS OF BRITTANY AND COUNTESS OF MONTFORT
FOUND AMONG HER BELONGINGS AT THE TIME OF HER DEATH

Tickhill, South Yorkshire, 1348

I had never spent Christmas alone before. First, it had been with my parents. Then the lovely celebrations with John on the Montfort estate. We had one Christmas together as a family after young John was born. Even in the years while John was held captive, the children and I were together.

Henri managed a Christmas feast as spectacular as any we'd ever had. And Sir William made the days leading up to Twelfth Night as festive as anyone could in a remote place like Tickhill. He hired musicians and mummers to come from Sheffield. On the eve of the New Year, he opened the castle for all the villagers to join us and lit a bonfire for people to dance around. For the benefit of everyone else, I put on a brave show of joy, but inside, the loneliness was tearing at my soul. So when that terrible letter arrived, I was already closer to despair than I'd ever imagined could be possible.

It snowed a lot that January, which only worsened the chill that gripped my heart. Henri and Aaliz tried mightily to help. I remember Henri telling me at some point that if I wanted to get a letter to John or to Amaury, he had ways to smuggle things out of the castle without the constable's knowledge. Even that couldn't penetrate the overwhelming grief that consumed me.

I remember nothing of what happened in that year of 1344. For me, it was a year of mourning – not for a death – Aaliz refused to let me wear weeds – but for a great loss nonetheless. It was not until the middle of the following year that I was jarred from my stupor. And once again, it was by a terrible betrayal.

CHAPTER THIRTY-THREE

Tickhill, South Yorkshire, 1 June 1345

As the days grew warmer in the late Yorkshire spring, Aaliz had begun insisting that her mistress spend more time outdoors. In the middle of May, she'd reported, "I found some bluebells under the trees by the south wall. Let's go have a look." Then, a week later, she announced, "The first strawberries are ready in the garden, madame. Let's go collect some. I'll bet Cook will give us some cream to go with them." Though she wasn't really heartened by the idea of nature's rebirth, Jeanne had little choice but to go along since Aaliz would give her no peace otherwise. And she had to admit the strawberries were delicious.

Today, Aaliz had dragged her to the garden to cut flowers to brighten up her sitting room. Cornflowers and columbines were still in full bloom. Here and there, a few poppies and daisies were just starting to flower. The rose bushes that weren't already covered in blossoms were covered in buds that would soon add to the fragrant display. Surrounded by such loveliness, Jeanne couldn't help but feel somewhat cheered.

Their basket filled, they were making their way back to the entrance when Henri came through the door. "Ah, there you are, madame. Sir William would like to have a word. He says there's news of your husband."

"After all this time?" Jeanne asked. "Do you have any inkling what it might be, Henri?"

"No, madame. Only that Sir William thinks you'll be eager to know."

"Very well. Aaliz, take the flowers upstairs and work your usual magic. Henri, let's go find out what the news is."

Sir William was waiting in his study with three glasses of wine standing on the sideboard. "One for you as well, Henri. I think your mistress will want you to hear this too." The constable took his own glass as Henri handed one to Jeanne and took the third for himself. "Now, shall we sit?"

When they were all comfortably seated, Sir William raised his glass. "To the arrival of summer. May it be as pleasant as the one just past." Jeanne joined the toast, despite having absolutely no recollection of what the previous summer had been like.

"Now," the constable continued, "I've had a messenger this morning with news of your husband, my lady. He found a way, sometime in the spring, to escape the house imprisonment imposed by the French king and has made his way to England."

Jeanne could feel all the gloom of the past year and a half falling away. "John? Here in England? Since the spring? Where? Why hasn't he come to me?"

"One question at a time, my dear. The letter I received says nothing about when he arrived or where he went. Only that he is currently lodging with the Archbishop of Canterbury at Lambeth Palace. Or at least he was there when the letter was written. His purpose in being there was to do homage to Edward, as King of France, for Brittany. That has been accomplished."

"That's wonderful news!" Jeanne actually sounded happy, even to herself, for the first time in months. "That means Edward has affirmed his continued support to help John retake the duchy."

"It would seem so," said Sir William.

"Surely it must also mean that John will collect his family to return to Brittany with him."

"That I cannot say. The letter goes on to say that your husband reached an agreement with Edward that the children are to be brought up to succeed to the ducal crown and that suitable marriages will be arranged for them from among the English nobility. The king's own infant daughter, Mary, has been suggested for your son."

Jeanne had the distinct feeling there was something the constable wasn't telling her. "What does 'brought up to succeed to the ducal crown' mean, Sir William?" She was certain she saw the man flinch at her question.

"The letter says, my lady, that your children have been made wards of King Edward."

"*What?!*" Jeanne couldn't disguise her shock.

Henri looked worried. He and Aaliz were only just now getting the duchess back to her former self. Would this throw her back into the depths of despair? Would she start throwing things here in Sir William's study?

"What else does the letter say, Constable?" she asked.

"Nothing more, my lady. It is remarkably devoid of explanations, though one would have thought the sender would be aware that you would press for such details."

"Oh, I've no doubt the sender is aware but is following instructions. Humor me, Sir William. Is the sender perchance the Lord Privy Seal?"

"He once held that title. He is now Lord Chancellor."

"Following instructions." She took another sip of wine then pushed the glass aside. "Then, Sir William, since there's nothing more you can tell me, I'll take my leave. I have flowers to arrange." She rose and made for the door, Henri close on her heels.

He followed her to her sitting room. Uncertain what to make of her calm demeanor, he opened the door for her and stepped inside as she crossed to look out the little window.

"I don't understand him, Henri. Is John so desperate for Edward's help that he'd give away his own children to get it? And without even asking me?"

"I don't know, madame."

"Have things gone that badly in Brittany?"

"I don't know that either, unfortunately."

"We've had no word from Amaury while I was . . . whatever I was? No letters that you've withheld, knowing I couldn't cope with what they might contain?"

"No, madame."

Jeanne turned away from the window. "Are you holding something back from me even now, Henri?"

He stepped into the corridor to look around then came back inside the room and closed the door. "Perhaps you don't remember, my lady, that I told you I have ways to smuggle messages in and out without the constable's knowledge. I hope you'll forgive me. I took the liberty of sending a message to Lord de Clisson telling him of your distress and seeking his help."

"Oh, Henri, there's nothing to forgive. That was truly a kindness. Did he reply?"

"Only that de Blois was still ignoring the truce, pursuing the Montfortist forces everywhere and regaining territory. They needed the duke to lead them, and your husband was still hampered by Philip's restrictions on his movements. Much as Lord de Clisson would have liked to help, he had no choice but to stay and defend his own holdings."

"Things must be dire indeed." She sat in her favorite chair, staring at her hands in her lap. "If only John had talked with me about what he intended to do . . . what he must have *had* to do. Am I wrong, Henri, to think Edward prevented him from coming here?"

"That's not for me to say, madame."

"But what do you think?"

"That madame is most likely right as usual."

She stared at her hands again for several long moments. "If I were to write to John, Henri, could you smuggle the letter out?"

"Do you know where to send it?"

"Sir William said he was last at Lambeth Palace."

"Are you sure you want to do that, madame? That's right in the teeth of the viper. Assuming my messenger could even get through to deliver it, might it not give the king an excuse to place even more restrictions on you?"

"I *want* to do it more than anything. But you make a fair point. If John had to surrender our children, what chance would he have of getting me free of this dreadful place? And I want that most fervently as well."

"We would all like to return home, madame."

"Then, from today, Henri, let's make that our goal, you and I. I have no idea at this moment how we'll do it. But it wouldn't be the first thing we've done that people thought was impossible."

. . . . .

October 1345

Little news got through to Tickhill about what was happening in Brittany during the summer. Even fewer opportunities presented themselves to escape their confinement. Jeanne preferred to think of it as the right opportunity not having appeared. Henri was more inclined to think of it as no opportunities at all.

They'd heard that most of the south coast of Brittany was back in Montfortist control and that only Quimper remained to be retaken.

On the eve of the feast day of Saint Luke, Jeanne was surprised when Henri appeared in her sitting room, bearing a tray of food, well before the usual hour for the evening meal. "It occurred to me, madame, that you might enjoy dining here this evening as the chilly rain all day has left the dining hall feeling a bit drafty."

"How thoughtful of you, Henri."

He placed the tray on the sideboard and busied himself serving a plate for her and filling a goblet from the wine pitcher that was always present. Then, as he always did when she dined alone, he moved one of the side tables alongside her favorite chair and arranged everything on it just as he would if serving formally downstairs. But tonight, he added one thing more – a letter. "It also occurred to me, madame, that you might enjoy an accompaniment to your meal."

"Ah, Henri, not just thoughtful but sly as well." She smiled. "And absolutely correct." His hint of a smile told her that he relished her praise.

As soon as he left, she picked up the letter. The seal was de Clisson, but the handwriting was unfamiliar. Her curiosity was piqued. What she found inside was the last thing she expected.

My dear Duchess,

*I'm taking the risk of writing to you – not knowing if this will even reach you – because I fear that no one will give you the news. In fact, as I understand things, those who **should** bring you the news may be at pains to keep it from* *you. With a heavy heart, I must tell you that your husband, John, was called to God on the 26th day of the month just past.*

He had laid siege to Quimper, intending to remove the last of the Blois adherents from the south coast, but his assault met heavy resistance, costing many lives. And as he was attempting to regroup, de Blois arrived with his army, forcing your husband to retreat in haste.

They managed to escape and fled to Hennebont, as a safe haven for contemplating their next move. Your husband was, at the time, in good health and uninjured.

Sadly, that state of affairs didn't last. He fell most seriously ill and was unable to recover. That he died in the place you so gloriously defended makes his loss all the more poignant.

I know you will grieve as deeply as I did when my own dear Olivier was so violently taken from me by that whoreson Philip of Valois. Not a day passes that I don't take some step to exact revenge on him for Olivier's execution. He may have stripped me of all my titles and lands, but he couldn't take my spirit. With the money I had hidden away, I've purchased a small fleet, and, alongside my devoted seamen, I'm harassing French ships wherever they sail. Every French vessel I send to the depths of the sea – every French ship we capture and take its cargo – every French seaman we send rowing for shore while we sail away is a message to Philip that he should never have trifled with me. In your husband's honor, the next boatload of Frenchmen I capture will be put ashore at Hennebont with my fervent hope that the people there make sure those men never make it home.

My dear Duchess, it is thanks to your example that I've had the confidence to follow this path. Your courage has been an inspiration, as it should be for every Breton who breathes God's sweet air. I know in my soul that you will triumph in the end and that your beloved husband will be cheering you on from his lofty vantage point at God's side.

Jeanne de Clisson
Written on the feast day of Saint Francis of Assisi

Henri and Aaliz found her an hour later, staring into what was left of the fire, tears streaming down her cheeks, the letter in her lap, her food and wine untouched. Henri took the letter and read it, then whispered to Aaliz. "There's no need to whisper," said Jeanne softly. "We have no secrets among the three of us."

"Oh, madame." Aaliz sank to the floor in front of her mistress and laid her head in Jeanne's lap. "He was the best of men."

"Indeed he was, my lady," said Henri.

"I wonder," said Jeanne, "if our children have been told? I only hope whoever tells them is kind."

"Perhaps we'll learn in due course, madame," said Henri.

"Most likely not," said Jeanne, "but I'm grateful for your thought." She found a handkerchief in her pocket and dried her eyes and cheeks.

"Are you alright, madame?" asked Henri.

"No, Henri. But it won't be like last time. I can't promise you won't find me crying now and again." She stroked Aaliz's hair. "But I won't descend into the depths of hell. I can't. With John gone, Brittany needs me more than ever, so I have to have my wits about me if we're to find a way out of this place." Another tear escaped and begin to roll down her cheek. "But I *so* wish I could have seen him one last time."

FROM THE WRITINGS OF JEANNE DE FLANDRE, DUCHESS OF BRITTANY AND COUNTESS OF MONTFORT

FOUND AMONG HER BELONGINGS AT THE TIME OF HER DEATH

Tickhill, South Yorkshire, 1348

John's death left me truly alone in the world. Oh, I had Henri and Aaliz, and kinder, more loyal people there could never be. And I did cry for John – and for me. Our lives had held so much hope. And so much love for one another.

Sometimes I would rail at God for allowing it all to be rent asunder. More often, I railed at Jeanne de Penthièvre for being the agent of our misfortune. But no amount of railing could change the fact that I was alone, confined against my will, penniless, and bereft of any recourse to change my situation. So I railed at Edward Plantagenet for his duplicity and hoped it was costing him a king's ransom to provide for the proper maintenance of my household.

*And when I realized that was something that actually **was** within my control, I made a game of spending England's money. Nothing so audacious that it would be obvious what I was doing, but a constant stream of needs. Three new gowns straightaway – after all, I had only the wardrobe I'd arrived with – and then a new gown every couple of months. Only beeswax candles, even for the kitchen. A new set of clothing for every servant. The best herbs and spices for Cook – I developed quite a liking for ginger, which, if not worth a king's ransom, could easily cost as much as a good ewe. A musician or a bard or* *a juggler to entertain at the evening meal once a month. A craftsman to repair the window in my sitting room so it wasn't so drafty in winter.*

Henri recognized straightaway what I was up to and seemed to take a great deal of pleasure from playing along. And, in truth, it lifted everyone's spirits and kept us all from going mad with boredom.

CHAPTER THIRTY-FOUR

In mid-January of the New Year, they got a new minder. Sir William Frank was replaced as constable by Sir Thomas de Haukeston. The two men could not have been more different. Whereas Frank viewed his role as guard and guardian, Haukeston behaved more like a host. Jeanne was sure he was also a custodian, but he didn't wear that aspect overtly. Frank always declined Jeanne's invitations to dine with her. Haukeston accepted with enthusiasm and turned out to be quite a pleasant conversationalist. In many ways, he reminded her of John. About the same stature, clean-shaven, with the same streaks of gray beginning to show in his hair, though that hair was a bit lighter than John's had been. But it was the kindness in his eyes and the way he didn't patronize her no matter what they were discussing that won her over, despite the fact that he was, nonetheless, her gaoler.

Since she'd recovered from the loss of her children, she'd taken up the habit of visiting the stables frequently. Frank wouldn't condone her riding outside the walls, even escorted by his men, and there really wasn't enough room within the walls for a horse to stretch its legs, so she'd had to content herself with making friends with the beasts, brushing and grooming them, and sneaking them apples or carrots from the kitchen. Even in winter, if the weather was fair, it was common to see her walking from stall to stall, talking to horses and stable boys alike. Sometimes Aaliz came with her for a change of scenery even though she was rather afraid of horses.

The weather had been consistently miserable since Haukeston's arrival, making visits to the stables unappealing. But when late February brought a series of sunny days and much of the snow melted, they had both been cooped up indoors for so long that Aaliz didn't protest when Jeanne insisted they visit the horses together. Jeanne was having a pleasant conversation with her favorite mare when she heard bootsteps approaching and turned to see Sir Thomas making his way down the line of stalls. "So you talk to them too, I see," he said.

"Of course. They quite enjoy it, I think," said Jeanne.

"Frank didn't tell me you were a horsewoman."

"That's because he never allowed me to go riding, so he wouldn't know."

"You ride well?"

"Better than lots of men," Aaliz chimed in. "She had a fine charger when we were in Hennebont. Rode him when she led the raid that set fire to the French camp."

"A woman who rides war horses?" Sir Thomas sounded incredulous. "This I have to see." He called out to the nearest stable boy. "You, there. Saddle my horse for the lady here."

"But, sir, we got no side saddles."

"Don't be silly, lad," Jeanne chided him. "No one puts a side saddle on a war horse. Saddle him properly."

The stable boy looked befuddled and just stood there, uncertain what to do. "Well, go on, lad," Haukeston said. "Do as the lady says. And saddle another horse for me. We're going riding."

It wasn't long before the lad returned leading a fine chestnut stallion. "Oh, my, aren't you a beauty?" Jeanne said, taking the reins and stroking the horse's muzzle. "We're going to get along just fine, aren't we?" The horse nickered and flicked his tail. She led him over to a mounting block and climbed into the saddle while Sir Thomas mounted the big grey that had been brought up for him.

When they returned an hour later, Jeanne's face was flushed and her hands cold from the still-chilly air, but she was the happiest she'd been since she'd arrived in England. "That was most exhilarating, sir," she told her companion. Then, leaning forward to stroke the horse's neck, she added, "And you are a joy to ride." She jumped down off the horse's back and gave the reins to the stable boy.

"And you, madame," said Haukeston as he handed over his own mount, "are a marvel on horseback. If you'd like, I'll get you a fine animal of your own."

"You'd allow me to go riding outside the walls?"

"Well, accompanied, of course. Either me or some of my men. We can't have you riding off to God knows where when you don't know anything about the countryside, now, can we?"

Jeanne laughed. He was still her gaoler, even if he *was* an amiable one. "That would be lovely, sir. Can I choose the horse?"

Sir Thomas laughed aloud. "Why not? But there's one condition."

She cocked her head, wondering what kind of restriction he was going to demand. Was she going to be relegated to a broken-down plough horse? "And what's the condition?"

"You can't have mine, no matter how much you like him."

In the end, after riding several candidates, she chose the mare whose nose she'd been stroking when Sir Thomas first approached. They had an affinity for one another, the horse seeming to know what Jeanne wanted even before she asked for it. But more importantly, the mare was fast – which might be important if one of those opportunities she and Henri kept hoping for should ever present itself.

Winter gave way to spring soon thereafter, and Sir Thomas was as good as his word – and as often as not, her companion for pleasant rides exploring the countryside. She rode every day that the weather was fair, and it almost felt like freedom. Almost. It was impossible not to notice the armed men who were ever-present. At least when Haukeston came along, they kept a greater distance.

Sir Thomas treated the villagers to a great celebration at the castle for Midsummer's Day. And when Saint Swithun's Day dawned fair, the villagers organized their own modest fête. Just the sort of thing Jeanne would have contributed to in the days when she had money, so it saddened her to be unable to do so now. Ever resourceful, Henri cajoled the cook to bake some honey cakes for his mistress to take to the festivities.

Around the time of the Hunter's Moon, they heard the news of Edward's great victory at Crécy, an utter humiliation for Philip VI. All of

England celebrated, including even the little village of Tickhill. And while England celebrated, Edward besieged Calais.

But there was no news from Brittany. And as fall gave way to winter and the old year to a new one, Jeanne became increasingly concerned that her family and all she'd sacrificed to ensure her son's future were being forgotten. It was time to search more diligently for that elusive opportunity.

CHAPTER THIRTY-FIVE

Rarely do longed-for opportunities present themselves in the guise one is expecting. Nor do they announce themselves from the ramparts for all to hear. But if one knows what to look for . . .

Thanks to Sir Thomas's affability, the inhabitants of Tickhill Castle got regular news on the progress of England's war. The siege of Calais dragged on, even as spring flowers sprung up all over the English countryside. The upper classes groused a bit about the taxes they had to pay to finance such a massive undertaking, but the complaints were only half-hearted. Everyone seemed to agree with the king that Calais was a prize worth taking – a jewel for the English crown. The pope tried to mediate a solution to end the siege, but neither Edward nor Philip would deign to speak to the papal emissaries.

But if Calais was what everyone was talking about, it was Sir Thomas's offhand remark over supper one evening in early June that caught Jeanne's attention. She had been speculating about how long Calais might hold out when he said, "And that's not the only siege Edward's running at the moment."

"Oh?"

"Thomas Dagworth's got an army camped outside La Roche-Derrien doing much the same thing."

So there *was* something happening in Brittany. Jeanne managed to keep her expression and her tone bland. "Then I wish him good fortune."

"He'll need it. If my information is right, he's outnumbered four or five to one."

"But surely he has archers, doesn't he? I mean, doesn't that reduce the odds?"

"Madame is a wealth of surprises." Sir Thomas gave her an approving smile.

"I saw for myself, in Hennebont, what two hundred longbowmen could do against a much larger army – how they could completely change the battle."

"Ah, yes. De Mauny's little force that helped you win the day. I rather think that battle is going to become the stuff of legends. You may even become part of the legend yourself." He raised his glass to her but didn't voice a toast.

That night, she lay awake thinking about Sir Thomas's words. The fighting in Brittany hadn't waned, as she'd feared. La Roche-Derrien was in the heart of Penthièvre. If this Thomas Dagworth had been ordered to take it, then the army holed up there was almost certainly under Charles de Blois's command. If Dagworth could prevail, it would breathe new life into her cause. She would need to find a way to learn the outcome without Haukeston becoming suspicious of her interest.

She needn't have worried. Sir Thomas maintained a keen interest in what was going on with Edward's wars in France.

One evening in early July, she came down to the evening meal to discover a feast the likes of which she hadn't seen in many months – perhaps not even since the night her erstwhile friend King Edward had toasted her as the Heroine of Hennebont. Henri stood beside the table, beaming. The table top was covered with all manner of dishes, even including a roast pheasant. Her finest jeweled goblets that she'd brought with her to England stood at each place, already filled with wine. She couldn't suppress a little gasp of surprise. "Henri, I . . . what's the occasion?"

"The occasion, my dear lady," Sir Thomas replied as he strode into the dining hall, "is to celebrate a victory."

"A victory? Whose?"

"Why, yours, of course."

"Mine?"

Henri held her chair for her as Haukeston took his own place across the table. "Well, technically, Thomas Dagworth's, but yours nevertheless."

"You mean?" She didn't dare utter the words for fear she might be wrong.

"I mean that La Roche-Derrien has fallen."

"Oh, my God. When? No, wait. When doesn't matter. You're certain?" She could barely take it in. Could it be that the winds had finally spun the weathercock in her favor again?

"Absolutely."

"Then we should toast Sir Thomas Dagworth."

"Indeed we should," said Haukeston, "but not just yet."

Jeanne looked puzzled. "I don't understand."

"There's more, my dear. Dagworth has returned to England, bringing a prisoner with him. Shall I tell you who that prisoner is?" The constable was clearly enjoying himself.

"I think maybe you should, sir, unless you want me to die from suspense."

Haukeston laughed heartily. "Well, now, we can't have you dying before you get to celebrate your victory. That prisoner is none other than Charles de Blois himself. And that, my dear lady, is why I say the victory is yours."

Jeanne had never fainted in her life. But she was suddenly so lightheaded, she feared it might be about to happen for the first time. Charles taken prisoner? How that must have heartened the Montfortists!

Sir Thomas raised his goblet. "To the Duchess."

"I think, Sir Thomas," Jeanne said, "the toast should be 'To Brittany.'"

"To Brittany," he echoed.

After they'd drunk the toast, she added, "For as long as this lasts."

"Why would you say that, my dear?"

"Because it's true. Yes, Charles is a prisoner now. But we both know he'll be ransomed and back in the fray in no time at all."

"So you might think. But I'm given to understand that his ransom is to be five hundred thousand *écus*."

"Five hundred thousand? That's a *staggering* sum."

"Which will take quite some time to raise. So his stay on this side of the Channel may be quite a bit longer than he expects. King Edward's gift to you, I think, for giving him Brittany. Without it, he could never have reclaimed Normandy much less be so close to capturing Calais."

"I—" She started to react then bit her tongue.

"You what, my dear?"

"Nothing. I simply don't know what to say."

But later that evening, while Aaliz snored softly on her palette, Jeanne tossed and turned and fumed. *Giving him Brittany? The* **arrogance** *of the man!* His part of the agreement had been to help her regain Brittany for her husband and her son. She hadn't cared what he did once John's title was secure, but she hadn't turned over her entire treasury for him to run roughshod over her family's interests. It was time for her to return. This was no time for Jeanne de Penthièvre to have free rein.

The following morning, she told Henri they could no longer hope for an opportunity to escape. They had to make one.

CHAPTER THIRTY-SIX

Calais fell at the beginning of August and a formal truce had been signed by the end of September. Both kings disbanded their armies, and Edward replaced the entire population of Calais with English citizens. By the end of October, he was back in England.

On the eve of Saint Elizabeth's day, Henri asked his mistress to walk with him in the garden to discuss household matters. "I think there are some asters still in bloom," he remarked as they walked past the rose bushes that were already bereft of their summer glory. Jeanne was puzzled. This was completely out of character. But she went along.

Once they were on the far side of the garden, Henri revealed his true purpose. "There are things afoot, madame. Breton nobles who want to bring you home to rule in your son's name. Their planning, it seems, is well advanced."

"How do you know this, Henri?" She spoke softly even though there was no one within earshot.

"Perhaps it's better that you not know, my lady." He paused but continued when she didn't press. "Will you trust me in this?"

"Of course, Henri."

"All I know so far is that the Breton agents are already on English soil for the purpose of devising a scheme for your escape. I have no idea when there will be more information, so I suggest we discuss all household matters *en plein air* for the present – a new habit we're adopting to break up the monotony of life."

"I quite agree. Does every third day seem appropriate to you?"

"That will do nicely, madame. And should anything out of the ordinary arise, I will, of course, ask you to join me here."

"And what shall we do if it rains?"

"One must inventory the wine cellar from time to time. Footsteps echo loudly in those undercrofts, so we would know if we were about to be disturbed."

Six days later, the asters were beginning to look rather sad, but not so Henri's mood. "I've learned that the Bretons landed at Hull and are now in the vicinity of Pontefract. Their leader goes by the name of Warmer de Giston, and he's expected in Doncaster before the end of the week. That's all I know for the moment, madame."

"It's enough, Henri. Our job now is to be patient."

There was no further news when they next met. With the possibility of escape from this hell-hole so tantalizingly close, Jeanne found herself having to take her own advice on the merits of patience . . . and of taking pains to ensure her manner with everyone – especially Haukeston – revealed nothing of the excitement she felt inside.

What there was three days later was an abundance of rain. "Which makes it quite a natural thing," Henri assured her, "to choose this day for determining when we will need another barrel of wine." She watched as he placed an inkpot and quill atop one of the barrels and opened his ledger. "Perhaps madame would be interested in this while I make a record of the stores."

The folded page bore no seal. She almost ripped the paper in her eagerness to see the words it bore.

Your loyal supporters are close by and our plans have been made. Be ready. Do not change your daily habits. But from now on, be sure that the people you value most are always at your side. We will not be able to give you any warning. We will act when we deem the circumstances most favorable.

Warmer de Giston

When Henri finished his notations and cleaned the tip of his quill, she proffered him the letter. "I've already read it, madame. But I will take it for burning. No sign of this must be found in your presence. Not even the ash."

"Then know this, Henri. I'll contrive to keep Aaliz with me, even when we go riding . . . though how I'm going to get past her fear of horses, I don't quite know at the moment. But I need to rely on you to find your own way to always be close by. No matter what happens, I need you both."

He returned the letter to its hiding place inside the ledger and picked up the quill and ink pot. "When we left Nantes, I swore a solemn oath to your husband that I'd look after you. I'm a man of my word, my lady." She gave him a quick peck on the cheek and watched as his entire face turned scarlet. "I believe," he said, leading the way out of the cellar, "that Sir Thomas will need to bring in another barrel if he intends to have lavish celebrations for Twelfth Night."

And then the waiting began. First, the jittery anticipation of something about to happen. Then the calm acceptance that it was all out of her control and no amount of eagerness would make it happen any sooner. And finally, when ten days had passed with no further news and no sign of rescuers, a sad resignation to the possibility that her hopes might be dashed . . . that the plotters might have been discovered and all their plans thwarted.

With his usual ingenuity, Henri solved her problem of Aaliz's fear of horses by turning their rides into an occasion for enjoying the midday meal outdoors in a meadow or along the banks of a stream. Which, naturally, required a wagon to transport the food, the blankets for spreading on the ground, and someone to assist him in serving the meal. Sir Thomas accompanied them the first time, but then declared that eating outdoors reminded him too much of his experience in siege camps, so he'd leave them to it if they somehow found this enjoyable. Leave them to it with their usual escorts, of course, who always ate several yards away to be close to their grazing horses should they need to leap into action.

The weather remained unseasonably warm, but Jeanne knew the chill winds of winter could arrive at any time, putting an end to their little outings. She awoke on Wednesday before the first Sunday of Advent with a strange sense of something momentous about to happen. Dismissing it as no more than recognition of the import of the coming season, she joined in Aaliz's delight that the sun was shining, the air was still warm, and Henri had promised they could eat beside her favorite stream that noon.

The reason Jeanne loved this little stream so much was because it was rocky and the sounds of the water gurgling over and around the rocks seemed almost like having musicians to entertain them while they ate. Today, though, that music suddenly had a new accompaniment. Hoofbeats approaching fast. "Into the wagon – quick as you can," Henri said then lifted Jeanne and Aaliz into the back and threw blankets over them. As he climbed into the driver's seat, he admonished, "Stay down. Stay hidden. It may be a rough ride."

Jeanne could hear the sound of riders all around now and an unfamiliar voice. "Warmer de Giston. Follow me." And then Henri's voice calling to the horses as the wagon lurched forward. And the sounds of their escorts shouting – she could imagine them scrambling onto their horses. Then the sounds of armed men clashing – receding into the distance. Jeanne and Aaliz clung to each other under the blankets as the wagon careened along at breakneck speed. How long could the horses keep up this pace?

When Jeanne thought the animals must soon drop dead in their traces from sheer exhaustion, the wagon finally slowed. That's when she heard hoofbeats approaching from behind. Their escorts catching up with them to haul them back to Tickhill? But when the wagon kept moving forward at the pace of a walk, she reasoned that the new arrivals were those who had stayed behind to prevent any pursuit.

Under the blankets, she had no sense of time or place or even what direction they might be traveling. From the bumpiness of the ride, she guessed they were on little-used country lanes with the ruts and potholes formed by heavy wagons and bad weather. At long last, the sounds of wagon wheels and horseshoes on stone told her they might have reached their destination. And then the wagon came to a stop.

Much as she wanted a look at the new surroundings, Henri's whispered "Just a bit farther now" kept her from throwing off the blanket. The wagon moved again and she could no longer feel the warmth of the sun. When it stopped for a second time, Henri said, "You can come out now."

She tossed away the blanket and jumped to her feet. They were in a barn or stable of some sort – a very fine one, so wherever this was, the owner must be a person of means. Aaliz was still in hiding. "We're safe now, Aaliz. Henri's right – you can come out." Jeanne sat on the side of the wagon and swung her legs over to put her feet on top of the wheel. A man standing below lifted her down then doffed his cap and bowed. "Warmer de Giston, my lady duchess, at your service. Welcome to Pontefract."

· · · · ·

Leeds Castle, 29 November 1347

"That *bloody* woman!" Edward raged. "Why can't she just enjoy the pleasant life I provide for her and quit making trouble?" If they could have quietly wandered away without the king's permission, everyone in the presence chamber would have done so. As it was, their only recourse was to look out the windows, study the tapestries, or contemplate their own fingernails.

Everyone, that is, except Sir Thomas de Haukeston, who'd had the unenviable task of delivering the news of the escape. Eventually, Edward stopped pacing back and forth in front of his throne and faced Sir Thomas. "How could you have let this happen, Haukeston?"

"With all due respect, Sire, my men did their job. She's never alone without guards. We had no hint at all of anything afoot. They descended on my men from nowhere, grabbed the duchess and her companions, and overwhelmed the guards. It was more than a quarter of an hour before we were able to pursue them and by then, they'd seemingly disappeared."

"So you say." Edward was not at all mollified. "We'll talk more about this later."

Haukeston bowed. "Yes, Your Grace."

Edward sat back down on the throne as Sir Thomas backed slowly away toward the side of the room. "Someone fetch John Bourdon here," Edward ordered to the room in general. Those nearest the door rushed to comply. No one wanted to risk another display of the king's temper.

It couldn't have been more than a quarter of an hour before Bourdon arrived, but to those enduring the silence in the chamber, it might as well have been half a lifetime. At long last, the doors opened and the sergeant-at-arms strode in. "You sent for me, Your Grace?"

"I have a job for you, Sergeant. Find the Duchess of Brittany, her companions, and the conspirators who stole her away and bring them here to me. Every last one of them. And without delay. Do I make myself clear?"

"Perfectly, Sire," Bourdon replied.

"Sir Thomas here will tell you everything he knows that might help to find them. Every detail. Do I make myself clear, Haukeston?"

"Perfectly, Sire." Haukeston echoed the sergeant.

"Then get to it, man. They mustn't be allowed to leave these shores."

"Aye, Your Grace." Bourdon bowed and made for the door. Haukeston followed, eager to escape Edward's presence until he was in a better frame of mind.

•   •   •   •   •

Pontefract Castle, 29 November 1347

They had passed a comfortable enough night, Jeanne and Aaliz sharing a small room with two narrow, low beds that might have been sleeping quarters for stable boys. Henri had slept in the company of de Giston's men. Once everyone had taken care of the morning necessaries, Henri and de Giston joined the women in their small room.

"I had scouts out all night, my lady," de Giston told them," and there's no sign of pursuit. But never doubt for a moment that they'll come looking for us. So we're going to stay here for a few days – long enough for them to have searched the area and decided we're not here. Then we'll make for the coast. The ship that brought us here is waiting to take you home."

"Pardon me for doubting you, sir," said Jeanne, "but don't you think they'll be searching the ports as well?"

"Of course they will. But we landed in Hull. And our ship put back out to sea just as soon as they loaded a few bales of wool. At the moment, they're standing off Grimsby. I won't risk having them come into port where they'd be recognized. We'll have to row out to them."

"And what about whoever you hire to do the rowing?"

"For enough gold florins, I'm sure they'll be happy to keep their mouths shut. Besides . . . before they could get back to port and raise the alarm, we'll be long gone. The captain will raise sail when he spots my signal from the boat, so he can get underway as soon as the last of us climbs aboard."

"You seem to have everything worked out, sir," said Jeanne.

"Your safety isn't to be trifled with, Duchess. You're needed in Brittany."

"So how many days must we wait here?"

"Today and two more. If my scouts are satisfied that the searchers have moved on, then it will be time to leave. But for those three days, you must keep to yourself here – and your steward here with you. Except for sleeping hours, of course. We mustn't risk your being seen."

"In which case, Henri can share our quarters for sleeping if you can arrange something decent for him to sleep on. He would never take advantage of either of us."

"As you wish, madame. I'll see to it straightaway."

"It'll be a bit crowded in here, Henri . . . Aaliz," said Jeanne, "but it's only for a short time, and we can keep each other company."

They spent the next two days in the little room, leaving the door open for light during the day but shutting it at night. De Giston brought them food and drink twice a day – bread, chunks of cheese, bits of dried venison, and small ale. They marked the passage of time by the sound of the bells from the nearby priory.

•   •   •   •   •

Outside Ackworth Village, 1 December 1347

"Where to tomorrow, Sergeant?" asked the squire as he banked the campfire for the night.

"Alright, men, gather round," Bourdon called out. When they'd assembled, he began giving instructions for the following day. "My gut still tells me they'll try to find sanctuary in a religious house until they think we've given up the search. We didn't find them in Doncaster and we've searched Monk Bretton Priory. So in the morning, we head for Pontefract.

It's a good place to hide out before making a run for Hull and a waiting ship. First the priory, then the castle. Same as today at Monk Bretton. Herd all the monks into the chapel and keep them under guard while we search. If we don't find them at the priory, then two of you will stay and keep the monks from leaving to warn the castle while the rest of us search there."

"What if they're already on their way to Hull?" someone asked.

"I've sent a message to the harbor master to prevent any sailings until I give the word. Now, get a good night's sleep. I have a feeling in my bones we're closing in on them."

.   .   .   .   .

Pontefract Castle, 2 December 1347

"Something's wrong," Jeanne spoke softly to her companions.

"What makes you say that?" Henri asked.

"The priory bells. They haven't sounded Sext."

"Perhaps it's not time yet," said Aaliz.

"No, they're late. De Giston always changes the guard at midday, and he did that some time ago."

"Maybe he's changed the routine?" Henri offered.

"I don't think so," said Jeanne.

"Well, how would he know when to change the guard if he's not going by the bells?" asked Aaliz.

"I don't know. Maybe he's using an hourglass. It doesn't matter. But something's wrong. I'm sure of it."

No one spoke for several moments. Finally, Henri said, "I think perhaps we should close the door. We'll be in the dark, but if anything's amiss, we might be safer."

"Yes, do, Henri," said Jeanne. "Aaliz, come sit beside me." Jeanne patted the bed to her left. Aaliz didn't hesitate. "You too, Henri . . ." Jeanne patted the bed on her right. ". . . if you can make your way back here in the dark."

After a bit of stumbling, Henri managed to find his way. Jeanne took one of their hands in each of hers, praying that either she was wrong or their hiding place would protect them. For a long time, she could hear nothing but the sound of their breathing. Then suddenly there was the sound of horseshoes on stone. Was it de Giston's men? Or someone else? She squeezed the hands of her companions and they squeezed back.

Then men's voices, but she couldn't make out if she'd heard them before or even what they were saying. They seemed to be going off in a different direction. And for a while, the world went quiet again. Could it be that the danger was past? That the next sound they heard would be de Giston telling them there was no longer anything to worry about?

All three of them flinched at once when the priory bells started ringing. Not the familiar tolling of the monastic hour but something wilder that sounded like an alarm. And as the bells kept clanging, they were joined by the sound of voices and bootsteps coming back in the direction of the barn. Shouted orders. "Search every inch of the place." The commotion coming closer and closer. Jeanne tightened her grip on her companions' hands.

Then, without warning, the door of the little room flew open and the light was almost blinding, so accustomed had their eyes grown to the dark, and in the doorway stood a tall man. "The Duchess of Brittany, I presume."

Jeanne refused to act the role of a fugitive being captured. She stood straight and tall, smoothed her skirts, and said, "Who would like to know?"

"John Bourdon. Sergeant-at-arms to His Grace Edward III. The king would like a word with you."

He stepped into the room and took hold of her arm, but she jerked it free. "How *dare* you take such liberties, Sergeant?" She turned to her companions. "Aaliz . . . Henri . . . come along. It seems the king would like us to pay a visit." She brushed past Bourdon and out into the open barn, her servants right behind her, then added in a voice loud enough to ensure Bourdon couldn't fail to hear, "Though his manner of delivering the message is exceedingly rude."

There was nothing for it – she had to comply. All of de Giston's men had been rounded up and were being held in one corner of the barn while a wagon and a small carriage were being readied. Once the horses were hitched, de Giston's men were loaded into the wagon and Bourdon barked,

"You three . . . inside the carriage." Henri held the door for the women then joined them inside.

· · · · ·

Leeds Castle, 3 December 1347

It was Bourdon himself who led them into Edward's presence chamber shortly after midday. Jeanne bristled when Bourdon was announced but *she* was *not*. As she followed the sergeant toward the throne, she took stock of her surroundings. De Giston and his men stood under guard next to one wall. Aaliz and Henri were with a separate guard near them. Quite a number of nobles stood here and there. She recognized the Earl of Arundel. Off to one side, near a window, was Sir Thomas de Haukeston.

Bourdon bowed. "As you ordered, Your Grace, the Duchess of Brittany and her entourage."

Edward smiled. "Well done, Bourdon." Bourdon bowed again and stepped aside. "And now for you, Jeanne de Montfort. What do you have to say for yourself?"

"Only that it seems apparent that the people of Brittany desire my return to my homeland."

"They've certainly gone to great lengths to spirit you away. Surely you've not grown weary of my hospitality."

Hospitality? How dare he? She seethed but decided it might not be the opportune time for a show of temper. "It seems that I have very little say in the matter, sir."

"And what, madame, was your role in plotting this little escapade?"

"My role, sir?"

"Who did you write to? Who did you ask to organize those conspirators standing back there under guard? How did you arrange to have a ship sent for you? There had to be a ship, of course, to get that lot into my kingdom."

"I'm sure you know as well as I do, sir, that I'm not at liberty to write to anyone or to arrange anything." She would spar with him all day long, if need be. After all, she outranked everyone in this room except Edward himself.

"Hmph. You expect me to believe that someone like you would not be clever enough to find ways to achieve her ends?"

"What I expect is that you have people watching my every move and that if I had done any of those things you accuse me of, you would already know about it. So I believe that the mere fact that you have to ask is proof that I've done nothing of the sort." *No matter how much I've wanted to*, she added to herself.

Edward stroked his chin. Then he changed tacks. "What say you, Arundel? Should I send her back to the home I've given her at Tickhill?"

"If all the conspirators have been rounded up, Sire, then it seems the threat is past."

"And you, Warwick?"

"I concur, Your Grace."

"Very well. Haukeston?"

Sir Thomas hurried over from his spot by the window. "Your Grace?"

"Take the lady home. And keep her there."

"As you wish, Sire." Haukeston bowed.

"As for the rest of them . . ." Edward gestured to the back of the room where Henri and Aaliz waited alongside de Giston and his men. ". . . they're to remain in custody for now until I decide what to try them for."

Jeanne's temper boiled. She could *not* let him get away with this. "Wait just a minute, Sir Thomas. I'm not going anywhere without my servants." Gasps sounded all around the room.

Edward sat up straighter on the throne. "Did I hear you right, madame?"

His tone wasn't quite menacing, but she knew she was risking an explosion of his famous temper. It didn't matter. She owed it to Henri and Aaliz. "You did indeed, sir. You've taken my liberty. You've taken my children. You prevented my husband from seeing me when he was here. By the Blessed Virgin, you've even taken my duchy. But you will **not** take my servants. I will not take **one** step from this place until they're released to go with me."

The entire room held its collective breath, waiting for the king's reaction. Jeanne watched the muscles of his neck tighten and braced herself for the outburst.

Finally, he broke the silence. "And how am I to know they weren't involved in the plot if they're not put on trial and questioned under oath?"

"You can take *my* word for it, Your Grace."

He met her gaze and they stared at each other, neither willing to look away. When it seemed this might go on for the rest of the afternoon, Sir Thomas cleared his throat. "If I may, Your Grace."

"What is it, Haukeston?"

"It's my opinion that you can believe the lady. Those two are always at her side. I've never had cause to distrust either of them."

"Very well, let the servants go. Now, Haukeston, get them all out of here. And you, madame, don't give me reason regret this."

They spent that night at an inn in Wakefield and were back at Tickhill just after sundown the following day. There had been little conversation during the journey, each of them having much to occupy their own thoughts. But when they prepared to part ways in the entrance hall of the castle, Jeanne said quietly, "I'm grateful, Sir Thomas, for your courage."

"Then I'm sure, madame, that you won't give *me* reason to regret it."

She gave him a reassuring smile. "There's something I've long wanted to ask you, Sir Thomas. Why do *you* think Edward refuses to let me go home? Why does he insist on keeping me here in what amounts to house imprisonment?"

"I can't pretend to know his mind, madame . . . only that it must suit his purposes."

"Then why do the people around him think he does it?"

Haukeston hesitated, seemingly uncertain how to answer. "It pains me to say this, my dear, but you deserve the truth. Some think you must be mad."

"And Edward allows them to believe this?"

"He offers neither affirmation nor denial."

"But I've not been given the test for madness. Surely that is known."

"How would it be, madame, if the king doesn't proclaim it?"

"And yet he allows men to believe I'm bereft of my senses."

"Again, madame, I know only that it must suit his purposes."

"Which are?"

"It's not my place to speculate, madame."

"But you said I deserve the truth. Surely you must have thoughts of your own."

Again, Haukeston hestated – far longer this time. "I think, my dear, that if the king doesn't declare a reason for your confinement then he cannot be challenged over it by anyone except yourself. And he cannot risk any challenge to his greater purpose."

It was Jeanne's turn to pause, mulling his words in her mind. At long last, she said, "Then I think, Sir Thomas, it must be my task to set the record straight."

Haukeston merely smiled.

Jeanne climbed the stairs to her apartment deep in thought. Sir Thomas had just confirmed what she'd already come to believe. She would never be allowed to return to the places where her heart lay. Where she walked side-by-side with her beloved John. Where she gave her people a reason to believe. And she would never be allowed to lie beside her husband when death finally claimed her. The weathercock had finally spun its head away from her, never to show her its face again. As she reached the top of the stairs and turned down the corridor toward her bedchamber, she finally allowed herself to articulate in her mind what she'd been pushing away for so many months. *What began as a dispute over who could call himself Duke of Brittany, is now about something else entirely. It's about who can call himself King of France. And it's far, far from over.*

Author's Notes

The War of the Breton Succession (1341-1365) is an early phase of the Hundred Years War between France and England. It's sometimes known as *La guerre des deux Jeannes* – the war of the two Joans – after the two women at the heart of the conflict. Jeanne de Penthièvre, the wife of Charles de Blois, claimed her right to the duchy as the only child of a full brother of Duke John III. Jeanne de Flandre was the wife of John de Montfort, the half-brother of John III named as his successor in John III's will, and the indomitable force behind the Montfortist cause.

This dispute might never have escalated into such a lengthy fight had it not been for the growing conflict between Edward III of England and Philip VI of France over rights to the French Crown. When all three of Philip IV's sons died childless, the crown passed to Philip of Valois, Philip IV's nephew, who was seen in France as the nearest living male relative to Philip IV. Edward, however, was confident he had the superior claim, being the direct grandson of Philip IV. But Edward's claim came through his mother, Isabella – Philip IV's daughter – and France adhered to Salic Law, which asserts that inheritance does not pass via female bloodlines. Nevertheless, in 1338, Edward declared himself King of France.

The situation in Brittany had parallels. As the duchy was a fief of the French Crown, it was subject to French law. But Bretons had long been fiercely protective of their own customs and maintained a variation on Salic Law. In Brittany, the ducal title normally passed to the nearest direct male descendant. But in the case where there was no direct male descendant, the title could be inherited through the female line or even pass directly to a woman if there was no eligible male heir at all. When Duke John III died childless, the succession was complicated by his long-standing grudge against his father's second family and by his well-known vacillation over naming his successor.

The irony of the War of the Breton Succession is that both Edward and Philip aligned with the side that represented exactly the opposite of the principle they adhered to in the dispute over the French Crown – Edward with the Montforts, Philip with Jeanne de Penthièvre's faction. Of course, it was all far more complicated than that, but what we would today call the optics of the situation are impossible to overlook.

By the time the first Treaty of Guérande was signed in 1365, many of the principals responsible for the war were dead. Edward III, of course, was still alive. John de Montfort died in 1345. Charles de Blois was taken prisoner by the English in 1347 and held for years until his enormous ransom was finally paid and he was released in 1356. Charles was indeed the paradox the old duke called a "strange duck" in this story. When he returned to France, he decided to make a barefoot pilgrimage in winter from La Roche-Derrien to Tréguier Cathedral to honor Saint Ivo of Kermartin. But all that piety didn't stop him from ordering the massacre of thousands of innocent civilians following the sieges of Quimper and Guérande. Charles was killed during the Battle of Auray in 1364.

Philip VI died in 1350 and was succeeded by his son (who was Duke of Normandy at the time of this story), John II. John was captured by the English at the Battle of Poitiers. He was allowed to return to France to raise his ransom while his son, Louis, was held as a hostage at Calais. When Louis escaped, John voluntarily returned to England and died there in 1364, leaving Charles V on the throne.

The two Jeannes, however, were both still alive. Jeanne de Flandre is believed to have died in 1374. Jeanne de Penthièvre lived until 1384. By the time of the Treaty of Guérande that definitively acknowledged the Montforts' son, John, as Duke of Brittany, that John was a widower, having married Edward III's daughter Mary, who died of a mysterious illness just two months after the marriage. Thirteen months after the signing of the treaty, John would marry Lady Joan Holland, who would be known as Duchess of Brittany from the time of her marriage, though, according to the terms of the treaty, Jeanne de Penthièvre was still permitted to use the title.

Names

Jeanne was a common name in Francophone countries at the time – witness Jeanne de Flandre, Jeanne de Penthièvre, Jeanne de Savoie (the old duke's wife), Jeanne de Clisson, and, at the opposite end of the Hundred Years War, Jeanne d'Arc. It is almost always rendered in English as Joan. But occasionally, for reasons that I've been unable to determine, English texts render it as Joanna, and such is the case with Jeanne de Flandre (Joanna of Flanders). I certainly haven't delved deeply into why because it wasn't pertinent to the narrative. I mention it here only for those who might choose to do their own study of the War of the Breton Succession and encounter that translation. Oddly, many of those English texts render Jeanne de Penthièvre only in the original French.

John de Montfort as well as his half-brother (the old duke) and his son would all have borne the name Jean.

So why did I choose to use the French for the women's names and the English translation for the men? For the women, I wanted to be true to the context of the story as The War of the Two Jeannes, and Joanna versus Jeanne just didn't feel right. The choice for the men's names was a nod to practicality. Two Jeannes and three Jeans would have created a nightmare for an audiobook narrator, not to mention how problematic it might have been for audiobook listeners, especially if they have little or no knowledge of French. Readers are free to take issue with these choices, but at least you know my rationale.

The Fate of Jeanne de Flandre

Jeanne de Flandre might have gone down as just a small footnote in the epic of the Hundred Years War had it not been for the writings of Jean Froissart. Froissart was a great admirer of Jeanne de Flandre and included her exploits in his *Chronicles*, a contemporaneous history of the Hundred Years War.

There are, however, a number of inconsistencies in the various accounts of her life. Jonathan Sumption, in his modern history of the Hundred Years War, attributes the burning of the French army camp outside Hennebont to an unauthorized attack on the town by Genoese and Spanish troops within that army who were overwhelmed by the defenders, who then burned part of the camp. Others tell of the camp having been largely abandoned for an unexplained reason and Jeanne de Flandre leading the raiding party that set the camp ablaze – and getting caught outside the walls when the French returned. It was from that exploit that she gained the moniker of *Jeanne de la Flamme* (or sometimes *Jeanne la Flamme*). Even within those latter accounts, the number of men she led differs – some say thirty, some say three hundred. Since Jeanne apparently did not have a very large force with her inside the walls of Hennebont, the smaller number seems much more plausible and also fits better with the idea that she didn't lose a substantial portion of her army in the escape.

Another inconsistency concerns Jeanne's departure to England. Some accounts say that she accompanied Edward when he returned home. Others have her, apparently traveling independently, landing somewhere in Devon and then making her way to London.

But the biggest inconsistency of all arises from what happened to her in late 1343. It's generally agreed that she was celebrated upon her arrival in England, even at court. The disagreement arises over why she was sent to Tickhill Castle and confined there. Many historians assert that she went mad. But madness was far from the only reason that medieval women – especially intelligent and strong-willed ones – were confined by the men surrounding them. Custodial confinement happened far more frequently than many people may know. The most famous example, of course, is Eleanor of Aquitaine's confinement by her husband, Henry II.

In her book *Joanna of Flanders: Heroine and Exile*, Julie Sarpy makes a compelling case that this is precisely what happened to Jeanne de Flandre. In Edward III's grand strategy for his designs on the French Crown, Jeanne and her Montfortist cause had given him the opening he needed to establish English control over Brittany. But with that accomplished, he had no further use for her, and her own goal of returning to lead the Montfortists was an unwanted distraction to his objectives in northern France.

Sarpy points out that English law of the time required a test for madness before someone could be confined. Her research found no evidence that Jeanne was ever administered the prescribed test. Sarpy also found numerous entries in Edward III's records for assignment of custodial responsibility for Jeanne de Flandre to specific individuals and of payments to those individuals for her upkeep. Sarpy points to the specific language used in those records as evidence that Jeanne was merely in custody and not deemed mentally deficient.

That he simply wanted her out of the way is further evidenced by the fact that he took control of the Montfort children. Edward was playing a long game in France, and raising the future Duke of Brittany in the English court was the ideal way to guarantee where that duke's loyalty would lie when he reached his majority.

Jeanne's short-lived escape from Tickhill is documented, though there is less known about who informed Edward of her flight or the details of how she was recovered – only that it was John Bourdon who was sent to retrieve her. Sarpy asserts that all the servants who left with her and all the Bretons who engineered the escape were imprisoned by Edward for some unknown fate. I preferred to think that it would be within Jeanne's character for her to fight for the servants who were closest to her.

Speaking of servants, Sarpy asserts that Jeanne would have had a very large household with her, including ladies-in-waiting, servants, and all the people who would normally surround an aristocrat of her stature. I made the decision that incorporating such an extensive cast of characters into the narrative would add unnecessary complication and distract from the story's focus on Jeanne herself. Readers should feel free to imagine any number of people around her while still keeping their attention on those closest to her.

After the escape, Jeanne was returned to Tickhill and the custody of Sir Thomas de Haukeston until his death in late 1357. Richard Charles, a yeoman to Queen Philippa, was then appointed Constable of Tickhill Castle for about a year, after which time responsibility for Jeanne was assigned to John Delves, who was the Deputy Justice of Chester. This begins a different type of custody for her – one in which she wasn't confined in a single location but was moved from place to place with the household of her custodian, wherever the custodian's assignments might take him. As such, she was first moved to Chester Castle, later to High Peak Castle in Derbyshire, likely to the manor of Walton on Trent, and quite possibly to Doddington Castle in Cheshire when John Delves died and his wife Isabel took over as custodian for a brief period of time.

She most likely died at Tickhill Castle sometime in 1374. There's reason to believe she was still alive in February 1374 when a payment for her upkeep was made to Godfrey Foljambe.

Jeanne did see her son one more time before she died. In 1360, he was sent to Chester Castle to recuperate from an illness prior to his marriage to Mary of Waltham, Edward III's daughter. Jeanne happened to be at Chester Castle at the time, in the custody of John Delves.

And she lived long enough to see her cause vindicated and her son restored to his proper place as Duke of Brittany.

I've found no evidence that Jeanne left any written record of her recollections of the events of the war. If she did, her writings have been lost or destroyed. That said, it seemed to me completely within the scope of her character that she would be determined to do whatever she could to ensure that the truth of her story came to light. So her writings are a product of my imagination, but one I like to think she would have approved of.

Characters

Aaliz and Henri, Durant and Kerveil, Raoul, Canon Gregoire, and the various mayors are all fictitious. But readers may be surprised to learn that quite a number of the incidental characters are actually real.

We know the name of the Montfort children's nurse from records in The National Archives of Britain. The household accounts of Queen Philippa include payments to the nurse, Perota de Britannie, for the care of the Montfort children

The man who served as Edward III's Lord Privy Seal at the time of this story was Robert de Offord – sometimes cited as Robert de Ufford. But it appears Offord and Ufford were likely two different families and the Lord Privy Seal was a member of the de Offord family. He did indeed become Lord Chancellor.

Jeanne de Clisson and her exploits are also real. She took up piracy after her husband's execution as revenge against Philip VI.

Warmer de Giston was also real, though there is some question as to whether his name was actually Warmer, Warier, or Warnier – or even if that was perhaps a pseudonym to obscure his real identity. Most accounts render the name as Warmer. Whoever he was, he disappears from history after his failed attempt to liberate Jeanne de Flandre and return her to Brittany.

John Bourdon – the man charged with recapturing the escapees – was a trusted sergeant-at-arms in Edward III's household who had a reputation for recovering fugitives.

The names of the constables of Tickhill and Jeanne's other custodians are known from Edward III's account records, which have entries of payments to these individuals for her upkeep.

Some things you just can't make up

One of the joys of writing historical fiction comes from the things that align in almost magical ways to augment the story. Is it serendipity? Or the fact that one is looking at things in hindsight? Most likely a bit of both. These are some of my favorites in this book.

The proximity of the fall of Champtoceaux to the feast day of Saint Jude (sometimes thought of as the patron of lost causes) provided the perfect metaphor to carry through to the sieges of Hennebont and Brest.

It should be no surprise that there would be a church dedicated to the patron saint of mariners (Saint Clement) in an important port such as Sandwich, but it was nice to be able to have Edward hear mass there before setting sail for Brittany. One might postulate that his prayers fell on deaf ears, since his voyage wound up being plagued with gales and bad weather and it took him three weeks to get to Brest, but I chose not to play with that idea. Instead, it was more fun to discover that the date of his sailing was the feast day of the much-beloved Saint Francis of Assisi.

It's documented that Edward III finally arrived in Brittany on the 26th of October 1342. What a lovely coincidence that the date is also the feast day of Saint Alfred the Great! Did Edward actually think his designs on France had any parallel to Alfred's vision for a united England? There's no way to know. But it certainly was fun to imagine such thoughts in his head.

While it's known that Edward returned to England (following the signing of the Truce of Malestroit) toward the end of February 1343, I didn't find an exact date. What I did find was Saint Honorina (*Sainte Honorine* in French), who had strong connections both to Normandy (Edward's ancestral homeland) and Conflans (where the edict disinheriting John de Montfort was signed). How convenient that her feast day falls on February 27!

ACKNOWLEDGMENTS

My interest in the Edwardian phase of the Hundred Years War was initially piqued by my reading of Bernard Cornwell's Grail Quest Series, which follows a fictional character from the siege of La Roche-Derrien through the great battle of Crécy and the siege of Calais, all the way to the battle of Poitiers. If you haven't read that series, I highly recommend it. Cornwell is a master of bringing the epic moments of history to life by placing his fictional characters in the middle of those grand events.

While looking for a story that might follow on from the events of *The Rest of His Days* (and already having an interest in the period), I discovered Jeanne de Flandre and her role in the disputed succession to the ducal crown of Brittany – which, of course, became Edward III's foot in the door in his dispute with Philip VI over the succession to the kingdom of France. Hers was a story that seemed worth exploring.

Some historians have bought into the conventional wisdom that Jeanne went mad while she was in England, hence her confinement to a series of custodians at Tickhill Castle and later in other locations. If one thinks, however, about other instances of highly capable women who were confined against their will when they "got in the way" of the men surrounding them, madness seems like a rather pat excuse. Julie Sarpy's book *Joanna of Flanders: Heroine and Exile* proved to be a great resource for insight into the what, how, and why of Edward III's confinement of Jeanne de Flandre and sheds light on why the madness theory is at best, unsubstantiated, and more likely, completely inaccurate.

For much of the detail of the important events of the War of the Breton succession, I relied on Johnathan Sumption's in-depth history of the Hundred Years War, in particular the first volume entitled *The Hundred*

Years War I: Trial by Battle. The bibliography in this volume attests to the extensive research that went into the compilation of the text.

Without the writings of Jean Froissart, Jeanne de Flandre's story might have been lost to history. I freely admit to not having read his *Chronicles* myself, having relied on secondary sources that derive much from Froissart's writings. Perhaps I'll put that on my TBR list for some future time – there might be other interesting stories within the *Chronicles* that could be fodder for another novel.

A special acknowledgment this time goes to a reader who contributed to this book. I was mulling over several possible names for the captain of the men-at-arms who came from the Montfort estate, so I ran a contest for my newsletter subscribers to make the choice. With her kind permission to use her name, I extend my thanks to Amber Rose McDaniel, who won the contest, for choosing Durant as the captain's name.

Behind every good author, there's always a good editor, and I'm fortunate to have Linda Kirwin in my court. Thank you, Linda, for everything you do.

Thanks, as always, to my publisher, Black Rose Writing, for your continued support.

And thank *you*, dear readers, for bringing these stories into your lives. I hope you've had as much pleasure reading or listening to them as I've had in bringing them to life.

About the Author

Pamela Taylor brings her love of history to the art of storytelling. An avid reader of historical fact and fiction, she finds the past offers rich sources for character, ambiance, and plot that allow readers to escape into a world totally unlike their daily lives. She shares her home with two Pembroke Welsh Corgis who remind her frequently that a dog walk is the best way to find inspiration for that next chapter.

OTHER TITLES BY PAMELA TAYLOR

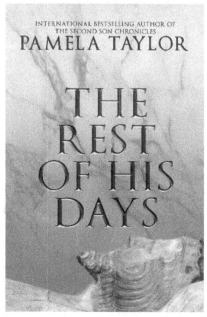

Note from Pamela Taylor

Word-of-mouth is crucial for any author to succeed. If you enjoyed *From Tickhill, 1348*, please leave a review online—anywhere you are able. Even if it's just a sentence or two. It would make all the difference and would be very much appreciated.

Thanks!
Pamela Taylor

We hope you enjoyed reading this title from:

www.blackrosewriting.com

Subscribe to our mailing list – *The Rosevine* – and receive **FREE** books, daily deals, and stay current with news about upcoming releases and our hottest authors.
Scan the QR code below to sign up.

Already a subscriber? Please accept a sincere thank you for being a fan of Black Rose Writing authors.

View other Black Rose Writing titles at
www.blackrosewriting.com/books and use promo code
PRINT to receive a **20% discount** when purchasing.

Printed in the USA
CPSIA information can be obtained
at www.ICGtesting.com
JSHW020808290924
70599JS00001B/19